SPRINKLE
CHEESE

She's pregnant, and she will find him.

for Derek

SPRINKLE CHEESE

Russell Helms

SIJ BOOKS

copyright © Russell Helms, 2017

printed in the United States

Please request permission to copy material
from this book.

First edition as *Sprinkle Cheese;* originally
published in 2015 as *The Ground Catches
Everything.*

sij books
booksbysij@gmail.com

CONTENTS

Bobby stopped his medications a month prior to visiting Thailand. He imagined the pills made him paranoid and anxious, plus he hadn't been truthful on the application about his medical history, so he couldn't be seen taking prescription meds. The Peace Corps orientation in San Francisco had passed in a blur. Everyone commented on his cedar-colored hair. He'd often found himself the last person in a room and not clear on where everyone went. San Francisco had seemed like a movie set. It was too cold for April. His roommate looked to be thirteen. Bobby's thoughts revolved around the prostitutes and addicts with HIV he would be working with in Bangkok. He imagined knife fights, gangs, yellow flowers, and gonorrhea. When the plane landed at Narita in Tokyo, he hadn't eaten in over twenty-four hours. He was skinny and needed to eat. He watched men huddle over bowls of soup and wanted to buy a Coke but was afraid. He fell in love with a young woman sitting across from him. Her skin was that of an old bruise, her hair long and midnight black. She was listening to a Walkman with a million-mile look in her eyes. His feet hurt. He felt caged and then overwhelmed with freedom.

In Bangkok, the night air flowed as if from a cooling oven. After an eternity of flying, the group of eighteen new volunteers split up into vans. Bobby, in jeans and a blue tee-shirt, sat by a window behind Beaver, the Peace Corps coordinator with a fifties haircut. The van climbed ramps, zoomed over bridges, slipped between narrow walls, and dropped into labyrinthine tunnels. There were motorcycles, cars, and trucks. It was after ten o'clock and all was a vague dark in an empty city of ten million. The ride seemed to last a lifetime, endless shifting onto tracks of road that went nowhere among a lifeless bog of buildings. Time shrank. Light came to sharp points. He had nothing to say to the female volunteer beside him. He tried and tried but nothing came. He felt his silence making a noise. A tidal wave curled in his chest. He clenched his fists beneath his thighs.

He imagined Helen Keller at the water pump. "Wah wah." He laughed and pinched himself.

Just a half mile from the Chao Phraya River, the Dusit Thani hotel stood ramrod straight. There was a zoo nearby and a palace. The exhausted hotel staff wore stiff white shirts but managed bright smiles you could crawl into. The elevator doors were patterned in faux gold. Bobby's new roommate looked like a finger puppet. Their narrow room faced a busy street. The blinking lights and motorcycles with chainsaw engines looked like toys. He mused, gazing over the rambunctious traffic. There was work to do in Bangkok, good work. He drank a warm can of lemon Lipton iced tea. His eyes hardened into little quail eggs. His roommate made a dozen phone calls to the States. Orientation began at 8:30 in the morning. Every thirty seconds, a tiny red light blipped near the ceiling. The air conditioner blew the entire endless night, cycling, *whum, whum, whum, whum.* He pulled the stiff sheet to his ears with eyes fixed on the blinking dot.

Bobby felt great, wider than wide awake. Bangkok was a juicy red tomato, and everyone seemed to have had breakfast except him. He ate a thumb-sized banana from a bowl in the cold conference room. The room was incredibly blue and hurt his eyes. He didn't recognize anyone. Everyone wore a nametag except for him.

"Bobby?" said Beaver. He held out a plastic-sheathed badge.

Bobby examined the pin's brass mechanism. "Yes?" He palmed the nametag and looked around the room. A young woman waved at him. She looked to be in her twenties, her face framed in tight black curls. He waved back. She seemed like an old friend he'd known all his life. He saw a water pitcher, and Beaver talked as ice clacked in a glass.

There were introductions, a piece of paper with important phone numbers, a schedule for language classes that would begin after lunch, a little speech on courtesy and safety, a reminder of the new no-no for volunteers— riding motorcycles *Verboten!* Beaver wandered about the room, going from one side of the semicircle to the other, gesturing his long arms. His haircut looked homemade. A Thai woman with perfect posture named Suchanad opened the glass door. Beaver explained that Suchanad was a nurse, a coordinator working with the Peace Corps and the Thai government. She wore an impeccable, tan pants suit. She looked like a movie star. She had long legs and her smile caused Bobby to examine his hands. She spoke terrible English.

"Haroo body," she said.

No one moved. Someone coughed. Bobby's right testicle crawled into his abdomen.

"Let's take a ten-minute break and then we'll have a little fun," said Beaver.

Bobby wanted to say something. He slipped out, though, and wound up back in his room, gasping for air. He felt trapped beneath a frozen lake with only one nostril breaking the surface. He drank a warm orange soda. The beds hadn't been made. The AC hummed like an electric tank. He had to pee. His hand shook, and he made little puddles on the floor. His chest trembled. He breathed deep, in and out, in and out, missing his grandparents, Chester and Clara. He imagined their neighbor's pond. He saw Chester leaning on his hoe by the garden. He smelled okra frying on the brown electric stove in the cabin's tiny kitchen.

Tears gathered in his head but seemed stuck. As a kid, the summers with Chester and Clara had been his salvation, his reward for breathing the other nine months of the year.

Moving from Army base to Army base had been hell. They always, always, moved at Christmas, so he was the new kid, over and over. That last night by the pond when he was fifteen, the sky silver with a pink sun clawing at the horizon. His parents were packing the bronze Mercury Bobcat, ready to leave early the next day and cart him back to Texas. He'd felt his heart inch out of his throat and wallow into the mud beneath the cattails, and he'd just left it there for safekeeping until the next summer rolled around. "Wave goodbye, Bobby." Wadded up in the back of that damn Bobcat, seats folded down, the hatchback slammed shut. He was on an eggcrate mattress wedged between a hard suitcase and the window. Eighteen hours to Fort Hood with a stop in Bossier City, Louisiana, he had wanted to die.

The elevator door opened and two volunteers were chatting about heroin. With his hand in his pocket, Bobby pinched himself hard to keep from laughing.

"You've got to be careful," said one. "You know, about who you smoke it with." He looked grim.

"Yeah, not with just anybody. Play it safe and whatever, dude," said the other, tapping his fingers on the metal rail.

"I'll smoke it anywhere, anytime, with anybody," said Bobby. He'd never even seen heroin. "Hell, I'll do it right here and now. Handcuffed. Blindfolded." His voice came out kind of angry.

The two guys looked at each other and nodded at Bobby. "You do that," said one.

"Bet your black ass I will," said Bobby. He felt his fists clenching. The doors opened.

"I'm not black," said the guy.

"Your jeans are black," said Bobby. As he said each word, he regretted each one. He took a deep breath, straightened the crooked look on his face, and re-entered the cold, blue room. The shades had been opened and it felt light and airy. The outside rushed up to the window edges, and he sat as far from the glass as he could.

"Looks like everyone's here," said Beaver. He patted his leg three times. "Bobby, want to move closer to the group?"

Bobby grabbed his chair to his bottom and walked bent over to the end of the semicircle. He wasn't sure if the chair was attached to him or not.

"Okay," said Beaver. "We're going to start off with a little exercise, a get-to-know-one-another game."

Bobby watched, fascinated, as one volunteer after another fell backwards into Beaver's arms. The trust game. A dizziness built in his gut, waiting for his turn.

"Let's shift gears," said Beaver. He wore wrinkled brown pants.

Disappointed that he didn't get to fall into Beaver's arms, Bobby mentally shifted gears on a giant red tractor. The seat was big enough to hold a dozen people. He could barely move the huge gear lever. He pushed his feet against the tight carpet and grunted.

"Bobby?" said Beaver.

"Yes, Beaver," said Bobby.

Everyone laughed, even the guys from the elevator. Suchanad nodded with bright eyes.

Bobby felt crushed, then elated, then crushed. Beaver motioned for him, reached into a small laundry bag, and withdrew a length of white rope. He looked Bobby in the eye. He held up the rope for everyone to see. Suchanad giggled. He tied the rope to Bobby's leg then wrapped it up to his waist. Beaver stared at Bobby, who stood stock still, waiting for something to happen. Beaver wound the rope up Bobby's torso and stopped at his neck.

"Can I put this laundry bag over your head?" said Beaver.

"Sure thing, Beaver," said Bobby. Everyone laughed again, but not quite as hard as the first time.

Beaver looked puzzled. He unwound the rope. "You didn't resist at all, Bobby. You didn't even fidget." He looked concerned. "You really trusted me, didn't you?" said Beaver.

"Not really," said Bobby. "I just let you tie me up. I didn't trust you for a hot second."

A thick silence settled at eye level in the room.

After the little trust game with Beaver, Bobby panicked. He fled to his room and gobbled forty milligrams of Prozac. He'd hidden ten of the pastel green-and-white capsules inside a blue sock. Within half an hour his pupils blew wide open, his worldview quadrupled, he yawned every thirty seconds, and he felt a renewed vigor for his mission in Thailand. He stared out the window at a pack of motorcycles straining at a red light. A man in a uniform directed traffic with a beer bottle. Bobby imagined the traffic cop's cheap clock radio, saw how he washed his face each morning with a thin rag and cool water from a porcelain basin while his two daughters with pigtails slept in a hammock. He had a bad tooth but never complained.

Bobby invited himself to lunch with his roommate and a couple of other guys. The cute volunteer with the tight curls joined them, Patsy. He imagined the conversation went well, that he hadn't raised any hackles or alarmed anyone. He ate something that looked like a boiled morning glory vine and tasted like collard greens. "This'd be good with cornbread," he'd said, feeling a rush of normalcy in his bones.

That afternoon was free unless anyone wanted to visit Mercy Mission, a healthcare center in one of the slums. Like Bobby, most of the Peace Corps volunteers would be working with the Ministry of Health, and this would be a little taste.

Beaver's powers of persuasion reeled in three volunteers brave enough to penetrate the real City of Angels. Bobby was raring to go. Since it was a small group, Beaver opted for a taxi that, with some coaxing, held two up front and three in the back. Packs of motorbikes fought for the rarefied real estate behind each traffic light. Even inside the cab, the city's roar dimmed the blasting AC and Thai talk radio. In the back seat, Bobby squeezed between Patsy and a guy with thin curly locks that spilled over the top of a flat head.

"Teddy," said Bobby. He pointed at Teddy's name badge.

"Yes. Is it Bobby?" said Teddy.

"Twenty-four, seven," said Bobby. His mind went blank. Teddy looked like a frog. The taxi zoomed toward Victory Monument with its traffic roundabout and elevated trains. All of Bangkok fed the traffic whirlpool creating a maelstrom of diesel fumes.

"We're headed to Khlong Toey," said Beaver.

He explained that Khlong Toey was the slum of all slums in Bangkok, known for its slaughterhouses and abject poverty. Death ran from the faucets according to Beaver. Part of the work the Mercy Mission performed there was providing hospice care for people living with HIV and AIDS. Heroin and prostitution, he said. Everywhere, all the time. Orphans without legs, slum fires, bellies full of roundworms, pinworms, tapeworms, little bugs that crawled up your privates and made you blind, decapitation with oyster shells, rape with poisonous snakes impaled on ax handles.

"Twenty four seven," said Bobby. It was all he could think of other than "Have a nice day" or "Two for a dollar." He shook his head, trying to rid his thoughts of the candy he used to steal as a child, Bit-o-Honey, Payday. Sprinkle cheese, cheese powder in a shakeable tube. He mouthed the words, "I like sprinkle cheese."

Beaver talked over his shoulder. The taxi merged from one expressway to another. Bobby saw a sign for Skin Hospital. "It's cosmetic and not for burns," said Beaver. Patsy and Beaver seemed to know each other. She said that only Catholics killed pigs in Khlong Toey. Muslims could kill everything but the pigs, and the Buddhists kept their hands clean of it all. Beaver nodded. Lots of poor Thai, Lao, and Cambodian Catholics lived in the vast slum and did most of the slaughtering. The taxi driver looked at the address Beaver had written. He didn't speak English and was nervous about being in the slum. Beaver spoke Thai, but how well Bobby couldn't tell. The taxi veered down a hole through piles of junk disguised as houses. A single blue roof jumped out from the sheets of rust.

"Damrong Phiphat?" said the driver. He waved his hand over the dashboard, casting a protective spell.

"Sprinkle cheese," said Bobby.

The taxi jerked to a stop and blared its horn. A shirtless brown man, a young man, with long twisted hair wobbled in the middle of the narrow lane. He vomited. Strings of mucous billowed from the bubblewand of his lips. The driver muttered and squeaked around the wavering tattooed skeleton. Kids and young women leaned from doorways without doors. Down an alleyway, a green hammock held boxes. A naked boy with his fingers in his mouth stood in a yellow plastic bucket.

"Have a nice day," said Bobby.

"Stop! *Yùt yang!*" said Beaver. "*Teeny.*"

The driver hesitated and pulled over. "*Têe nêe?*" he said.

"Yes. *Teeny,*" said Beaver. He pointed toward the large, white building they had just passed.

"Twenty-four seven," said Bobby.

Teddy stroked the leading edge of his forehead. Patsy frowned and caught Beaver's concerned eye.

Inside the hospice, a wick'd air freshener in front of a red-bladed plastic fan battled stale excrement and garlic-laced urine.

The ward glowed dim, lit only with sunlight. The ceilings hung very low, and the tile floor looked very clean. The beds were a mishmash of styles surrounded by sky-blue curtains tied back like hair ribbons. In the warm room, tidy living corpses of sharp jaws, shoulders, and hips trembled beneath thin sheets and clean torn blankets.

A thin moan was the only sound other than the fan's whir and the *chug chug* of an ancient IV pump. Two slender young men in white moved from bed to bed, murmuring like birds, adjusting pillows. A nurse in aqua scrubs drew

back a gauzy curtain. She wore a loose mask
and latex gloves, as did Bobby and the others.
She spoke in Thai to one of the male assistants. Her voice was clear, sing songy, and quite
beautiful. Her name was Silliporn.

"He has die," she said. And there lay a dark
brown man of bones covered with moles and
lesions. He was naked except for a thin, papery
diaper that swallowed him. His cracked lips
drew back over long, yellow teeth. Dry, injec-
tion-molded eyes stared through the ceiling at
a point several galaxies distant. She tugged the
curtain closed.

No phones rang. Packs of doctors in white
coats and thousand-dollar stethoscopes did
not interrupt the silence. A pigeon landed on a
windowsill, looked in, and burst away leaving a
single gray feather.

Silliporn's smile broke through and Bobby's
knees buckled. He fought back a hurricane of
tears. He felt his diaphragm receding, a tsuna-
mi pushing an ocean of helplessness into his
chest. She was gorgeous, and he wanted to give
the dead man mouth to mouth. He wanted to
give Silliporn all of his money, what little he
had. He wanted to put on scrubs and work in
the hospice for the rest of his life. He would
marry Silliporn and they would adopt HIV-in-
fected orphans from the slum. He put his hand
in his back pocket and pinched himself. His
eyes found those of a woman with no hair. Her
thin gown draped into the valley of her pelvis,
hips towering like the walls of a circular can-

yon. A small wooden Pinocchio marionette clung to her rail. Her mouth crept into a Q.

"I'm sorry," said Bobby.

The woman who made the Q with her mouth had been a dancer in Patpong, said Silliporn. Her name was May. She'd been trafficked into the sex trade by her parents from a village in the Cardamom Mountains of Cambodia. As Silliporn continued the tour, she spoke of bondage, heroin, and the plague of *yaa baa*, street meth. Two other patients had died that week and would be cremated at a nearby Buddhist temple. She floated her hand around the room of sixteen living dead as if arranging beautiful chilies around a cancerous tumor to make it more attractive.

Before leaving the hospice, while helping Silliporn and her two assistants lift the chrysalis of the dead man into the yellow "goodbye" box, Bobby made up his mind to visit Patpong that very night, the sex part of the HIV equation, and begin his research. He'd watched patients with full-blown AIDS die on his nursing unit back home, bathed them, placed pads to catch the postmortem flow of fluids, closed jaws with rips of gauze for the open caskets, drew their eyes shut to prepare them for the dark journey home, and wrapped them in clean morgue sheets. They died hermetically sealed in their rooms, surrounded by nurses gloved and masked, mouths and throats blown apart with fulminating herpes, ribs sucking skin to the spine, eyes yellowed from liver failure, blind from cytomegalovirus, skin knotted with the purple wounds of Kaposi's sarcoma. His mind spun. You can't backhand something like HIV. You don't play tiddlywinks with it hoping to win, you have to embrace it, and then you have to murder it.

Back at the hotel, Bobby discovered that others had already planned a trip. Patpong was famous they said. People came from all over the world to get laid and watch sex shows. Officially, prostitution was illegal in Thailand, but the money... Billions. Curse the hordes of horny men sweating red-faced in the short-time hotels. Coconuts can make you rich but nothing compares to warehouses of virgins in plaid and high heels. The hunger. The horror. The revenue. Bobby showered, ate five skewers of *moo satay* slathered in peanut sauce from a street vendor, rubbed some complimentary menthol talcum powder into his sparse chest hair, drank a liter of warm bottled water, then brushed his teeth with Pepsodent from home. His stomach felt light and airy. The world seemed brighter than it had in a long time. He took a long beautiful pee. His roommate asked where he was going. Bobby didn't hear him.

He met the others in the lobby, five in all. Patsy was there. She, Bobby, and some guy in a kilt took one taxi. Bobby rode up front with the driver. The driver slid his mint-green toothpick around and looked at Bobby with tired, puffy eyes.

"Patpong Road," said Bobby, as if he'd been born there.

"Patpong?" said the driver. His shirt pocket gaped open and Bobby tried to look inside.

"Patpong Road," said Bobby.

"Ok," said the driver. "Ping pong ball?" He laughed.

"*Yin-dee-dauy-na,*" said Bobby.

The driver chuckled.

"You said, Congratulations," said Patsy.

"He did?" said Bobby. It was dark. The world was tiny.

"No, you did."

"Oh." Bobby thought about Clara and Chester.

A tear glistened. Motorcycles with rip-saw engines screamed past. The taxi raced up ramps, zigzagged on elevated roads, and snuck through alleys, one mirror folded in. A woman with a boy's haircut leaned out of a souped-up red Nissan and threw up on the road.

"For Pete's sake."

The taxi slipped into a new darkness splattered with pricks of light and baubles of neon. Perched above the clamor and chaos, standing statuesque inside a glassed guard station, a Thai official in a brown uniform and reflective safety vest looked out over the gentle waves of trinket vendors cloaked beneath awnings that reached out, almost touching, from either side of the narrow lane. Stall after stall lit with blinding fluorescent tubes lined the way to raw oysters, cock, pussy, and ass. There was a young man in a pink shirt and earphones selling husked ears of fat, yellow, roasted corn. He smiled without end. In the distance, a neon dick thirty-feet high spurted tidy neon drops of liquid love at the hard moon.

Weird dolls, trays of watches, stalls stacked with shoes and purses—Bobby, Patsy, and the guy in a kilt moved with the crowds. The other two volunteers were nowhere to be seen. "Hotel California" wafted from a club through a thin veil of long beads. A "Hot Stuff for Lovers" poster hung crooked in the window beneath a neon Singha beer sign. Bobby stared. Girls in white bikinis squirmed on top of a bar. A short, thick man with a mole between his eyes pushed a piece of paper in his face. Another man in a suit by the door motioned him to come in. Patsy was talking. A woman in a miniskirt put her hand in Bobby's pocket and looked him in the eyes.

"Move!" said Patsy. "Go, go!" She said something in Thai to the woman with her hand in Bobby's pocket.

Bobby looked up through a narrow slit at the night sky. The lane was becoming an alley. Tarps, umbrellas, and plastic sheets formed a tunnel. Clubs on either side balanced on top of more clubs. The woman pulled a piece of gum from his pocket. Bobby held his arms up like he was being robbed.

"Bobby, what is wrong with you?" said Patsy. "Move."

"Sexy show, five hundred baht," said the

thick man with the mole. He produced a book of tickets and fanned them with his thumb. "You like pussy? Ping pong in pussy?" He moved as they moved. A tattoo of a fuzzy elephant covered his forearm. He wore two watches and a waxy string necklace with a shiny lug nut on it. A vertical scar pitted his throat.

Pink Floyd floated from another club, this one with a bar outside. Two leggy young ladies faced the passersby, doling out fall-inside-me smiles.

"He's a tout," said Patsy. She grimaced at their shadow who seemed dead set on taking them somewhere. "He'll follow us and the price'll get lower. Just keep walking."

"A toot?" said Bobby. He stepped in a thin rivulet of something wet. He eyeballed a tall woman in hot pants who looked Scandinavian. He saw her banana breasts swinging through the blousy arm of her top.

"Four hundred baht. Four hundred. Pussy darts. You like sexy?" Mole eye looked tired. He had a swift haircut.

"This is crazy," said Kilt Guy. "Have you been here before?" A family of four from the Isle of Wight perused necklaces and t-shirts.

"Yes," said Patsy. She hurled some harsh words at the tout walking backward in front of them.

Bobby smelled sex. He watched a lone white guy with rumpled brown hair in shorts and flipflops. A sleek woman in a black satin dress with a slit up to her kidney was eating him alive. Her gaze slipped and for a brief second she was Bobby's best friend. She pushed the guy's hands away and an improbable slew of disjointed, syllables slaughtered him. He looked dead. He looked ten thousand miles from home, winter when it should be summer, women becoming men, children with the balls of soldiers, and beer stronger than wine. He had come to play and be amazed, but now it was just a struggle to breathe.

"Two hundred," said Mole Eye. "Free drink. Sexy, sexy, ping pong." He pulled out a new ticket book, identical to the last, except for the price. He fanned the tickets. "Two hundred, two hundred. Pussy. You like pussy? You like oyster?"

Stevie Wonder played from a stairwell speaker. Bobby looked up. "Hotel Glory" flashed red. An old guy dressed in creased slacks descended red-carpeted stairs. He looked rattled. His belt was unbuckled.

"All right guys. I think this is our best shot. That's as low as he's gonna go. Don't count on the free drink, though," said Patsy.

Kilt Guy looked stunned. A man in a black suit took their money and Mole Eye disappeared. *Do a little dance, make a little love...* Bobby felt the music in his bones, especially his hyoid bone. A pink light flooded the upper part of the stairwell. A woman with footlong eyelashes motioned them up. "Come. Come. Come. Come." She looked wicked.

"I hope this satisfies your curiosity," said

Patsy.

"What?" said Bobby. The music hammered his throat. "You drink too much diet soda."

"What?" said Patsy.

Inside, darkness ran to the edge of a bar where hot, swirling colors committed suicide. Music pumped, *thump, thump, thud.* Topless young ladies in neon-orange hot pants worked the shadowy booths and dim tables. They looked like sisters to Bobby, sisters working the family business.

"They have on and off switches," said Bobby.

Kilt Guy stood behind his barstool. "What?"

"He means the hookers turn it on when they come in here and turn it off when they leave," said Patsy. She already had her free drink, Sprite in a tiny plastic champagne glass.

"No. Their smiles," said Bobby. "On, off, on, off." He worked hard at getting the big picture. A nice-looking family with two teenage boys sat at the nearest table. They looked Greek to Bobby. Single guys in hip t-shirts cloistered themselves in the booths. Behind the bar was a raised wooden platform, the stage.

A short woman in a killer miniskirt with sparkles leaned into Bobby from the side. She smelled like gardenia air freshener. Lush skid-marks of black satin lined her horse-sized eyes.

"Four hundred fifty horsepower of maximum destruction," said Bobby.

"Belle. My name is Belle," she said, dragging "Belle" across a quarter-mile of melting pavement. She squeezed Bobby's bicep. "Beef-cake," she said. "Mmm, beefy cake."

Bobby thought about how birds fly in swirling clouds, splitting and merging. He couldn't get that Primus song about Jerry the racecar driver out of his head. Beefcake reminded him of Brunswick stew from a can. *Libby's, Libby's, Libby's, on the label, label, label. You'll like it, like it, like it, on the table, table, table.*

Patsy rolled her eyes. She fluffed her tight curls and took a tiny sip of her Sprite. Kilt Guy drank his Coke in a single gulp.

"Your wallet's bulging out the back of your dress," said Bobby.

Kilt Guy felt his crotch. Bobby reached and handed him the wallet. "Jesus Christ," said Kilt Guy.

"Dog will hunt," said Bobby. How did it all work? Who got the money? The music shifted and bright lights lifted the shadows for three seconds. Where did you go to screw? Did the girls carry condoms, knives? Did they take birth control? Were they tested for HIV? The sad woman behind the bar with the microphone lacked spark. She lacked *joie de vivre.*

"Show's starting." Patsy leaned forward on her bar stool.

"She lacks joy de veever," said Bobby.

"Belle. I am Beeeeeeeellllllle." Belle put Bobby's arm around her waist and he let it stay there.

"Welcome, Thailand!" said the barmaid who lacked joy. "Who is visitor Thailand?" she barked into the microphone. Weak cheers lifted from the noisy gloom. She approached Bobby. "Sexy balls!" A spotlight turned on over Bobby's head. "You are name is?" She leaned across to hear what Bobby's name was and wrote something down.

Lights jiggled over the stage and an eerie ballad of bamboo flutes and high-strung violins played. A woman in a white robe appeared from the far side, climbed the stage, and did her best to insinuate a major cultural event. The robe slid from her thin, smooth body. Lights blinked without rhyme. She sauntered back and forth, black hair sliding down her back like water. She smiled and pointed toward Bobby, popping her bikini top off with a finger. The bottom followed suit. She leaned over backwards into a perfect C and received a magic marker in her vagina.

For a full minute she labored, dipping the marker down with her hips to the paper. Bobby drained his Singha and ordered another. The lights went up and the naked author picked up her handiwork. "Welcum Ruby! Thailand!"

The lackluster barmaid presented the poster to Bobby with a smile that said *Thank You!* "Five hundred baht," she said.

"What?" said Bobby.

"He's not Ruby," said Kilt Guy.

"Yes, you Ruby," said the barmaid. "You pay."

"You better pay," said Patsy. She looked around.

"Hell no," said Bobby. He wanted to pay, but not be forced to pay.

Belle backed away until he did the right thing.

"Four hundred baht. You pay," said the barmaid. The teeth in her mouth looked fake.

A stocky man with long sideburns and wearing loose jeans appeared. Belle slipped farther away. The barmaid retreated. Def Leppard boomed. A woman in a silver bikini stepped on stage in silver high heels. An old guy at the bar with a red face and a skipper hat handed the barmaid a bill. She lifted her red t-shirt that read *Angel*. The old man leaned across and latched on like a newborn for five seconds.

The stocky man asked Bobby why he did not pay. Bobby couldn't hear him. The man motioned for Bobby to follow and Bobby ignored him. The man touched his shoulder and signaled again. Bobby sized him up.

The leggy stripper stripped. She undulated like Istanbul.

The thick man moved to the door and waved Bobby over with small hands on fat arms. He looked tired.

On stage, a ping-pong ball dropped out.

"Ouch," said Kilt Guy.

Patsy handed the barmaid a twenty-dollar bill and pointed at Bobby.

The ping-pong balls crested one by one. The bucket held five gallons. One missed and stuck where it fell. Bobby's entire being buzzed with the seamlessness of it all. The barmaid went to her knees behind the bar. The thick man disappeared down the stairwell. The old skipper humped the bar. Patsy made a sour face.

"Jesus Hangnail Christ," said Bobby. The bucket was full of ping-pong balls and the song cut to dead silence followed by polite applause. Ping-pong lady *wai'd* the audience and waved like Miss America. A wave of fear swept Bobby's torso, back and forth, sideways. His ribs contracted. He gripped the bar edge and let his head drop. He caught his eye on a beer bottle and yelled. Belle swept to his side and made a fuss over him. Deep Purple—and another woman on stage, flat on her back. Two assistants maneuvered a dart tube into her birth canal. Bobby's head lolled up and down. He choked back a yodel. The woman on stage clenched her thighs and a balloon popped over the skipper's head.

"Belle. My name Beeeeeeeelllllle."

Bobby felt empty, as Belle led him away. Another balloon popped. Patsy gave Bobby a death look. Kilt Guy, gripping his wallet between his knees, didn't even know Bobby was leaving.

Bobby paid the guy at the door three hundred baht, about eight dollars. He didn't quite understand what the bar fine was all about and just paid it. Belle dog-walked him on an invisible leash down the long, narrow stairs. In the lane outside, Bobby followed in Belle's wake, parting the masses. Her tight, yellow miniskirt looked impossible. She smiled over her shoulder and became a stunning cartoon.

Bobby floated. He felt naked. He was in a movie. The clubs were props. The slow weaving tourists were actors. Everything made puppet sounds. Then they were going in circles. The alley had no access to the sky. Sounds stopped in mid-air. "Hello Puss. Hello Puss," said a tall man with a pipe-cleaner mustache.

Neon signs: Pretty Lady, Carnival, Paris, VIP, and Golden Cock everywhere. A woman, dead three times over, held out a mocha hand with two coins in her palm. She picked her nose with the other.

Bobby worried about his grandmother Clara's blood pressure. A stripe of panic snaked around his neck. She needed to drink more water. The beer in Thailand was really strong. Belle's hands were really strong.

"Come, come," said Belle. Her voice squirreled out of her mouth as she led him past a line of supermodels posing on red, plastic chairs. "No look," she told him and yanked.

Up cement stairs with a mangled steel railing and dried carnations, the world dropped away down a blood-red corridor. Had they gone inside something? The red carpet didn't match the red walls. A motorcycle sat propped behind a low counter. A man in a suit and tie stood. A woman with a bouffant hairdo remained seated. Bobby glanced at a framed sign written in Thai with what seemed to be prices. His two thousand baht was running out fast.

He missed his cat, Merk. Merk had a decent home with Clara and Chester, but he only had one eye and Bobby worried he'd get hit by a car.

The short-time hotel proprietor yelled at Belle. Bobby flinched. Belle yelled back and then gave Bobby a tremendous smile. Bobby imagined he was on a squat houseboat without gas, nudging the spillway of a roaring dam. The short hallway intersected a long dark corridor. Red carpet, exposed in puddles of weak light, appeared every fifteen feet. Bobby touched the curtains, which were the fronts of the rooms. Numbers printed in marker on white laminated cards hung from shower hooks. He heard slaps and cursing.

"You like?" said Belle. Number 47. She pushed Bobby through a slit in the dusky fabric that reminded him of choir robes.

Her shoulder-length hair looked solid in the flickering fluorescent light. She plugged in a cheap air conditioner mounted high on the wall. Bobby pushed on the curtain and it moved. The room was clean, with just a single bed against the wall, next to a doll-size sink. Belle spit into a plastic garbage can lined with a black bag. She checked her makeup in the mirror. She squeezed her breasts, forcing them up high. She put Bobby's hand on one.

"You want smoke?" she said. She gripped a tiny sequined purse and spit again.

Bobby stared at her, at the room. He smelled coffee, but it was something else. "Smoke?" said Bobby. He heard footfalls.

"No fuck me," said Belle. "Smoke cock." She reached for Bobby's pants.

The curtain jerked open and the proprietor in his suit popped in. "Show time! Show time!"

Bobby froze and put two and two together. The proprietor tapped his watch, a cheap watch. Belle exploded and slammed a rusty bucket of Thai word knives over his head.

The curtain jerked closed. "Sexy Belle. Sexy Balls. Beefy, beefy," said Belle. She led Bobby to the bed and sat down. She took his hand and placed it on her breast. "You like?" Her other hand was searching. "Are you boring?"

Sounds of arguing down the hall. Everything seemed vague. The veins on Belle's hands were huge, pipelike, and opal. She was unbuckling his belt. The blue of her veins reminded him of the belly of a catfish. He'd left the condoms at the hotel. Belle's long fingers with perfect nails finished in French tips were undoing his zipper.

"Smoke. Mmm, for Sexy Balls."

That tight dress. Her breast so firm. She was working his jeans, probably down. His wallet was in his front pocket and then it was in her hand. She tossed it on the bed. Those eyelashes. That makeup.

"Welcum Ruby, Thailand. Mmmm." She went to her knees and made him sit. "Mmmm. Are you boring?"

The air conditioner cycled and changed pitch, humming louder. Bobby noticed a bobbypin on the floor near the curtain. If he'd been in church, it would've been funny. But he wasn't in church. He was in the grimiest red-light district in Bangkok. The air conditioner coughed and shot a stream of water into the garbage can.

"Happy Ruby," said Belle. She hocked and spit in the sink. "Welcum, Thailand." Belle zipped Bobby, shook him, and shoved him through the curtain into the hall. Stairs. A long walk. Stairs. Bobby recognized the bar as a robot recognizes a string of zeros and ones. Patsy welcomed him back with a sneer. On stage, the theme song from *Shaft* cast a groovy glaze on a scarecrow woman smoking a cigarette with her vagina.

"Shaft!" went the backup singers.

"In context, *Shaft* is a sobriquet," said Bobby. He made quote marks with his fingers. "Kind of like a charcoal briquette."

"Can ya dig it?" said Isaac Hayes.

"I sure can," said Bobby. He felt as black as the ace of spades. He could smell Belle's pancake makeup.

Kilt Guy sat on the edge of the barstool with his knees stuck together. Lights swirled. Belle dragged Bobby to a booth, where she draped on him like a Sunday morning hangover. A bottle of beer for Bobby and a soft drink for Belle appeared. Bobby watched the topless waitress walk away in her cupcake-liner skirt.

"Beeelle," said Belle into Bobby's ear. "I am Beeellllllle." She grabbed his crotch. She'd seen the bills left in his wallet.

Bobby moved her hand to the vinyl seat. The dancer on stage crab-walked while smoking with her canal. *Shaft* petered out and five seconds of chairs scraping and patrons coughing lasted for a full five minutes.

"Sexy balls," said Belle.

"If I was a preacher, you'd make a good wife," said Bobby.

"You want more smoke?" said Belle. She reached for his crotch again.

"Dammit," said Bobby. He drained his beer. "I'm just trying to get it, that's all. Research."

The dancer plucked the burning cigarette from her groin, put it to her mouth, took a puff, and bowed.

Belle dug her claws in. "Are you boring?" and grappled him back into the booth.

"A look of consternation just crossed my face," said Bobby. "If I had a steering wheel, I'd grip it."

The lights swirled and a woman in a white hotel robe climbed the little ladder onto the stage. The old man who'd gotten a blowjob at the bar staggered out of what looked to be a closet and resumed his slouch on the stool. The moony woman on stage sashayed in bare feet. A man in his fifties wearing a "Belong to Hotel" bathrobe joined her.

"Christ," said Bobby. He looked at Belle's perfect hands, bigger than his own, her face hot with makeup, like a geisha doing Pantone.

The robed man shuffled. His eyes looked dark and saggy as he undressed his partner.

Bobby imagined a sloth peeling a banana.

"He sells t-shirts and belt buckles and has to get back to his cart," Bobby told Belle. "People call him Ned. His daughter's dead with TB and he takes care of her three children, all in wheelchairs. That woman's his wife. She owes money to Laotian card sharks and is working it off here. The only way he can see her is to have sex with her during the show. They chain her to a bed during the day. Her name is Brenda."

Belle nodded, excited that Bobby was so animated. "Sexy Beeellle," she said. "Sexy balls. Beefcake."

"Brunswick stew," said Bobby.

In a loose-fitting bathing suit, Brenda assumed ridiculous poses. Her breasts flopped from the sides of her top. A little sag of flesh pooched below her bellybutton. Her short curly hair made her face seem fat. Sad Ned stepped out of his underwear and snagged it on a toenail. They entwined, managing passionate glances.

"They look like two beavers halfway through an oak tree," said Bobby. He wondered how Clara was getting along. He could see her stirring a pot of pinto beans and Chester reading a *National Geographic* from 1973 for the hundredth time.

Ned lay his woman down and, on his knees, rolled a condom onto his tired flesh. With her cake on the plate, Ned carved his enslaved wife Brenda for two minutes, twisting her hips this way and that. The soulful Thai ballad whispered to an end and the pair stood and bowed.

"Belong to hotel," said Bobby.

Belle grabbed the loops of Bobby's jeans as he fought his way to the exit. He imagined his mother in the street below calling his name, not angry, but concerned. She used to call him in at night, past dark, after dinner, to come inside for Bible Study before they got ready for bed. Every night she would read an inspirational passage from that little square Baptist book called *Open Windows*. And after that came the reading of missionary names for that day, their birthdays—Doug Jansen, Philippines; Mary Ann Gerber, China; Paul Truelove, El Salvador. He'd felt like his mother was praying for the whole world sometimes, that she was filling the empty spot left by his dad with the names of those missionaries, rock stars for God able to reach and fill their tiny living room with hope. He'd felt it in his bones, too, especially when she bowed her head, closed her eyes, and prayed. A kind of warmth, an acceptance that the world was big and cruel but that there were hard-working people out there smoothing the wrinkles, easing the pain.

The next morning, Bobby hustled to the hotel lobby, wearing hemmed jean shorts and a baggy yellow t-shirt. Patpong Road and Belle had left him swimming, but Jatuchak Market sounded like genuine fun. There was nothing else to do on a Sunday morning and the volunteers had the day to themselves. He expected the whole group was going, but only five peo-ple showed, not including Patsy or Kilt Guy. Bobby couldn't remember anyone's name and just tagged along. The heat felt good. The sun looked tiny but focused. The roar of traffic drowned conversation, which put him at ease.

Bobby struggled in behind the others through the middle door of a packed red-and-white bus. He caught his shoulder on the frame, picked up a long stripe of grease on his shirt, and grabbed a pole. Everyone looked sad and hardened to their lonely lives. When the bus stopped, he followed the group and changed buses with them. Monks in saffron robes dotted the crowds. He wondered if they were wearing underwear. The city was endless, layered with diesel fumes, and on the brink of collapsing. There were more people on the bus than in the church cemetery back home. The bus stopped and he got off last, running to catch up with the group, which had already decided to split and part ways. He attached himself to the perimeter of two girls and a guy. The other two lazed off together with dreamy looks.

Bobby remembered making friends with two kids in the Smoky Mountains. He was camping with Clara and Chester in Elkmont, right by the creek. The kids had paired off at the campfire. The girl had pigtails and apple cheeks. The boy had neat bangs, braces, and an innertube built for two. "Looks like they're sharing an innertube," said Bobby. He pointed at the departing couple.

"What?" said the tall girl. A heavy daypack strained her shoulders and she leaned forward.

A three-wheeled *tuk-tuk* fringed in velvet edged around them. The driver pointed into the cab. "Velly, velly," he said. He revved his 650cc engine. "Good, good."

Bobby shook his head *No* and admired the tall girl's feet. The skin looked healthy. He could see the tendons to her toes running across the top and a delta of firm blue veins.

"We're just going to wander around if you want to hang with us," said the guy. He looked like a medical student.

"Where's your stethoscope?" said Bobby.

"What?"

"What is this place?" said Bobby.

"It's a giant outdoor market that's supposed to only be open on weekends," said the other girl. She had freckles, sunburned shoulders, and a willful dispensation.

"You have a willful dispensation," said Bobby. He couldn't focus on the market or imagine its dimensions. He needed a hot-air balloon to see it all from a distance. He used to ride the chairlift first thing at Six Flags in order to get the big picture.

There were a few side glances.

"Cool," said the medical student.

"Are you from Alabama?" said the freckled girl.

"Yep," said Bobby. "Got my first pair of shoes right before I came over." He stayed a step or so behind as the group ventured into the first ribbon of stalls. To absorb the mounting stimuli, Bobby divided the throngs of people into those who were resting and those who were walking. Anything that moved belonged to the walking and vice versa. "That woman just made the transition from resting to walking."

"What?" said the freckled girl. She looked ahead to her friends.

Bobby watched the woman in question sit back down then stand again, changing her category each time. He examined her little stacked tables that held hundreds of colorful wind-up toys. She smiled and twisted a plastic key. A tiny two-car train went around a tiny track. The whole thing fit in her hand.

"One zero zero baht," said the lady. A large gap split her bottom front teeth.

Bobby imagined her knitting oven mitts in the middle of a freeway. He looked down the narrow alley. Cubicles of trinkets crushed each side. Haphazard awnings met in the middle blocking out most of the sky. The freckled girl and her friends had disappeared.

Bobby picked up a miniature Pinocchio marionette. "I, am, iron, man," he whispered.

"One zero zero baht," said the lady. She rolled up her t-shirt and exposed her midriff. Her face looked thirty but her belly looked eighteen.

Bobby shook his head and walked away.

"Nine zero baht," the lady called. Her voice

reminded Bobby of an electric shaver.

He passed through endless toys, handmade flowers, and glass-encased Buddha shrines. Young people in love sipped slushy soda pop from clear plastic bags through straws. It seemed to be noon. In the few open spaces, the heat felt hotter, but he could breathe better. He worried that he had a thermometer in his mouth and brushed his lips every minute or so to check. Helen Keller jokes ran through his head. *How did Helen Keller burn her fingers?*

"Wah wah," he said to no one. "Wah wah." He made himself laugh and had to bend over with hands on thighs to recover.

He looked at shoes. He looked at polished rocks. He looked at medical supplies: bedpans, unopened bags of IV fluid, and syringes with needles. He dropped a five-dollar bill into a can at the feet of a young girl trying to play the violin. He saw a toucan. He saw muscled fighting cocks. He saw beef tongues roasting. He saw a café and sat down as if commanded to do so. He saw the menu in pictures beneath a piece of scratched glass on the table. Squiggles and numbers. One photo looked like soup. He pointed to the soup and it came within seconds along with a Coke in a bottle. In a scalding gray broth floated thumb-size octopi. He waited. He drank his Coke and waited. He put a spoonful in his mouth and it wouldn't go down.

Bobby draped a gauzy paper napkin over the awful soup and handed the scrawled check and a 50-baht note to the waiter. The waiter jabbered. He was old, skinny, and wore a long t-shirt that said "No Problem!"

"How much? Gee baht?" said Bobby.

The waiter poked his finger at the scribbles on the check. "Pay this amount, cuntsucker," he said in Thai.

Bobby looked at the check again. The writing looked like dust clouds.

"I'm sorry," said Bobby. He looked into the unhappy crowd streaming past. The waiter machinegunned him with language. Bobby stood and reached for his wallet. "There's a lot of pinched faces and folded arms out there," he said.

"Stupid farang," said the waiter in Thai.

"When the roll is called up yonder, will you be there?" Bobby gave the waiter another 50 baht.

"Bye bye," said the waiter. "Bye bye."

A familiar face passed. "Silliporn?"

She turned. "Oh! Surprise to me!" she said.

"To God be the glory," said Bobby. His head felt light. He touched his mouth. Sweat ran down his back. "Silliporn?" She looked like a schoolgirl in her blue skirt and sleeveless pullover.

"Silliporn, yes. You name Ruby, right?" She motioned for him to follow.

"Yes, Ruby my name." He bumped into an old woman. "Mi scusi, pardon. Uh, no, me name Bobby." He weaved through the crowds with her. She turned left and right and left and right.

"You like this many things?" She gestured

toward a stall of pop-art flipflops.

"Oh, sure, very much. Maybe I'm lost." His voice eked out through a straw. He smelled cat pee.

"You are losing?" She smiled nonstop. "Where is your Beaver?"

Bobby thought for a minute. "He's at the hotel, I guess, doing whatever a Beaver does. Are you off today? From Mercy Mission? You guys do great work. Big work." He made hand motions indicating big. His feet felt tight in his shoes. Kittens mewled from woven baskets. Wooden pens squirmed with guinea pigs.

"My father here," said Silliporn. "I show you him."

The cramped stalls opened into a kingdom of tiny dog stores. Chihuahuas stacked in crates panted. Itsybitsy pugs wobbled and fell over on tables covered with red felt. Feeble electric fans moved the hot air around. A pink strap slipped from Silliporn's shoulder. Bobby stumbled.

Silliporn *wai'd* a stocky man with a gangster haircut and tight red t-shirt, an Asian sock-hop punk caught in a time warp. He held up a fat St. Bernard puppy and stroked it with folded cheesecloth. The dog had a stitched incision on its belly. A dozen other brown and white puppies lay on their sides, gasping to keep cool. Bobby thought he saw a dead one in a bag on the floor. Silliporn slouched with crossed arms and plied her father with edgy phrases. Bobby slid his hands in his pockets and felt for his wallet. He checked his pockets again. He looked around. He checked his pockets again. Everyone and everything went out of focus. The wallet was in his hand. Silliporn's father handed off a droopy puppy to a young girl with a cartoon backpack who disappeared into the shifting throngs. Silliporn frowned and took her father's place in the tiny store made of cages and tables. He put a yellow toothpick in his mouth, picked up the bag with the dead puppy in it, and brushed against Bobby without a word.

After an hour, still dazed, Bobby wandered away from Silliporn's family business in the bowels of Jatuchak. He needed to get back to the hotel. She was coming that night for dinner! He walked and walked. He stopped and browsed at leather sandals held together with carpet tacks. He was about to buy a pair and then panicked, dropping the shoes onto the cement floor.

"Bend over and shit in your mouth," said the vendor in Thai.

"She'll be riding six white horses when she comes," said Bobby. He popped into a lane with sky above. A one-legged man in a wheelchair, selling lottery tickets from a suitcase, ran over his foot. "The devil's in the details," said Bobby. He saw a Prozac squashed on the pavement. He scanned for the tall clock tower at the entrance that Silliporn had told him to look for. He saw people wearing backpacks backwards. Carnival music played on a toy piano. A child screamed,

"Mommy!" Mommy!" in English. An old woman carried a clear, plastic bag filled with danger-yellow chicken feet. Surrounded by containers of spice, a man wearing a surgical mask stir-fried noodles on a round, steel grill. He clanged and smacked, flinging powders and chopped things at blinding speed.

"Pull forward and guide your vehicle toward the light," said Bobby.

A woman approached him holding a fuzzy baby duck. She wore a tight, black miniskirt. Her giant breasts bulged. She blew on the duck, standing up its airy down. Bobby put his hands in his pockets, looked away, began to run, and then walked again. He saw books. They were Bibles. A tiny, drawn man with guitar-string neck cords nodded at him. "Come see," he said.

Bobby gazed at the piles of Bibles. A young Korean man wearing a backward backpack sidled beside him.

"You are Christy-an?" said the young man.

"Kristy Ann?" said Bobby.

"Yes, Jealous Lice," said the man. He smiled as big as heaven.

"Do you like speed skating?" said Bobby.

"Yes," said the man, his smile spreading beyond heaven's gates.

"Maybe you can help me. I'm lost."

"Oh you are wrost to be redeemed?"

The Bible salesman opened a red Bible to a colorful illustration of Samson dismembering infidels with the jawbone of a donkey.

"Redeemed? Is it double coupon day?" Bobby looked at the Bible salesman and laughed. Sweat burned his eyes. His feet felt disconnected from his ankles. He had a headache. He felt a mustache growing and disappearing on his upper lip.

"You must wash in the Jealous blood," said the man. "Jealous Lice to give you bread life."

"Get right or get left." Bobby touched his mouth. "Seven days without church makes one weak."

"This good news, I tell you." Little webs of saliva crept into the corners of his mouth.

"What's the good news? You've got the syllabic language and speed skating, what more could you want?"

"You will die to Hell," said the young man.

"That's pretty good news," said Bobby, "considering the options."

"You know Beely Graham?"

"Is he a character in *The Hobbit?*"

"One hundred baht," said the Bible salesman.

Bobby noticed the old man had a wooden leg with a beige mannequin foot and walked away. He tried to remember the name of his hotel. A *tuk-tuk* pulled up. The driver motioned Bobby to get in. The sun looked to be the size of a dime. He saw men in brown uniforms. Then he heard someone speaking English and followed the sound. He thought he'd wandered into a police station, but the uniforms, metal desks, and plainness of it all shouted military. A man beside a black telephone spoke in single syllables.

"Ah, be, ce de, eh, eff," said Bobby. A round clock displayed military time. "Lost. English." Bobby felt terrible. He resolved to learn Thai and the languages of all bordering countries. "Here…" He pointed at the ground. "Few days."

The sharp-jawed man glared at him. "Stupid farang," he said in Thai. He shouted to the back. "Hey, Colonel, come up here and look at this donkey dick."

"Just call me Sprinkle Cheese," said Bobby.

A short man in camo with a black belt designed to hold hand grenades appeared. "Haroo," he said. He had three-day bangs on a precision flat-top.

"Dusit Thani," said Bobby. "My hotel. Lost." He pinched himself through his pockets. He strained to focus. He saw the man in camouflage as the Helper.

"You write," said the Helper.

Bobby wrote Hotel Dusit Thani on a piece of green paper.

The Helper studied it for a minute. Somebody important walked by and everyone went stiff for five seconds. Bobby saluted. Two guys with helmets and machineguns walked in and stared.

"Twenty-four seven," said Bobby.

"I know, come come," said the Helper. "Let me dump this idiot back at his hotel before he gets hurt," he said in Thai to the guy at the desk.

Bobby followed the Helper outside and watched him mount a 250cc Kawasaki. He thought about the ban on volunteers riding motorcycles. At the orientation in San Francisco, the Peace Corps official leading the welcome seminar had made it very clear that, although volunteers in the past had been allowed to ride motorcycles, beginning that very year, a no-motorcycle policy had been implemented and that violation of the new rule would result in termination. End of story. Motorcycle-related accidents had become the number one cause of morbidity and mortality among Peace Corps' volunteers worldwide. Should he bother to explain this to the Helper or just hop on? He hopped on, pressed his ankle to the hot muffler, and leapt off.

"You okey dokey?" said the Helper.

Bobby took three deep breaths and carefully remounted the back seat. "Okey dokey," said Bobby.

At the hotel, Bobby handed his forbidden motorcycle ride a one hundred–baht note. "Thank you, sir." The Helper shook his head *No* and roared off without looking back. The hotel sucked Bobby in and led him to his room.

"What happened to your leg?" said Bobby's finger-puppet roommate. He lounged on the bed watching Thai MTV.

"I burned it in Sarasota, Florida." Bobby saw his roommate in his old age, wearing headphones and sweeping a playground with a metal detector. "Sometimes you find bullets, but it's usually just cans."

"What?"

"I got lost and the Helper gave me a ride back to the hotel," said Bobby. He moved in front of the air conditioner. He looked at the crimson mark on his leg tinged with soot. "Damn muffler."

His roommate coughed and said, "Muffler?"

"It wasn't the muffler's fault," said Bobby.

"What?" The room phone bleeped. "Sure, he's here," said the roommate.

"What?" said Bobby.

"That was Patsy, just asking if you were here."

"Well, I'm here."

There was a knock on the door and there stood Beaver.

"Bobby, we need to speak with you downstairs."

Bobby looked into the hallway beyond Beaver. "How many shekels changed hands. Forty seven?" He put his hand to his mouth, checking for a thermometer. He tried to straighten the smile on his face into something serious.

"I saw you get off the motorcycle. So did a couple of other people. You were warned."

"But did you see me get on?"

"You were riding on a motorcycle. You know the rules."

"How do you know I got on it? You said we

couldn't get on but nothing about getting off." Bobby was ready to discuss the issue until the end of time. He pressed his hands together. The left one always seemed stronger. "Bobby wonders if there are cameras in the hotel room," said Bobby.

"This is serious, Mr. Hartwig. Take a few minutes, but we need to talk."

"Mr. Beaver, was it really me or someone who looked like me?"

Beaver cleared his throat and asked Bobby's roommate if he needed anything. The roommate hopped out of bed and said he needed some fresh air. Bobby followed them into the hall.

"I've met an angel!" Bobby yelled. Tears came to his eyes. "Her name is Seafoam! She takes care of the dying! She comes up to here." He made a line on his chest at the level of his heart. "People with AIDS. Poor people with no place to go. Addicts. Sex workers. She pulls her hair straight back, but these wisps of hair hang down and hide her ears." He choked and lost his voice.

Beaver and the roommate disappeared into the elevator.

"Silliporn," said Bobby.

That night, following an interrogation and transmission of the motorcycle-riding facts by Beaver to the Peace Corps' bigwigs in Washington, D.C., Bobby enjoyed the most fabulous meal of his life with Silliporn at the hotel restaurant, Loka, a Thai-Indian fusion bistro. Green papaya salad followed by that killer masala. For dessert she had the curried sago with yams, which she ate with a tiny elegant spoon. He devoured the pistachio gelato. The meal with drinks cost Bobby over 2,000 baht, about half of his Peace Corps' monthly stipend.

Sipping a shot of Johnny Walker Black, Bobby stared at the fine down on Silliporn's arms. She looked royal sitting in the gleaming lacquered chair. He wanted to push the hair back over her ears to see them. He was at a loss, now that the check lay paid on the table. In Hindi, *loka* referred to a type of heaven.

"Kob khun ka," said Silliporn, intonating her voice high and low. She touched Bobby's hand and gave his thigh a squeeze under the table.

He was pretty sure she'd said thank you. "You're welcome." A lump formed in his throat and his chest felt like dried coral. He looked around the soft-lit room with only two other couples still dining. Their waitress, dressed in a lime-green embroidered jacket, stood in the same spot she had been in the entire evening, waiting for a nod from her tables.

"Do you want to go for a walk?" said Bobby. He touched the electric candle.

"Go for walk?"

"Walk. Around the hotel?"

"Okay."

Bobby's roommate had moved out, just disappeared. The pieces were coming together and flying apart.

That morning, the US Ambassador screamed up to the hotel on a red 1130cc BMW touring motorcycle and greeted the volunteers. Bobby asked him where his helmet was. Beaver pulled Bobby aside and told him that he had been administratively separated and to keep a low profile. The Ambassador would meet them later across the river at another hotel, at a banquet where fried chicken would be served. Patsy encouraged Bobby to walk with them, to keep his spirits up. Bobby returned to his room and put on his only pair of dress pants and a short-sleeve white shirt with buttons up the front. He felt sacrificial, like the new kid in gym class. His stomach felt sour. He was going home for riding a damn motorcycle.

"You ever read that story called 'The Swimmer,'" said Bobby, talking way too fast.

Patsy nodded a maybe.

"This rich guy gets drunk and decides to leave a party and swim home through the neighborhood pools." Bobby saw a dandelion growing in a sidewalk crack. "I'm pretty sure it was all a dream. That he fell into the pool at the party and drowned. The rest was just a hallucination as he died." He laughed.

Patsy nodded.

"He's dead when the story starts." The traffic on the busy road assumed the shape of parallel trains. Sweat ran down Bobby's back and belly.

Patsy nodded. She wore clean white sneakers and a short dress. "Who wrote it?"

"Rhymes with Beaver," said Bobby. He followed the splintered group of volunteers onto the Thanon Ratchawithi Bridge. He smelled the river and then saw it.

"There's the hotel," said Patsy. She fingered a tall, icy-white building in the distance as the melting wreck of noon raged. On the bridge, motorcycles, trucks, cars, and three-wheeled *tuk-tuks* blurred in opposite directions. Bobby lingered near the middle and stared at the water clawing below. The Chao Phraya River boiled as it flowed, splitting Bangkok's middle—a dirty yellow snake flushing into the Gulf of Siam twenty-five miles south.

From the steel bridge, Bobby shifted his gaze to three small boats lazing on the river—thin open kayaks, tiny boats cushioned in foamy brown currents of trash, captained by stick figures wearing hats wider than the gunwales. The paddlers foraged plastic water bottles, scorched bras, and boards swollen with rusty nails. A dog's head sloshed under the bridge.

Along the river's banks, zigzag stairs tumbled to piers of weathered wood that fingered out to small ships with vast hulls and tiny wheelhouses. Between the vessels, markets selling coconuts and condoms bobbed on tethered rafts. A squat woman appeared topside a dirty white trawler, a boat large enough to take on a rough sea. She lowered a bucket and pulled in a slopping haul of chewy water. Maybe the trawler was empty. Maybe prostitutes swelled its holds, doped with *yaa baa,* dreaming of the hills to the north.

Sweat glazed Bobby's back. The lunch banquet seemed pointless now. He'd been "administratively separated" from the Peace Corps. Fired. Canned like tuna. He'd been in Bangkok for just a week. He was supposed to have been gone for two years. He'd given away his books, had a tooth pulled, a root canal on another, and lied about his medical history to get in. A fever ached in his stomach. Most of the volunteers had moved on, satisfied with the view and eager for air conditioning. There'd been talk of fried chicken. He untied his shoes. Traffic buzzed behind him.

"Hold on. I'll be right back," said Bobby to a cloud of gnats. The din of the city narrowed to a pencil point.

"What are you doing?" said Patsy.

He remembered the previous night with the beautiful nurse Silliporn who cared for the dying. Or maybe it had been a dream. The green papaya salad, he had only imagined. Pistachio ice cream could never be unforgettable, right? The way she pulled her hair back, the wisps over her ears, the fine down on her arms. There had been lotus seeds, and she had come back to his room after a magical walk past unseen palaces. For thirty years, the narrow roads crisscrossing the universe had brought him here to this spot on the Thanon Ratchawithi Bridge.

The heat, humidity, and sweat were an extension of the river below. There was no other choice. He focused on the dog's head sloshing in brown foam, bobbing toward the tiny boats and jumped.

An ancient river mariner tied Bobby to the side of his tiny trash boat with a huge black strap. Bobby's head went under, then popped back up. The river man laughed at a squatting woman selling starfruit on a floating dock. He pulled Bobby's head up by the hair. "He's a bad swimmer," he said in Thai.

Bobby vomited river water. In the sky, two fading jet contrails formed a white convex X stretching as far as he could see. It gave him an idea for a tattoo. He imagined a hockey team using glue sticks. He saw a mule nodding its head in Tennessee. He wondered if the brain was a single yellow wire. He shivered and vomited again. Thai sentences crisscrossed the air, bouncing slingshot tones of high and low.

He went back to the purple evening when the Sugg's barn caught fire. Moans came from the loft. He imagined his dad and that bastard Sammy as two ants lapping a drop of nectar from a summer mushroom and then it all started to look like a convenience store. Porn magazines behind him, cigarettes over his head. The cash register with the bubble-pop buttons. A wall of drink coolers off to his left next to an island chock-full of cups, lids, coffee, doughnuts, and spinning hot dogs. The Zima cooler display. The red tape on the door to measure people with guns and knives. He could see the big display of sprinkle cheese. Why they sold so much sprinkle cheese he couldn't figure. He guessed it was a kind of magic, cheese from a cardboard can that you could shake on spaghetti, green beans, toast, or a mayonnaise sandwich. Some people ate it straight from their hand in the parking lot. Bobby had poured motor oil at the base of the stairs going to the barn loft. He couldn't find a match. He'd heard yelling, heard something heavy thud to the ground, and discovered his naked father curled in the dirt.

"One is always next to zero," said Bobby, looking up at the great X in the sky.

"Get that monkey turd out of here!" screamed the old lady selling starfruit. She pretend-kicked Bobby in the ribs. "Stick a banana in his ass and throw him back in."

Four laughing teenage boys dragged and carried Bobby up a maze of plank and wire walkways. Some people put their hands over their mouths. Others laughed. Bobby cataloged each one as his eyes met theirs. "Two for a dollar," he said. "Lick it right from your hand like a summer mushroom."

The laughing boys rested at a wobbling metal landing behind a gutted building that used to be a warehouse for processing river lobster. One smoked a found cigarette. One scratched his balls. The other ate a stolen starfruit. "What's that?" said a little girl pretending

to sell flowers. "Trash from the river," said one.
  "If a nuclear bomb helps just one person
then I think it's worth it," said Bobby.

Silliporn Wongmalasith emerged from the underground train at Lat Phrao station, the hot smell of two-stroke motorcycle engines mixing with sweet coconut. The yellow Bangkok sun felt nice on her slender arms, arms tired from bathing patients, turning them, feeding them broths and rice, helping them into plain straightback chairs. She shaded her eyes to cross the street, walked two blocks, and then passed down a narrow lane beyond the coin laundry to a four-story lime-green apartment building as square as her father's jaw. She slipped by the long, red vehicle gate on wheels, open just enough for her slight figure. To avoid contamination of the fragile patients she cared for at Mercy Mission, she changed into scrubs there and wore her street clothes home, today a pair of dark blue linen pants and a pink print top decorated with orange blossoms. From the street, on a tiny open balcony, she could see where her mother had rotated her father's pants and shirts on hangers from the closet to air them. He disliked any hint of detergent, but liked the smell of the sun. He insisted on it. The two-bedroom apartment was in the vicinity of Jatujak, less than half a kilometer from the teeming outdoor market where Silliporn's father ran a dog shop, specializing in St. Bernard puppies.

Once up the stairs and inside the tiny living room, she found her mother playing *Gao Gae* on the phone with a friend who worked a desk job at an insurance company. Stacks of green, white, red, and blue chips sat in piles on a wooden TV tray beside her mother's favorite leather chair. She dealt herself three cards. The TV ran without volume, a commercial for foot deodorant spray. Silliporn's mother only left the apartment in the company of her husband, Chanarong, better known by his nickname Khun Phaen. He traveled often, making her outings infrequent.

Silliporn entered the small white-tiled bathroom and brushed back her brilliant hair from her ears. She was pregnant. She was sure of it now. An echo, a tiny voice beneath her breastbone told her so. It had been two weeks since meeting Bobby, the American, the Peace Corps volunteer. He was to have been in Thailand for two years, but now he was gone. Their one dinner together she held onto as a dream, even though her father had beat her when she came home at three in the morning. Where was Bobby? *Ah-la-ba-ma?* She had an address for him, but that was all. She would write him a letter, but should she tell him she was pregnant? She knew what her father's reaction would be if he found out. The more she thought about Bobby, the more his absence weighed on her.

"Silliporn! *Ma!*" her father called from the bedroom.

She heard a zipper, shoes hitting the floor. Silliporn cringed. He wanted a massage before his afternoon nap.

55

Bright bright Alabama sunshine emptied through bare windows onto floorboards groaning beneath Bobby's feet. There was the smell of new paint. A double bed jammed into the back bedroom. Bobby's stuff lay scattered on a thin, blue spread—a pair of jeans, two t-shirts, a tiny flashlight, passport, discharge papers from the Peace Corps, and four bottles with pills.

Nine months prior, he'd left his grandparents' old house for Bangkok, but they'd moved into town during his brief absence. The old place was too far from town without him around, they'd said. Bobby had loved their old cabin in the pine woods, the garden, the neighbor's pond that teemed with bream and bullfrogs. Since his father had disappeared when he was seventeen, and as his mother had faded away at the nursing home, Bobby had lived with his grandparents. He took care of Chester and Clara, mowing their two-acre lawn, sweeping pine straw from the roof and driveway, and plowing up their rich red garden dirt each first week of May.

Moving from Army base to Army base until he was sixteen had sucked oceans for Bobby. After finishing high school, he'd had a vague notion that he wanted to help people and gave it his best shot, becoming an RN with a two-year diploma from the nearby community college. In the back of his mind, he was going to bring his mom back home, take care of her and take care of his grandparents, too. She'd given up, though, after his dad Robert came up missing. She'd let her spirit slip away with the fractured memories—Fort Benning, Fort Dix, Augsburg, Stuttgart, Fort Knox, Fort Rucker, Redstone Arsenal, Fort Hood. The respites back in Kuhlman near her own parents, while Robert went overseas by himself for solo tours of duty, had never been enough—and then that black-box year he survived Vietnam.

For seven years Bobby worked as an ICU nurse, driving the hour and ten minutes back and forth to Birmingham. He'd started off working nights then took a schedule working three to eleven. His last year, he'd snagged a plum, working twenty-four hours every week-end and getting paid for forty. Plenty of time to drive his grandparents around, buy groceries, trim the yellow bells, help with canning green beans, and even cook, especially after Clara broke her hip at Walmart. The Peace Corps had become his excuse to dip his toe into the world at large again, but Chester and Clara had not encouraged him.

And so, with spirits high, and goodbyes to everyone who mattered, Bobby had taken off for Thailand. But, now, back again, in his grandparents' new house, the floors complaining of his weight, the sun warming his face, the spectre of his missing father looming larger than ever.

An explosion rattled the windows.

Bobby wheeled and slammed his shoulder into the doorframe. He stumbled into his grandmother Clara, clutched her thin shoulders, danced with her, pushed his hand through a hole in the screen door—"Hell!"— and ran down the cement stairs to where Chester lay sprawled in the grass with his fly open. Bobby dug his knuckles into Chester's breastbone, an old ICU trick.

Chester mumbled. His eyes swam into place, and he moved his head side to side. "Did she crank?" He looked comfortable lying in the ankle-high grass. His hearing aid squealed.

"You got a black place on your forehead," said Bobby.

Watching from above in her white housecoat, Clara gripped the deck rail. A red toothpick lolled between her teeth.

"Sit up a minute." Bobby helped Chester to his knees. The hood on the old riding mower gaped open. He saw the air filter and a Mason jar tipped into the grass. "Did you pour gasoline in the carburetor?"

A dirty-white garbage truck pulled up, hissing its brakes.

"Where's my hat?" said Chester.

"Heck, I was gonna cut the grass for you."

"Bobby!" said Clara. "Tell the garbage man to wait." The screen door slammed.

"Got a cut on your arm, there." Bobby scratched his thigh.

The garbage man limped over, a wad of gauze with a brown stain clinging to his swollen jaw. "He need some oxygen?"

"You got some?" said Bobby.

"What?" said the garbage man.

"Bobby! Got chicken skins in it." Clara dangled a plastic bag of trash off the deck. "Lord, I thought he was dead. You reckon he needs an X-ray?"

Bobby's chest heaved as he tossed the sack into the garbage truck's maw. An army of maggots writhed in a scoop of milky liquid. A cockroach wiggled its feelers at him.

"Hey, Bobby," said the cockroach. "Missed you in church on Sunday."

"Did you learn anything new?" The garbage smelled like the river in Bangkok, and he gagged.

"Same old, same old," said the cockroach.

"Two for a dollar," said Bobby.

The next day, Bobby drove his grandparents' long car past their old cabin and turned into a dirt driveway. They wanted to visit their old neighbors, the Suggs, who they had lived next to for thirty years before moving into town. From what Bobby knew about Harold Suggs' new caretaker, Sammy Dushane, he might just punch his lights out. Mr. Harold deserved better. He'd had a stroke and the last thing he needed was a drug-dealing do-nothing taking care of him.

Beneath a mint-blue sky, the Suggs' square brick house drooped in the shade of the towering pines. Pine straw matted the roof, raisined with pinecones. The Cadillac stuck out from the carport like always, its maroon trunk faded pink. A shed sat off to the side behind the house, built after the old barn burned when Bobby was seventeen. Cicadas squalled like boiled babies from the surrounding woods.

"Watch out," said Bobby. He steadied Clara and guided her around an anthill spilling onto a colicky sidewalk. Somebody had jammed a banana into the fine red dirt. He paused, syncing the cicadas' heady drone to the grind of heavy guitars in his head.

"Fire ants," said Chester, coming up from behind.

"Red ants, yellow banana," said Bobby. He peered in the sliding door and saw Harold's wife Nadine tipped back in her recliner, the TV rumbling from within. He'd heard stories of how she used to be a hot babe when she was younger.

Nadine spied Bobby and fumbled for the stickshift on the side of the chair. "Sammy!" She hammered on the wooden lever and knocked her aluminum cane to the floor. "Well, foot."

Bobby slid the door open. The Suggs' kitchen, den, and living room ran together. He recognized Sammy Dushane coming through the back, trailing a cloud of smoke, just like high school. Sammy wore a white t-shirt with a pocket. He lived just outside Kuhlman at Candy Mountain apartments, a welfare complex dropped into a cow pasture where the old cotton gin used to be. His face looked forty, his eyes about eighteen, cowering beneath a mold of couch-brown hair that lay like plastic. The big-screen TV blared breaking news from the Iraq War, rehashing footage of Saddam Hussein's statue bending lower and lower. Harold snored in his recliner, oblivious to his company.

Sammy dotted Harold on the temples with his fingertips. "Hey, old man!"

"Harold! Wake up! Chester and Clara's come to visit!" Nadine rapped a glass of warm water on the lamp table and grinned. "How you, Bobby?"

"Pretty good."

Harold flinched. "Well, hey!" The stroke had knocked out his left side, but his gravelly voice still boomed, although with a slur. "Honey, why didn't you wake me?"

"Harold, I just did!" A tight yellow shift drew Nadine's scarred knees together.

"Chester, how the dickens are you?" Harold's head rested lower than his feet in the laid-back recliner.

"Alright, just out to see the country and stopped by." Chester leaned on his walking stick.

"And Clara? Come here and give me a hug." Harold grabbed the end of an armrest, pulled, and grunted. "Man, somebody get me the hell up!"

Everybody looked at Bobby and then at Sammy. Sammy had the face of a desert drifter is what Nadine had told Clara on the phone. Sammy flared his nostrils and pushed Harold's recliner vertical.

"Boy, you smell like cigarettes." Harold itched his leg through his pajama bottom.

"Y'all get a chair from the kitchen," said Nadine. She tugged at Harold's folded wheelchair.

"I'll get him in the wheelchair," said Bobby.

"No, he don't like that chair," said Sammy. "He likes to stay in that recliner. Don't you, Harold?"

"I'd like to get the hell up." Harold narrowed his eyes, then a lost look crossed his face. "Honey, did you make my lunch?"

"What? You done had a big lunch. Maybe Sammy'll make you a sandwich."

Harold gazed through the sliding glass door. "We got any more tomatoes?"

Bobby pulled the wheelchair next to the recliner. He noticed shaving cream in Sammy's ear.

"Lock them wheels," said Sammy. "Unless you want to lay him in the floor."

"I'll lock *your* wheels." Bobby felt purposeful, giddy.

"Bobby, maybe you ought to let Sammy handle it," said Clara.

"You ready, Mr. Harold. I'll count to three." Bobby pivoted Harold on his good leg and swung him into the wheelchair.

Sammy frowned, retreated to the kitchen, and pushed some dirty glasses around on the counter.

With Harold taken care of, Bobby pulled a couple of chairs in for Clara and Chester. He'd decided in the past two minutes that he'd move in and take care of Mr. Suggs and that Sammy had to go, hard luck be damned. He watched Sammy sulk for a minute and then wandered outside to breathe in his old stomping grounds. He sauntered over to his grandparents' old cabin. A retired nun had bought it with cash. He remembered the letter in the car from the nurse, Silliporn.

2-1, 2003

To Bobby Hartwig,

Hello you! I worry you and have some news because you not send me your telephone. Oh you are so making sad all times Bobby. You say enjoy my life and how? Yes I am pregnant and you are asking who is the father! Now I working some days less in the clinic but so many new nurses, and old ones too. My job good one but I fearing to lose it. Bobby you help me! My life is a better one before I meet you and now all changed and lonely and what do? Bobby Hartwig, I find you because I cannot wait. Hard get visa for USA, but I have some money...

He walked back and pulled out the photo she'd sent. It smelled like seashells and disco. His heart lifted and his breath with it. Curried skin browned in the hot Bangkok sun. Thick black hair sweeping over the top of her head, gathered in back, a loose strand covering her ear. Her perfect eyebrows making her look twelve even though she was twenty. Her trusting smile blanking the fear in his belly. Her breasts firm, swinging out ever so slightly when she moved. Yes, he'd met her the day before he was kicked out of the Peace Corps, had been struck by her presence at the AIDS hospice as she tended the dying, the poorest of the poor. And now she was pregnant with his child. The letter said so. He felt lost, tiny, and helpless. He counted on his fingers again. By now she was in her what? ninth or tenth month? *Jesus, Mary, Mother of God.*

A plug of pinecone thunked the hood as he walked away from the car. He folded the letter, pulled the yellow banana from the red dirt, and watched the ants go crazy. He smelled pine, pond, *lemongrass?* and that faint twinge of something burned.

After visiting the Suggs with his grandparents, Bobby had called Nadine with the good news that he wanted to move in and take care of Harold. His grandparents were getting up in years but were still able to care for themselves. He couldn't stand Sammy Dushane and from what he could tell, neither did Mr. Harold. Nadine was all for it, especially since all Bobby wanted was room and board. The next day, with Sammy standing right there beside her,

Nadine told Harold about Bobby moving in. A fly floundered through her wild ivory hair. Harold grunted his approval, staring out through the sliding glass door, but Sammy was caught off guard.

"What?" said Sammy.

The story on Sammy was that after his mama fell in a hay baler, he'd shown up at Child Heaven, the orphanage in Kuhlman run by Pastor Daly or PD as he was known to the Kuhlman police. Through the years, Sammy had wallowed through beatings and marathon cassette-tape sessions of the "Christian Jew Hour," never managing to make it back to the outside. Just prior to a promising visit by an older couple from Blowing Rock, North Carolina, he had developed a fulminating case of pink eye that melted his sly face into the gaze of a roasted suckling pig. He just looked too awful to adopt that day. Otherwise, he was generally considered good-looking, better looking even than Pastor Daly, who imagined himself a cross between Elvis and Jesus.

Sammy put his hand on his hip. "What did you say about Bobby Hartwig? Moving in here?" He'd rolled in late, as usual, in his busted-up minivan. He nibbled a raw pecan and scratched his thick sideburns. He wouldn't spend the night like Nadine wanted. "Bobby Hartwig? With the red hair? Hell he's as crazy as his daddy was."

Harold sat stone-faced in his hospital bed. He wore the heavy plaid shirt he'd slept in. A full plastic urinal dangled from the rail, and a thin blue pad hung off the mattress.

"Hell, he ain't no kid. He's damn near thirty years old," said Nadine. "I done talked to my daughter Debbie and she knows to send you a check for last week. And his hair ain't red. It's a funny kind of cedar color."

"What about paying me for today?"

"You ain't done nothing today," said Nadine.

"Honey?" said Harold.

"Hell, Bobby looked like he was on drugs." Sammy rocked her recliner from behind and stared at the TV. "You can't just send me out the door like this. I'm trying to do right these days."

Nadine looked at her feet. She hadn't thought through this part. "Bobby's gonna work for free. He's practically a doctor and our families have known each other since... since 1965. Plus, you steal, and you smoke when you ought to be working." She shuffled toward Harold's bed in the den.

Sammy pressed his hands to the sliding glass door. He stared at the front yard filled with stumps and trees. "You still calling me a thief! I drive out here and listen to you bitch all day!"

"Boy, I'll break your neck." Harold's voice resonated like there was no furniture in the room. His eyes chiseled Sammy a cheap tombstone. "Nadine, get my pistol."

Nadine huddled at the open back door,

remembering the rusty ax leaning against the house. "Get on out, Sammy Dushane. I'm calling the sheriff." She eyed the path to the phone.

From the driveway, a car door slammed.

"Damn you to hell," said Sammy.

Nadine speed-hobbled to the kitchen, dropped her glasses, and squinted to dial.

"Knock, knock!"

"Bobby, get in here!" said Nadine.

"What the hell's going on?" Bobby saw Sammy disappear through the sliding glass door.

"Let him go," said Nadine. Her false teeth wobbled in her mouth.

"Bobby, get my pistol, would you?" said Harold.

Bobby watched Sammy's minivan lurch backwards into the road. "I remember when he stole my glasses, not more than two days after I transferred into Kuhlman High School. Took 'em out of my gym locker. Told me that same day that he'd been to the eye doctor and had a pair of glasses that looked just like mine. I couldn't believe it."

"He stole your glasses?" said Nadine.

"Sure did, and wore them to school the next day. I think he believed it himself. The orphanage screwed him up."

"Well, he never did have a good life," said Harold. "From what I know." His head drooped.

Bobby took stock of the kitchen sink full of dirty plates and cups, the piles of wadded, dirty sheets, and put his things away in the tiny back bedroom, including his extra pair of jeans, his CBGB t-shirt, and two novels, both by dead Russians. His nursing license had expired, but he knew what Harold needed and had a plan. His first day passed in a blur, cleaning the house, getting Harold outside into the sun, and cooking a simple dinner of macaroni and cheese and fried ham. He imagined a small cabin of his own, Silliporn in a hammock, their love child clutching at white clover. He imagined water bills, little jars of baby food, and felt a dryness in his throat.

"You need the restroom before I get you in the bed?" said Bobby. Harold's thick gray hair resembled cut felt.

Wheel of Fortune was on. "The category is *foreign word*," said Pat Sajak. Debbie from Phoenix spun.

"Harold, get on the toilet," said Nadine.

"There is one T," said Pat.

"I'll get on it when I damn want to." Slumping in his wheelchair, Harold leaned forward.

"Harold, you're a paralytic."

"There is no P."

"The hell I can't. I can still move."

"Mr. Harold, let me help you. I want to help you."

"Bobby, I've had a long day."

"One S," said Pat.

"Hmm…T, S," said Delores from Wichita.

"Long day?" said Nadine. "Who's been

cooking and washing your sheets all day?"

"Not you, honey."

"All right, let's get you in bed," said Bobby.

"Don't drop me."

"Come on, big money," said Bobby.

Nadine's recliner faced away from the hospital bed. She tilted on her left side and watched Bobby maneuver Harold. She squinted and pushed her uppers in and out with her tongue. "You reckon that was Sammy calling during supper?"

"I don't know." Bobby lowered the bed. He locked the chair wheels, flipped the feet to the side, and hugged Harold under the armpits. "On three, big man."

"There is no R."

Harold pushed up on his good leg, moaned, and faltered. He stood a good five inches taller than Bobby. "Oh!"

"Shut up, Harold. He ain't gonna drop you. You gonna stretch him out, Bobby?"

"Well, that's what I'm about to do right now."

"I'd like to buy a vowel."

Nadine settled in her chair and turned up the volume. The cordless phone rang.

"I'd like to solve the puzzle."

Nadine changed the channel.

"Gonna start with your legs." Bobby took the paralyzed leg and bent it toward Harold's chest.

"Oh! Damn, man, take it easy."

Bobby backed off and decided to cut the

session short, to start off slow since it didn't look like Sammy had been keeping Harold limber at all. He propped him on his side with a blue foam wedge and raised the rails. "You need some water?" he said, but Harold was already snoring.

The cuckoo clock on the wall showed seven-thirty. The reality of long nights in the tiny back bedroom snuck up on Bobby. He had a needle and some black shoe polish in his room. He might as well get started on the tattoo he'd imagined while flat on his back on the pier in Bangkok. He turned off the ceiling light over Harold and switched on the wooden lamp with horses running on its shade. The 30-watt bulb soaked black shadows around Harold's bed. With Nadine jabbering on the phone to her buddy Claudette, Bobby said goodnight and closed his door.

He pulled out the photograph of Silliporn and felt the edges. Her dark eyes beneath perfect eyebrows. They looked into his soul. Was he really the father of her child? He wanted it to be so. He would need a real job, insurance, daycare. If he married her, would she be allowed to stay in the US? A charge settled between his stomach and backbone as he lay back on the spread.

Outside, cicadas trilled in the early morning heat. The toilet lid slammed in the tiny bathroom between Bobby's bedroom and Nadine's. She banged her cane against the waste bin and flushed the toilet twice. *Why don't he get the hell up?*

Bobby lingered on the edge of the bed and pulled on his old jeans. His neck hurt from the mushy mattress.

"Coffee's on!" Nadine shuffled through the house with a sale paper stuck to her houseshoe and stared at Harold. He was on his back with his chin propped in his good hand.

"I got to go." Harold spoke to the room.

Bobby walked in, rubbing his head. He saw the urinal half full, half spilled on the bed. "Crap. I'm sorry, Mr. Harold. Let's get you out of bed."

"Harold, can't Bobby get his coffee first?" said Nadine. "He just got up."

"I've got an urgency," said Harold.

Bobby cranked up the head of the bed, emptied the urinal, picked up the sheet, and covered Harold. He swung Harold's legs around. The wheelchair was just out of reach, and Harold teetered on the edge of the bed.

"Don't drop me."

"I'm not gonna drop you." The urinal bounced on the floor.

"Hell, man, be careful."

Nadine glued the phone to her face. "Claudette, I don't think Bobby checked on him all night." She squinted into an imaginary sun.

Bobby made a face. He got Harold in the chair and wheeled him into the restroom. Harold slumped on the toilet with his good hand resting on the handrail, fighting the gravity of his dragging left side.

"Call me when you're ready."

"Bobby, my feet's cold."

Bobby found a pair of gray socks, but then Harold's feet slipped on the cool tile. "Hold on."

"Bobby, I need some privacy."

Bobby yelled over his shoulder. "He got any slippers?"

"What!"

"Any slippers? His feet're cold."

"Look under my bed!"

"My feet's cold."

"Hold on, Mr. Harold. I'll be right back."

Nadine's king-size bed spread from wall to wall. The room smelled like penicillin and tired feet. On his knees, Bobby saw piles of stuff under the steel mattress frame. He pulled out a plastic shoebox filled with old pennies in slotted cards, examined a case of vanilla Ensure that'd expired a year ago, and found a new pair of men's slippers with a note from Harold's daughter wishing him a happy birthday. He then discovered a mammoth .45 with one bullet in the final chamber, silver with a black handle.

"Four hundred and fifty horsepower of maximum destruction," said Bobby to the gun. "Found the slippers!" He sat with his back against the bed, wondering what it would be like to get old, to be at the mercy of a caretaker. Even though Harold'd had a stroke, he was strong, filled with the desire to pass his days as he saw fit. Harold deserved Bobby's best. Bobby thought about his father, the photograph of him on an old bicycle, Bobby in a basket on the back. His father's wide grin, the beginning of a hollowness to the eyes.

The first couple of days went "okay," Bobby had told his grandfather. Bobby was easing into a routine with Harold and learning how to side-step Nadine when needed. The nurse came every two weeks to check Harold's blood-thinner level and write things down, but a nurse's aide, Rochelle, came twice a week to give him a bath. The doorbell rang.

"Hey Rochelle," said Nadine. "Come on in."

Short and lumpy, Rochelle wore white jeans and a clingy knit shirt. "Where's my baby this morning?" She dropped a big black purse on the table. A heavy keyring slunked to the floor. She ignored Bobby, spied Harold in the bathroom, and glanced at her tiny watch. "Honey, we got to get you scrubbed."

"Hey," said Harold. "How're you, Rochelle?"

"Running late. Got behind a log truck on these awful roads." She ran the water hot, rummaged for the wash pan, and found the liquid soap.

"Rochelle, this here's Bobby," said Nadine.

"Well, hey." She arranged her bath stuff on

the overbed table. "You done run Sammy off?"

"I think he ran himself off. Can I help you?"

"Help me? Well, Sammy said he could get me a computer real cheap. My daughter needs a computer and I don't know the first thing about it."

"Rochelle," said Harold. "I sure do need a bath."

Rochelle draped a blue pad over the clean sheet. "Just put him on up."

Bobby helped Harold sprawl on the bed with a towel over his middle. Rochelle got to work.

"Oh! Damn, Rochelle."

"Too hot, baby? That's what kills them germs." She scrubbed his face, bringing the blood to the surface.

"Hell!"

Rochelle chuckled, dipped her rag, wrung it, and went after his ears. "Hold still. I can't wash a wiggle worm."

Harold sputtered. Nadine stood back, leaning on her cane, fascinated, imagining someone giving her a bath. She grinned at Bobby toting dirty sheets and towels to the washing machine in the crammed garage.

Rochelle held Harold on his side with one hand and bathed the red creases on his back with the other. "You miss old Sammy?"

"Sammy? God help the poor bastard."

Rochelle laughed. "Where am I gonna get a computer then?"

"Sammy'll steal you blind, girl," said Nadine. "Bobby here's nearly a doctor and he don't smoke."

"Hmm? I wonder, though, if he can get me a computer for two hundred dollars. Roll on back now, Mr. Suggs." The pan of water sloshed filmy and lukewarm. She squeezed the rag and scoured Harold's arms, hands, and fingers.

Resigned to his fate, he watched Rochelle's bosom heave and wobble inside her maroon scrub top. "I'm growing a new leg." His eyebrows went up.

Rochelle pulled the towel back across his middle and rolled her eyes.

Rochelle brushed Harold's thick hair, combing it back to lend his angular face a younger look. His smooth cheeks looked like a little boy's ready for a school picture.

"That's a good looking man," said Rochelle.

"I'll get him outside today," said Bobby. "You want to, Mr. Harold? Get outside and get some sun?"

"Is it cold?" said Harold.

"Heck no, it's warm," said Bobby.

"I want to plant my tomatoes."

"Maybe we can look over the garden."

Rochelle packed away the plastic washpan and rattled her keys. "I got to be moving, y'all."

"Bye, Rochelle," said Nadine. "I'm sure Bobby here knows more about computers than old Sammy."

"Computers?" said Bobby.

"I need the bathroom," said Harold.

"Oh hell, Harold, what's wrong with you?" said Nadine.

Harold examined his paralyzed hand.

"I'll see y'all later."

Bobby rolled Harold into the bathroom while Nadine kicked a laundry basket into the kitchen. "Mr. Harold, holler for me when you're ready." The phone rang.

"Hey Claudette," said Nadine. Claudette was a card buddy from days gone by. Nadine covered the receiver. "While you're resting, Bobby." She pointed at the piled laundry basket with her cane.

Coffee grounds smeared the counter and stove. He stepped on a piece of cornbread from the night before. "Well shit." He looked in the dark fridge at the buttermilk, a pitcher of sweet tea, and a dozen plastic containers of leftovers. He closed the door and put some dirty plates in the sink. Just for the hell of it, he opened the dishwasher and stared at the cans of food and Ensure in there. It had been broken since Harold's stroke.

"That's right. Bobby. The Hartwigs' grandson," said Nadine. "Used to stay summers out here when they lived next door. Rode that orange minibike into the pond one time and nearly drowned. Real skinny. Kind of got a sharp nose on him."

Bobby checked the coffee maker and felt the outline of his nose. He'd started a tattoo on his bicep with the shoe polish, the idea he'd had in Thailand.

"Honey, I'm done!"

Nadine clamped her hand over the receiver. "Hey, Bobby, don't make more coffee…Harold! Bobby's coming…Claudette, he won't call Bobby. Calls me instead."

Bobby turned on the warmer under the dirty pot and squeaked past Nadine sitting spraddle-legged in a swivel chair. The chairs kind of matched the marigold stove.

"You ready, Mr. Harold?"

"I want Nadine. Honey!"

"Mr. Harold, Mrs. Nadine's on the phone."

"Who with?" His eyes ran to slits. "Is it Sammy?"

"No. A lady friend I think."

"Honey!" Harold shouted through Bobby. The bathroom had been put in since the stroke. The walk-in shower looked unused and echoed every little peep.

Bobby stepped back. "I'll be right there in the living room. Just call me when you're ready." He watched TV with the volume low. It was a morning show. A soldier's pregnant wife spoke to the clean-faced host. He had a surprise for her. She was trembling. A man with no legs said Hello from a hospital bed in Germany.

Bobby remembered one of his ICU patients, Mrs. Massey. She'd had a heart attack massive enough to kill an elephant. But she hadn't realized she'd had a heart attack. That was the trick. She was schizophrenic and bipolar. Thirty years of Thorazine and lithium had pickled her brain. She still thought she was a sales girl at

Parisians and liked to hold a red comb. Her skin was fleshy and snow white. When she spoke, the words labored out coated with a flat icing of hopefulness. "I need some scissors," she would tell Bobby, while tugging at her wrist restraints. "I need to cut these strings." She thought the Swan-Ganz line that reached into her heart through her subclavian vein was a long yellow bug. When Bobby pushed in syringes of ice-cold saline to measure her cardiac output, her eyes would get bigger than moons, and she'd make an awful low moan like a mole being slowly crushed.

"Honey, come here and wipe me!"

Bobby glanced at Nadine in the kitchen.

Her teeth shuffled before she could respond. "Harold, hold on! Claudette, let me call you back." She struggled to stand and thrashed the table legs with her cane. Claudette's husband Ike was a retired bigshot from the County landfill. Nadine clanked by Bobby, hopping with her bad hip. She'd already had both knees replaced.

"Babydoll?" said Harold. He looked like a whipped cocker spaniel.

"Oh Lord. Bend over." She wadded toilet paper around her hand like a glove. "Bobby!"

"I'm here."

She flushed and swiped her hands on a yellow hand towel. "He's needing his breakfast. I reckon I'll just eat what he eats." She limped into the living room and fell into the recliner with a sigh.

A distant memory crossed Harold's face and he locked eyes with Bobby. "Was it you who burned my barn down?"

Bobby's face turned red. He could still smell the smoke, the burning metal, the air filled with delicate wisps of burned hay. His father tumbling from the loft, naked.

Driving to his grandparents' house for his weekend break, about thirty minutes on back roads, Bobby passed the gated monastery entrance that'd always been there. He'd been raised Baptist like most everybody else and thought of the monks and nuns who lived there as characters from *The Hobbit*.

He pulled into the driveway. A Braves game ran just shy of full volume as he walked in.

"How'd it go?" said Clara. "Chester…Chester! Turn it down."

"Alright, I guess." Bobby settled on the couch.

"A woman called for you." She wiggled her toes in her white socks. "Chester couldn't hear so well."

"Who was it?"

Chester cleared his throat. "Sounded like a colored woman. Said her name was Shreveport." He tapped his fingers on the armrests.

"Shreveport? What'd she want?"

"She wanted you. Look! He missed that ball. Easy as pie." Clara clapped her hands.

"He don't miss many," said Chester.

Bobby glanced at the slow-motion replay,

a hard shot to third base. "I see poison ivy's getting on the back steps."

"Got her number here." Chester fumbled in a small bookshelf. "Awful long one."

"Honey, it's on your glasses."

"Oh." He retrieved a piece of envelope stuck in his glasses' frame that he used to shade his eyes.

"There's something else," said Clara.

Bobby looked at the number scrawled in pencil on the paper. The battery-operated clock clicked over the TV. His heart skipped a beat. "Where's Merk?" He headed for the door, looking for his cat.

"He'd crawled up in the driveway, son." Chester grimaced. "I found him like that."

"When?"

"Yesterday. I was always afraid he'd get hit," said Clara. "Mashed up by a car."

Bobby leaned against the door. He'd adopted Merk. Merk'd had one eye and scars all over his head.

"You left the hospital that one time because you was worried about him. Remember that? Had the police looking for you," said Clara.

"I put him in a bag." Chester put his footrest down. "In the basement, where it's cool. Son..."

Bobby had read a long ad in the classifieds about this cat who needed a home. The woman who ran the ad, Madeline Mix, rescued strays. Bobby had signed a long contract, promising to never let Merk out of the house. Mrs. Mix lay in bed with new titanium hips and lectured him on vaccinations, fresh foods, and cat love. A young woman in a lab coat had brought her a cup of pills and then given Merk a rabies shot.

The screen door air-braked shut behind Bobby.

Twenty minutes later, Clara stepped onto the deck and watched Bobby pat the dirt with a shovel. Her doo was a perfect lightbulb of silvery black hair. Tomorrow was church. "That's not too close to the gas line is it?"

"No." He looked around for stones to mark the grave.

"You put him in that little flower bed didn't you? With them strawberries." She waved at the neighbor across the road. She wondered where Bobby would be if he hadn't done that volunteer work in China or Taiwan or wherever it was he'd gone. "Bobby, you want me to fix some chicken and dumplings?"

He leaned on the shovel half buried in the mound of red dirt. "Sure."

"Come on in and watch the game. Maddux is pitching." She thought about how trouble followed from generation to generation just like the Bible said. "Now I don't want you going out tonight. I'll worry about you."

Bobby kicked a dirt clod. "Let me poison that ivy first." A small cloud drifted in a dimming purply sky. A mockingbird with a grass snake in its mouth lit on the neighbor's mailbox. An ice cream truck played the "Entertainer" from a block away. The happy-go-lucky piano notes tightened the air, made it harder to breathe. He put the shovel away and headed back inside. He might as well watch the ballgame and relax until he drove back to the Suggs the next day. He remembered Chester teaching him how to shoot a .22 rifle, the summers fishing, the fried okra and rice puddings. Clara made a killer rice pudding and left out the raisins to suit Bobby. If something were to happen to either of them, he would have to leave the Suggs. They had always been such cornerstones of his existence. The thought of them gone made his legs feel weak.

Sunday bloomed blue and stiff, warm to the touch with a tinge of malaise. The Suggs' screen door slammed.

"Bobby, you back?" Harold strained his eyes toward the kitchen.

"Hey, Mr. Harold." Bobby pressed his hand against the fridge. He saw Harold craning his neck, his graying head of hair above the recliner.

Nadine blocked Bobby's progress. "Sammy said he's gonna make you pay. He came by and raised hell. He's crazier than a June bug in a paper sack." Nadine wore bright red lipstick with a smear on her dentures.

"Let him try. Where does he live again? *Candyland?*"

"Candy Mountain," said Nadine. "Them welfare apartments for lazy people. Where the old cotton gin used to be that Harold ran. Sammy's a lowdown yellow-bellied snake."

Bobby frowned. "Let me get over here and say hello to Mr. Harold."

"We got laundry since you been gone, Bobby. With my knees, I can't wash like I used to."

"Bobby, please get this damn contraption off me." Harold squirmed in the recliner wearing a giant blue pad pinned like a diaper. His legs looked like toothpicks. A crocheted brown and orange blanket hung off his shoulder.

"I had to put that on him, Bobby. I can't lift him like you can. I sure am glad to see you, boy. I was afraid Sammy had a gun."

"Honey!" said Harold. "You need to put my pistol where I can reach it."

"Don't worry about that," said Bobby. "Let's get you in some sweat pants. You want the red ones?"

"Yeah. There some football games on, Bobby?"

Nadine leaned on her cane in the kitchen. "Harold, you done watched the Super Bowl. You know football's done over."

"I bought three tomato plants, big ones," said Bobby. He remembered watching Harold manhandle a rear-tine tiller, swinging it around to start a new row in the garden below the road. Those days were gone.

"I sure need to plant my tomatoes. Bobby, is my plow in the shed?"

"Bobby, turn down that damn TV." Nadine punched the phone and squinted. "Hey, Claudette."

Bobby dressed Harold, handed him a can of vanilla Ensure with a straw and rolled him out the back door in his wheelchair. He noticed the thinness of the skin on Harold's hands, the age spots. The outside air struck Bobby as agreeable, almost overpowering in its electric warmth and light. Bobby took a deep breath and regained his balance.

"Mr. Harold, let's get you some exercise before lunch." Bobby wheeled him to the front yard onto the raised cement shuffleboard court, half shaded in the pines. A wooden rail ran the perimeter. Nadine had made Harold build it after he retired, hoping to get Claudette and her husband Ike over more often. "I'll lift you up, and I want you to grab the rail. Let's give it a whirl."

"Bobby, I remember your crazy daddy. He liked to put sprinkle cheese on his eggs. Had a good heart, though—least until the war got hold of him."

Bobby paused, soaking in the detail. His dad had always put sprinkle cheese on just about everything. He pinched his lips and sighed.

A horn blew.

"Who the hell is that?" said Harold.

"When I say three, pull on the rail and push up on your good leg." Bobby grabbed Harold under the arms. "One, two, three."

"Oh my God, Bobby." Harold fell against the rail like he'd huffed paint on a roller coaster.

Bobby hooked his left arm. "Okay, back in

the chair."

Harold slumped and slid. His sweat pants squirreled a path through his privates. "Nadine!"

The red truck passed again and slowed in front of the house next door, backed, and stopped. Bobby saw Sammy Dushane in a tanktop with a two-by-four coming across the yard. It might as well have been that first day at Kuhlman High School—Bobby the new kid as always, moving into town smack dab in the middle of the school year, just like the rest of his humpteen dozen jolting moves across the country.

Bobby had always dreaded that first day, especially gym class. He knew from vast experience that gym class exercised demons. God had created gym class on a bad day. The dark, tiled dressing room with brown steel lockers. Wads of gum in the urinal. The tension, sitting there on the wooden bench swaddled in decades of body stench, waiting for the teacher with a whistle to call roll. The dirty jock strap came from behind then over his head. Bobby leaped, banged his head on a locker. Zip, Sammy didn't have a chance once Bobby got him doubled over, knees to his head, had him by the back of his hair, knees to the face, knees to the head. And now here was Sammy again, but this time Bobby could see him coming, in slow motion this time, clear, like watching an after-school TV movie.

"Bobby?" said Harold.

The day's heat had crept into the shade like a sick kitten. The cicadas' buzz swung drunk monkey from one patch of pines to the next. Sammy's narrow shoulders. A backwards ball-cap and old combat boots.

Bobby stumbled off the shuffleboard court, watching Sammy advance one frame at a time. "Get the fuck outta here!" Bobby felt his throat tighten and gripped a rusty ball-peen hammer he'd grabbed from the rail.

Sammy glanced back at the truck drifting into the grass. He swapped the board back and forth. Bobby circled.

Harold unlocked the right wheel and the chair swung out.

"You fucked up everything," said Sammy and swung the board at Bobby.

The truck's left rear wheel dropped into a hole by the drainpipe. Bobby ducked, Harold tipped over, and Bobby scrambled to catch the wheelchair. Harold's head banged the top rail.

"Mother of God!" said Harold.

The board bounced off Bobby's left arm and thigh. He yelled, spun, and swung the hammer wild. Five seconds of silence erupted into a cry of extreme hurt.

Inside, Nadine gabbed on the phone with Claudette while they watched *The Price is Right.*

"Hell, Claudette, Bobby sleeps as much as Harold. Once he gets Harold to bed, he disappears into his room...That's it, you just can't get good help these days. Lord almighty, Claudette, look at that fat bastard coming down the aisle…" Nadine dropped the phone. A man with a bloody face was smearing red handprints on the sliding glass door.

Bobby watched Sammy carom off the little porch and run back toward the road. His forearm throbbed.

Harold touched the bloody spot on his head.

"You okay?" said Bobby.

Sammy staggered to the truck and slid into the driver's seat. The truck's rear wheel spun against the pipe, spewing a white cloud of smoking rubber.

"An angry tire," said Bobby.

"I guess Sammy really does love Nadine," said Harold.

Bobby jostled Harold to the back door in his chair, his heart thudding, and stopped to catch his breath.

"Bobby!" Nadine yelled from her bedroom. Hunched on her hands and knees, with her nightgown above her waist, she couldn't get up. The gun wasn't where it was supposed to be.

"Jesus Christ, you alright?" He looked away from her marbled buttocks covered with small bruises.

"Get me up!"

He pulled her gown down. "I'm gonna grab you under the arms and then lay you on the bed."

"Where's Harold? Is he dead?"

"He ain't dead."

Nadine fell face first into a wad of bed-clothes. "Shit on toast, Bobby! Flip me over!"

"Bobby!" Harold yelled from the den. Blood trickled from a long paper-thin piece of skin shoved back at his hairline.

Bobby hobbled back to the den. "Just a cut. Just a cut." He dabbed Harold's face with a handtowel. "Damn blood thinners."

"You gonna call the sheriff?" Nadine held to the wall and struggled for breath.

"Give me the phone," said Harold.

Nadine limped to the glass door. "Who the hell was that?"

"That was Sammy," said Bobby.

"Sammy? You sure?"

"Sammy's an orphan," said Harold.

"Aren't we all?" said Bobby.

Within ten minutes, a patrol car pulled into the driveway next door as an ambulance bellowed in the distance. The neighbor, the retired nun, had called 911. Bobby rolled Harold into the kitchen and handed Nadine a piece of gauze soaked in peroxide. "Hold this on his head."

Sammy had been there that night the barn burned, the last night Bobby saw his dad alive. Despite the rough start in the gym locker room, Sammy and Bobby had started hanging out after school. Bobby's dad Robert had taken Sammy in, had felt sorry for him being the oldest orphan at Child Heaven, and had begun to imagine him as his own son or so it had seemed.

Harold looked at Nadine sideways. "Honey, do you love me?"

"Shut your pie hole and put this on your damn head." She assumed a serious look. "I hope Sammy ain't told the law we ain't paid him."

"Paid him for what?" said Harold.

Sheriff Earl Gaslight stepped into the yard with a porkchop-hand on his textured-grip pistol. Bobby went out the glass door.

"Hold it right there, Bud," said Sheriff Gaslight. "Go ahead and put your haynes out where I can see 'em."

"My haynes?" said Bobby.

"Haynes out!" Gaslight assumed the pose.

Bobby lifted his hands. He glimpsed the neighbor lady peeping around the corner of the old cabin next door. "Did you catch him?"

"Walk on down them steps," said Gaslight. He spread about as wide as he was tall. The radio on his shoulder crackled and buzzed.

Bobby winced and touched his thigh.

"Haynes up!"

"Up or out?" Bobby looked to the sky for answers, listened to the rising cicada chatter for clues.

Gaslight swept the yard with his gun and looked in the trees.

"You know he tried to bust my brains out?" said Bobby. "Hurt Mr. Harold, too." He stepped on the banana, very black now. It squirted. An ambulance shuddered to a stop on the road.

"See down," said Gaslight.

"Do what?" Bobby swung his foot through the mound of red dirt and ants swarmed his banana-creamed shoe.

"Haynes up! See down!" Gaslight cocked his revolver. "On the groan!"

Bobby kicked off his shoe and let his hands drop. The ants breached his ankle sock. They had been friends, he and Sammy, plugging anthills with cherry bombs. The red dust flying. Hot summers playing cards late into the night. Pink Floyd on the radio.

"Hey!" said Nadine.

Two paramedics expanded a stretcher like an ironing board. Gaslight spun. He spotted the woman next door, holding what looked to be a broom. His eye caught a squirrel jumping from a pine tree to the roof of the Suggs' house. He whirled back to Bobby whose hands weren't where they were supposed to be.

"Haynes up, boy!"

"You got it all wrong!" said Nadine.

A shot cracked through the pines, and the cicadas lulled for a good thirty seconds. On his back, Bobby forgot about the ants. Drifting, the world just drifted along, and there it was again, the sky. Contrails crossing, the same as in Bangkok, but sharper this time. *I'm looking through a hole in the sky…*That plodding guitar that pulled on his guts. It wasn't losing his father that bothered Bobby so much as losing him over and over again, to the tours of duty in Germany, Vietnam, and then that night the damn barn went down in flames, his dad falling out of the loft at his feet, a rope around his neck, and that other silhouette he'd seen moving with purpose in the smoke. Sammy Dushane.

Crowded in the kitchen, Sheriff Gaslight collected his thoughts. He dwelled on his asshole uncle, the county judge who'd pretty much groomed him to be Sheriff, a kind of repayment for past wrongs. He hated how he had to cover up for the Judge, produce fake search warrants, arrest decent folks just because they ran afoul of his uncle. That morning, Gaslight'd had too much coffee and accidentally tasered himself during a public safety demonstration at the elementary school.

Gaslight cleared his throat. "You want to press charges, Mrs. Suggs? Looks like he don't want to." He nodded at Bobby and sipped a glass of sweet tea. "They got him located over at Candy Mountain, so I got to get on over and get his story. If it is Sammy Dushane, he ain't got a leg to stand on. Tell you what, if I have to bust him for dope one more time, he'll get locked up for good."

"I just say let it go," said Bobby.

"Well, don't matter no how. I need to look him in the eye anyway." Gaslight looked thoughtful. "You know, Bobby, I knew your daddy. Went to high school with him. He never turn up?"

Bobby shook his head.

"Sammy was hopped up on dope," said Harold. A strap of white gauze circled his head.

"Well, Mr. Suggs, you sure you don't need the hospital?" said Gaslight.

"Hospital? Hell no."

Gaslight laughed and banged his tumbler on the table. "Well, let me get on over to them apartments and see what trouble looks like."

"Bobby, you gonna get that blood off the door before it dries hard?" said Nadine.

"Yes ma'am. You got any more glass cleaner?"

"No. Why don't you just use a rag?"

"Why don't you use the hose, Bobby?" said Harold.

Bobby nodded and slid the door open. On the glass, the two sets of bloody handprints looked nearly identical, the left hand showing only fingertips and the right a perfect impression of a palm. Bobby examined the creases, the distinct fingerprint whorls. He resisted an urge to smell the blood. He looked across the road to the pond and poor old Mrs. Massey materialized from nothing.

After two weeks in the coronary care unit, Mrs. Massey still had not died like everyone expected. Her heart was a ragged mess, going in and out of a stupendous variety of arrhythmias. The prolonged QT intervals on her electrocardiogram indicated imminent risk of sudden death. Her heart seemed only to be quivering just enough to barely perfuse her kidneys and send enough oxygen to her brain to sustain her weird delusions of swiping credit cards at Parisians. He still had her obituary notice, just twenty-nine words, in his wallet.

He found the stiff and faded hose wadded behind the prickly holly bush that grew beside the little brick stoop. The water bucked through the hose, coughing out pockets of fetid air. Flowing clear and cool, Bobby used his thumb to direct the water onto the glass. He dropped the hose, found a huge brown pinecone and scraped with it and rinsed until the blood was gone.

With the cool of morning lifting, a bullfrog leaped full stretch and brooped into the water, breaking the glass of pond scum, a living dead thing. Bobby rolled Harold onto a grassy flat place beside a stunted willow and locked the wheels.

"Sure is pretty." Harold shaded his eyes with his fist.

"Let's sit here for a few minutes and then go do some standing." Bobby limped along, watching tadpoles squiggle in his shadow. A shiny silver jet chugged across a spot of clear sky to the east. A horn blew.

Harold tried to look over his shoulder. "Who could that be, Bobby?"

"Black Trans Am. Pulled in the driveway." Bobby turned Harold's chair.

"Why, that's my Bee."

Bobby saw a blonde woman and a man with long hair and a beard. He hadn't seen Bee since high school. She'd been a freshman when he graduated.

"Hey, sweetheart!" Harold yelled. Bobby pushed, the chair swaying back and forth over the uneven ground.

"She married?"

"She's too pretty to get married."

As they crossed the narrow road, Bee bounded toward them. Bobby swallowed hard.

"Pawpaw!"

Bee's guy friend stayed put and stared up a pine tree like he might want to buy it.

Back inside, Nadine lounged in her housecoat and gown. "Gets me nervous, Claudette, them down at the pond, knowing what I know. But beggars can't be choosers. Clara's worried Bobby done took up with a colored woman somewhere. Ain't no white girl named Shreveport I ever heard of…Well, let me go, I hear car doors…"

"Hey, darling!" said Harold.

"Pawpaw, you look so good." Bee bent down, shielded her surging breasts with one hand, and gave Harold a big kiss on his hair. "Smell good, too."

"Hey, Bee." Bobby jammed his hands into the pockets of his torn hiking shorts.

"Good Lord, boy, you're skinny as Pawpaw." Bee's tight pigtails tickled her bare shoulders. She had the day off from the Chevy dealership where she directed customer calls and made coffee.

"We're both putting on some weight." He

tripped over Harold's footrest.

"That's Gaybert over there," said Bee. "He likes to fish."

Gaybert's hair hung over the collar of a clean mechanic's shirt. He tore down transmissions, shuttling between three different repair shops. He walked over and pulled a pack of hardpack Camels from his jean's waist, snapped it in his palm. "Nice to meet you, Mr. Suggs, sir."

"Gaybert!" said Harold. "Ha, that's an old timey name. You gonna fish, babydoll? You sure are welcome to fish, honey."

"Well, I'm just gonna visit with you." Bee patted his arm. "I hear you had some excitement."

"Bobby took care of some business." Harold coughed.

"Lord, look at that bruise on his arm." She pulled up Bobby's sleeve for a better look. "And your leg, too."

"Say," said Gaybert, "I'll just get on down and set up the poles." He pulled Bee close and kissed her forehead. She took his cigarette.

"God, these menthols suck." She handed it to Bobby.

Bobby held it at arm's length, not sure what to do.

Gaybert coughed and shifted his manhood with a hip stretch and waist tug. "Gonna be storming come Easter and that pine's aiming to fall." He motioned toward the fifty-foot white pine a dozen feet from the house.

"Let her fall," said Harold.

"You got a chainsaw, Mr. Suggs? I could get her down for you," said Gaybert.

"I've been thinking about that tree," said Bobby. He puffed the menthol. "I might be able to straighten it up with a come-along and some cable."

Gaybert looked disgusted.

"Okay, boys," said Bee. "Tree looks fine to me, leaning a little. Well maybe a lot."

"Might let some fresh air in the house when she falls," said Harold.

"Pawpaw, that's not nice."

"We're gonna do some practice-standing over there. Before the day gets away." Bobby pointed toward the shuffleboard court and raked his finger right across Bee's breast.

"Hey," said Bee.

Bobby froze, mumbled an apology, and then locked eyes with Gaybert.

That evening, Bobby sat on his squishy bed and leaned against the paneling. He scratched a needle through shoe polish, lay down another black line on his bicep, and jabbed like a sewing machine. A streak of mercurial blood rose and quivered. He dabbed with a tissue and surveyed the row of black dots. Bee had invited him out for Indian food in Birmingham. He felt like a match at a gas station.

Harold snored in the den. Nadine lounged in bed talking on the phone, thumbing through an old *Readers Digest.*

"Hold on, Claudette, I got another call."
Nadine squinted. "Hey, Clara? Can I call you
back? I got Claudette on the other line. I'll
have Bobby call you in a few minutes... She's
at the airport? Well don't that take the cake."
Nadine pushed a button. "Hold on, Claudette."
She held the phone to her chest. "Bobby!" She
thought about how nothing good ever held
together.

Damn. Bobby jammed the needle in the
shoe polish and threw back the tangled sheet.
A dog barked close to the house. He turned off
his light and pulled back the blinds. The woods
loomed dark. A shape moved.

Nadine smacked the paneling with her
cane. "Bobby!"

Bobby came into the hall, peeped in, and
saw Nadine's glory through her flimsy gown.
Parallel galaxies of grape-jelly veins bulged on
her legs. He felt woozy.

"You awake?" said Nadine. "Use that phone
in there. I just hope to God this don't compro-
mise on Harold. I'd hate to have to get Sammy
back out here." She smacked her lips.

The lamp behind Harold's bed cast the
living room into a sculpted shadow. Harold's
snore cranked then released in a long hacking
sigh. He balled his good hand to his chin.

On the phone, Clara told Bobby that
Shreveport was in Atlanta.

Bobby said, "Huh?"

"Is she a colored girl?" said Clara.

"A what?"

A single drop of blood welled and crawled down his bicep.

"She's having a baby. Her name's Shreveport. She's come from Tylenol," said Clara.

"Jesus Christ," said Bobby.

He tried calling the number that Clara gave him and nearly wound up ordering a set of knives seen only on TV. He looked at Silliporn's photo. He pulled out a dictionary and looked up pregnant. The next word was preheat. He paced out back and threw rocks at the mile-wide moon. It seemed so close and real. He could never see the image of the old man's face that was supposed to be there. He went back inside and looked up pregnant again. Silliporn was slender but had that hourglass look, healthy hips that asserted *I am fertile.* They'd had only one night together, a fantasy now. He'd run into her earlier that day after getting lost at the Jatuchak Market in the bowels of Bangkok, where her shady father ran a St. Bernard puppy mill. His nickname was Khun Phaen, after the handsome ill-fated commoner who pursued the lovely Wanthong in the epic poem revered by the Thai people.

What would the baby look like? If it turned out to be a girl, Bobby imagined the child as magic, another likeness of Silliporn. He slipped back into bed and dreamed of flying, leaping through the air with arm-waving bounds.

After the visiting nurse took Harold's temperature, Bobby called Clara again and had her reread the phone number that Silliporn had left. He figured she was on a bus somewhere between Atlanta and Birmingham. Maybe it was a cell phone she had called from. He wasn't sure. He dialed again, changing the 7 to a 1.

"Pizza Bowl, Placerville," said a weak voice.

Bobby stood. His heart raced. "Silliporn?"

"Seafoam?" said the voice. "Would you like to reserve a lane?"

Bobby sat down. "Do you have a birthing center?" The line went dead. He walked to the kitchen and spooned canned salmon over a fried egg. A flare-shaped bottle of hot sauce sat on the table. Toast jumped up too brown from the toaster.

"Turn off that stove eye, Bobby." Nadine slung a sopped rag across the counter, knocking crumbs and a spoon caked with peanut butter onto the floor. Her bottom trapped him against the cabinets.

He held up his arms and let her pass. "I'll get him set up before I go. He'll be alright till this afternoon."

"Good god, boy, I guess you wish you never set foot in China."

"Thailand." He looked out the screen door to the carport. "I quit wishing a long time ago."

"He's got a slight fever," said the nurse. "Ninety-nine nine."

"Honey," said Harold. "I don't feel good."

"Harold, be quiet, the nurse is telling something." Nadine squinted. "Is he sick?"

"I'm going to take a urine sample and do a blood draw," said the nurse. "Mr. Suggs, does your pee burn?"

"What's that?"

"It's a little cloudy."

"Gonna rain," said Harold. "My garden sure needs it."

Bobby laughed in the kitchen. "I bet he's got a urinary tract infection. He won't drink like I tell him. Mr. Harold, you got to drink more water." A car door slammed. "Breakfast's ready."

"Hey, y'all!" Bee waltzed in wearing short-shorts and a tight white t-shirt. A red band swept back her hair. Bobby smelled the urgency of yellow Dial soap. He stared at her unpierced ear lobes. The phone rang.

Nadine answered, made a face, and started to say something. Bobby heard the voice on the other end and wiped his hands on his jeans.

"I'll call if you need to pick up an antibiotic," said the nurse. She eyed Bee, then Bobby for a response.

"Do I smell salmon?" said Harold.

"I'll help you, Pawpaw." Bee wheeled him into the kitchen.

"Hi, baby. I'm sick."

"We're gonna fix you up." She poured him a cup of coffee. "Your breakfast's getting cold."

Nadine motioned to Bobby with the cordless phone.

Bobby held it with two hands, lingering in

front of the muted TV. A finned missile floated off an F-16 toward a magnified target, brown and grainy. Looked like awnings, a market maybe, piles of lentils hiding shoulder-mounted rockets dipped in anthrax. The screen went fuzzy followed by a commercial for allergy medication. A pretty girl with glasses and a runny nose. Side effects included glaucoma, skin rash, edema of the face and tongue, pruritus, urticaria, bronchospasm, wheezing, and vasculitis consistent with Churg-Strauss syndrome.

"Bobby Hotwig!" Bobby's chest went tight. Silliporn's voice rang in his ear with instant recognition. Her gaze at him from the across the table that night. The smooth skin around her eyes, toned arms, and that coy look, so innocent yet bullet-proof. He stammered. He stumbled into Bee. He couldn't find his keys.

Bobby had to get to Birmingham damn quick. He pumped three dollars of unleaded into his Buick Regal. The AC was broken, but the fan worked. Silliporn had first called from the bus stop in Anniston. Now she was in Birmingham. The gas needle roamed back and forth as the saggy roof felt bellydanced in the wind.

Headed to the interstate, Bobby ran a four-way stop near White Curd. Charlie Daniels sang about a wooly swamp on one station, funeral announcements with Jemson Handloser played on the other.

"We have a prayer request this morning for

the good folks down at the County Manor for the Aged," said Jemson. "The oxygen delivery truck from Mississippi was hit by a train and needless to say we should—"

Cruising at 85, Bobby popped in a Primus cassette and thought about Nadine's sheer nightgown. The sky glowered dull white like her hair. A fuzzy yellow sun broke through here and there in searchlight beams, spotlighting sections of earth *to be pummeled by the fist of God.* Two yellow butterflies whooshed over the car and he followed them in the rearview.

There were plenty of Asian folks at the nearby university, but only one at the Birmingham bus station. A dirty white man with a belly as pregnant as Silliporn's shadowed her. He owned a green motorcycle helmet and smelled like unwashed genitals. She'd already given a guy in a fur coat three dollars. She tried to lift her heavy suitcase. The pain in her lower back took her breath. Her stomach rumbled. Her head hurt. Her feet bulged in black loafers. She imagined her father in every corner, that he had figured it all out.

"Just killing time," said the smelly man who said his name was Loomis and that he liked Chinese food, especially sweet and sour chicken with red sauce. "Ooh, that's some good eating," he said. He fished an oatmeal pie out of his helmet and offered Silliporn a bite.

"No," said Silliporn. She looked left and right. She wanted to scream or cry. In Bangkok, the bus stations were open-air and fragrant with diesel wafting through kiosks piled high with treats and drinks. Thoughts of squid-flavored fish snacks watered her mouth. No sound came from the TV, just a silent game show. She needed the bathroom but feared leaving her suitcase.

"My mama likes eggrolls best, with that red sauce," said Loomis. "What's in that sauce anyhow? Is it ketchup? Mama died on a Greyhound bus, choked on peanuts, boiled peanuts, the kind you can eat shell and all. They weren't boiled proper is what the preacher said."

Silliporn scooted her suitcase toward the bathroom. Loomis jumped and offered to carry it. His big hand squeezed hers. "Oh," she said, and let him.

He walked right in the bathroom with her.

A woman yelled, "Hey!"

Silliporn flinched and stiff-armed the sink. She swallowed thick seawater and gagged. Loomis walked out backward, fascinated. She tried to hold back her hair. The woman stood by her, bracing her, and it just kept coming until Silliporn was empty. She groaned and panted. Her nose dripped.

"Oh, baby," said the lady. She turned on the sink faucet.

"Excuse to me," said Silliporn. She moaned.

"Lord, lord, lord," said the lady. A waxy keloid shaped like a fat caterpillar pulled her nose sideways. She handed a paper towel to Silliporn. "What's your name, honey?"

She wiped her mouth. "Silliporn."

"Seafoam?" said the lady. "That's a pretty name, Seafoam. Let's get you out of this mean toilet. You need some fresh air. And look at you heavy with that baby."

Silliporn grabbed her swollen belly and wept.

An olympic downpour throbbing with dull thunder pounded the interstate, and cars pulled to the side with flashers blinking. The Buick's windshield wipers scraped like a rubber doormat. Bobby smeared the fogged glass with a page from an atlas, a piece of Texas. The rain slacked to a dribble of fat drops, revealing a steaming stretch of interstate unfurling across the green hills. The cassette reached the end, *chk, chk, chk,* and flew out. Even before he'd hung up the phone that morning with Silliporn, he'd made up his mind to marry her. He'd decided the very same back in Bangkok, but he'd let her slip away in the confusion of his dismissal from the Peace Corps. He gripped the wheel, imagined going to one knee. Where would he buy a ring? He would need to borrow the money from his grandparents. She would look fabulous in white, her brown skin, her hair in her eyes just so. He felt warm and cold at the same time.

He got lucky and found street parking near a hotdog place wedged into a parking deck. His palms felt sweaty and dry. He cut the wheel deep. The power steering hissed.

He wondered if Silliporn liked chilidogs. He remembered the pistachio ice cream and clenched his teeth. A light breeze blew toasty humid through sidewalk gingko trees washing the air a leafy lime green. Loose newspaper skittered back and forth in front of the station. A tiny woman in a sleeveless cowrie-print dress ran across the street toward him. He dropped the quarter pinched between his thumb and index finger. The woman tripped, lost her sunglasses, and sprawled in slow motion.

"Silliporn!" Bobby lunged into the street. He felt her arms squeeze his legs, and then she was tying his shoe. "No, no. It's okay." She smelled like vomit and groaned at him with bright eyes pleading. He helped her onto the sidewalk, and she leaned into the Buick before arching back, hands pressing to her lower spine.

"Bobby Hotwig!" She gave him a quick prayer nod, the traditional *wai*, and fell into his arms.

"*Sawadee*," said Bobby. He couldn't remember if he was supposed to follow it with *ka* or *krap*. "You okay? Jesus, you're sick. You got luggage?" He saw a man with a suitcase waving a green motorcycle helmet coming across the street.

Silliporn pushed Bobby away, groaned, and made noises like a planet going flat. "*Mai... mai...mai...*"

"Is this your honey?" said Loomis. "I been watching her stuff."

"I appreciate your help, man, but we're getting' the hell out of here." The Buick's trunk popped and Bobby rearranged a tangle of jumper cables, a jack, and a bag of cat litter that'd been in the car when he bought it.

Loomis wanted a tip for his troubles.

"Let it go, brother," said Bobby. He felt like a pulled tooth.

A flock of men in suits and neat hair passed, amused and alarmed.

"There's an ATM just right over there," said Loomis. He grinned like it might be a joke.

Silliporn moaned inside the car. She leaned against the damp window. "Bobby Hotwig! Help to me, Bobby Hotwig!"

"Dammit!" Bobby grabbed the suitcase handle and yanked. It broke.

Loomis stepped back and reached deep into his back pocket.

Bobby's brain went purple. He read the name on his shirt pocket. "Loomis, you ever see two snakes fight!"

Silliporn's door squeaked open. "Bobby! I am deathing!" She braced her hands on her thighs.

"They grab each other's tails, start swallowing, and poof! Gone! Nothing but a knot in the air!"

Loomis dropped his helmet and stumbled backward.

"Jesus Hubert Humphrey Christ!" Bobby's heart pounded as he humped the suitcase into the trunk. Silliporn was crying into a pretty yellow handkerchief. His head thudded. His eyes hurt. Sweat soaked his armpits and poured down the small of his back. He took a deep breath. "Here's what we need. We need the hospital, A-S-A pronto P-D-Q." He swung her legs back into the car and buckled her in. His eyebrows dripped.

"Yes," said Silliporn. She went still, letting Bobby take over.

Her rich brown hands rested on her tight round belly. Her ankles looked puffy. She sniffled, so tiny sitting on the Buick's blue crushed-velvet seat.

"I being your mother," she said. A contraction knocked the breath from her.

Bobby held his breath until she took a full breath. "The windows don't work. I'm sorry." He pulled out the folded cardboard wedge holding his window up and it guillotined into the door.

Silliporn managed a few deep breaths. She stared at the dashboard that Bobby had spray-painted gold. She touched the car's sagging felt roof. "You Bobby Hotwig."

"Yes." He ran his hands over his thighs. "I am." He turned the key, found the fan speed that worked, and directed the vents toward her face.

"I become your mother," she said. She broke into a sob. Tears mixed with sweat clung to her cheeks.

Bobby looked for a tissue and handed her a napkin from Wendy's.

She took a deep breath. "Baby, *taa-rók,* coming."

From nowhere a traffic cop named Theodore rapped on Silliporn's window. She flinched and clutched Bobby's injured arm. "Oh, Bobby Hotwig, you have purple."

Theodore stepped in front of the car. His little golf cart idled behind them with a happy purr. "Sir, you gonna move or put some money in the meter?" His teeth looked loose. His face looked burned.

"I see what's going on," said Bobby. "You're a traffic cop. I'm the driver of this Buick Regal. You want to give me a ticket."

Then, a city cop named Darren, driving a patrol car, stopped with lights flashing, trapping the Buick. Darren hopped out. "Writing a ticket, Theodore?" He looked in at Bobby. "You know that young lady, sir?"

Theodore moved around to the back of the car.

Bobby felt bound with piano wire, free falling into a bottomless Antarctic crevasse. "Hey, man! She's about to have a baby right here and now. You can't give me a goddamn ticket!"

"Watch your language, sir," said Darren. He looked worried, like he had to set an example for Theodore.

Bobby turned the wheel toward the street, straining the power steering.

Darren jabbered something into his radio.

"Oh, Bobby Hotwig!" Another contraction grabbed Silliporn and pulled her down.

Bobby blinked to make sure everything was real, and huffed a deep, deep breath. "Sir, my lady friend here needs to get to the hospital."

Bobby stared at his hands. He turned on the blinker, indicating a turn into the street. He counted to ten in German.

Silliporn arched her back and uttered a languid shriek, the unmistakable sound of a woman giving birth. She grabbed her backside and her hands came up wet. Bobby noticed her eyes change. When he used to work the ICU, the eyes were always dead giveaways. The eyes knew first.

"We have to go now! Her name is Shreveport. She is about to have a baby. She comes from the far away land of Tylenol. I used to work at University Hospital and I'm taking her there whether you move or not!"

Silliporn panted. Her face pulled into a knot.

"Breathe," said Bobby. He mimicked a deep breath in and out. "My name is Bobby Hotwig. Breathe. That's right. In. Out."

"I'm calling ahead to the ER," said Theodore, putting his ticket book in his back pocket.

"No! Let me call," said Darren. He gripped the edge of Bobby's window and stared at Silliporn. He was in love with a waitress at China Buffet named Xi Ling and was on the verge of asking her out, but knew that it would go badly. "Follow me."

Bobby turned the key. Just clicks.

Silliporn pounded the dashboard with her

fists.

The patrol car shot forward with lights flashing.

"Dammit!" Bobby opened his door.

"Won't start?" said Theodore. "Get out and get on!"

Bobby hustled Silliporn onto the little bench seat beside Theodore. He grappled Silliporn's suitcase into his lap. A red light squircled round and round on top of the fiberglass roof, and the tiny vehicle's engine shrieked with purpose.

The phone rang at Bobby's grandparents' house. The Braves were down by two to the Expos.

"Chester. Turn it down," said Clara.

Chester nodded with a page from *National Geographic* shading his eyes. "Nadine?" said Clara.

Chester blinked his eyes. "You on the phone?"

Clara covered the receiver. "It's Nadine."

"My stomach's growling," said Chester. He sat up and knocked his magnifying glass on the carpet. "Has it stopped raining?" He tried to stand and fell back.

"Where could he be, Nadine? Why, that makes me worried." She put the phone against her Braves sweatshirt. "Bobby's went off to Birmingham to pick up that Shreveport woman."

"Birmingham?" said Chester. He wasn't sure what she was talking about. "There was a couple of them Mormon girls come by here today. Real friendly."

"Lord, Nadine, I suspected something," said Clara. "But he's so tight lipped and I don't press him. She must be that colored girl from Korea." She walked toward the TV. The phone cord stretched and tugged the phone out of her hand. "Shoot!"

"I asked them Mormon girls to come in and one of 'em wanted a glass of water. I didn't see any harm in it." Chester folded his hands and yawned.

The phone grease-pigged along the floor with Clara grabbing after it. Jose Vidro hit a homerun for the Expos, but he lost the bat. It winged into the stands and smacked a ten-year-old boy in the head.

Clara pulled the phone up by its cord. "Well, Nadine, some nurse over there got sweet on him. That's about all he told me. Never said she was colored. I just thought she was Chinese."

"I'm going to drive up to Jack's and get us a hamburger," said Chester. He was wearing his ballcap from the bank. "Where's them car keys?"

Clara shielded the phone. "Chester! Bobby's lady friend Shreveport from China is in Birmingham." She went back to the phone. "Well, Nadine, we're just lucky he's still alive."

What Clara was talking about sunk in, and Chester looked a little sick. Bobby'd made it back from China, or wherever the hell it was he'd gone, but not all of him. Bobby's daddy in

Vietnam and now Bobby.

Clara placed the phone in the cradle and watched Chester mumbling to himself. She wondered if something good was coming for Bobby, how he would handle it. He was a good guy, just a little mixed up.

Filling out the hospital paperwork sobered Bobby in a hurry. His hand shook as he signed the forms promising to pay all costs in full. *How much do you estimate you can pay per month toward the outstanding balance?* He wrote *$15*, pushed the papers through the slot, and a woman from 1955 stamped them. He saw the clock behind her, 3:46. A sour smell wafted from his running shoes, and his face felt sticky. His head throbbed.

"Are you the father?" said the woman. She wore cat-eye glasses. She blinked.

"I think so."

Bobby wanted to be the father. He'd wanted to marry Silliporn the moment he saw her at Mercy Mission in Bangkok.

With papers in hand, Bobby walked out of the hospital's discharge office to return to Silliporn's room. He knew the sprawling hospital like the back of his hand but had to stop on a walkway between buildings to gather his bearings. Traffic jerked back and forth in the street below. The ICU he had worked in was behind him in the East Tower. Maternity was in the older building, facing him. He touched the glass to make sure it was real and fell in behind a large man pushing a wheelchair. He watched a long, black, plastic comb in the man's back pocket bob up and down. Were there stairs he could take to Silliporn's floor? Was that Cheryl, a nurse he used to work with? Oil paintings of blurry flowers lined the corridor. He glanced at the prices over the shoulders of people crowding and bunching the hallway. A white coat touched his sleeve.

Silliporn.

The crowd pushed him into the cafeteria. His shoelace flapped. He smelled pizza and green beans. The ceiling hung very low and the paint looked new. He hurried past vending machines and pushed into another building through a set of double doors, the light going from bright to dim. He saw wood paneling, marble, and sturdy doors leading to the street. The humidity hit him. He saw orange traffic cones and a small bulldozer. A cop in a yellow vest directed traffic. Bobby hadn't held the screaming little baby boy, just glimpsed him in the nurse's arms as she rushed by. He walked around the block to gather his bearings and started over.

The emergency room appeared to his left and he remembered a shortcut to the main hallway where the elevators were. Inside, he meandered and took a back elevator he had once used to transport deceased patients to the basement morgue. The elevator was small. One night, late, perhaps two in the morning, alone with a gurney draped in white sheets, the dead man had been too tall. The doors kept hitting the body's feet and opening again. It took some muscle and swearing, but Bobby had managed to drag the man to a lopsided sitting position and get him to the basement.

But, what to name the baby? What to do now with his new family? With renewed vigor, he walked off the elevator and found the dry-erase board by the busy nursing station. This used to be his territory—bedpans, insulin, green Jell-O cubes. "Wongmalasith, Silliporn, room 432," he said to no one.

"Sir?" said a strapping nurse in blue scrubs.

"Ma'am?" said Bobby. A very fluorescent and very bright light killed every shadow in the place. A pack of men and women in white coats moved down the hall.

"Chandra?" said the strapping nurse. She motioned to a waiflike nurse scribbling on a chart. "Can you talk to this young man?"

"Are you here to see Miss Wong…malasith?" She jammed the chart into a carousel and picked up a bag of IV saline.

"Yes, I'm the father," said Bobby.

She looked at Chandra, then Bobby. "What do you know about the babies?"

"Babies?" Bobby put his hands in his pockets. His mouth felt hot and cold at the same time.

"Twins," said Chandra. "Sort of."

"What?" Bobby pinched his thighs through pocket liners.

Chandra said the doctor would speak with

him. He followed her down the hall. The door to Silliporn's room was wide and heavy and made of honey-colored wood. She sat in bed with her arm bent. Beside her, a man in blue scrubs thumped a tube of blood. Bobby saw two large wet spots on her loosely tied gown. Her eyes were closed.

The man left with his tubes of blood. Silliporn's eyes stayed shut as Chandra changed the bag of saline. The IV pump beeped and then resumed its chewing sound. Bobby peeked around the curtain at the bed next to the window. A woman as big as a refrigerator said, "Hi fella." She was eating blue cotton candy from a plastic bag.

Bobby turned back to Silliporn. She looked too beautiful in her wrinkled gown. He reached to touch her.

Silliporn's eyes opened. The wad of gauze in the crook of her arm sailed across the bed. "Bobby Hotwig!" She grabbed his neck and pulled herself toward him.

A hot flash struck his cheeks, and he felt his heart split. "Oh god, Silliporn. You okay?" He eased her down. "Oh my god. You have to relax. Are you thirsty? Your lips are dry...Lips dry." He licked his lips.

"She's getting her fluid through the IV," said Chandra. "But she can have water or apple juice. All natural, no drugs. Only the second time I've ever seen it go like that." She squeezed Silliporn's hand.

"I mother now. One is die." She wept and

grabbed Bobby's neck again. He fell into the
bed, soaking up breast milk and tears.

"The doctor should be by soon," said Chandra. "Just a mix of happy and sad. You okay,
honey?"

"I want see," said Silliporn.

"Was born dead?" said Bobby.

"Oh, dead, dead," said Silliporn.

Little Jenkins Phlai Ngam Wongmalasith
Hartwig, black hair, wide forehead, narrow
chin, fierce black eyes, his cheeks like the skin
of a ripe peach, wailed just like any other newborn US citizen cuddled in his mother's arms.
Silliporn had twenty-eight days left on her
tourist visa, one that had taken her fifty-eight
days and $100 to acquire. Bobby owed $5,563
to the hospital, $35 on a parking ticket, and
$150 to the towing company. A new starter for
the Buick was going to run him another $85.
And then there was the matter of a burial for
the dead twin.

Silliporn jostled Jenkins into position beneath her light-blue gown patterned with tiny
flowers. His eyes squeezed shut and his tiny
mouth searched. The gown's neck, although
tied loosely, caught her under the chin. She
tugged the cloth while Jenkins pumped his
tiny fists in the air. His mouth slid on and off
her engorged nipple covered in milky droplets,
then he latched on with a firm and vigorous
suck.

Bobby took a deep breath, pacing around

the bed, adjusting the sheet, lifting the IV tubing away from the pinch of the bed rail, fiddling with the curtain on its swishy ceiling track, the busy work of a new dad feeling helpless. He'd called Chester and Clara first, and then Bee for a ride to take them all back to Kuhlman. He was hoping that Bee would bring Gaybert along and that she wouldn't wear anything too revealing. He had the sense now, more than ever, that Silliporn was a very powerful human being despite her gentle demeanor. She had gone to a lot of trouble finding him, and although he welcomed her and Jenkins with open arms, her efficiency and poise had him a bit rattled. He felt under the gun, that a giant responsibility of unknown magnitude had settled upon him. It felt good, but it was terrifying as well.

"Bobby Hotwig." Silliporn motioned for him to help her sit up and relieve the strain on her back.

"This okay?" He supported her with a hand between her shoulder blades, his skin to her skin. His hands were shaking. She felt hot, smelled hot, like a long-distance runner. He turned at a knock on the door and went speechless.

"Oh my God! It's her," said Bee. She stepped into the room, wearing a short black skirt and sleeveless fitted top. A necklace with a small, machined piece of polished steel embedded with a ring of tiny white diamonds dented the taut fabric that spanned her breasts. A little red purse from T.J. Maxx dangled on a long strap between her bare, shaved legs. She'd had her long blonde hair cut. It was freshly washed and shimmery bounced as she moved.

"This is Bee," said Bobby. He swallowed. He eased a pillow behind Silliporn's back and pushed the button to raise her bed a bit.

"Bobby Hotwig!" said Silliporn.

The bed rose until Silliporn's eyes were level with Bee's. The bed made a clicking noise, unable to rise higher.

"Bee's here to help us," Bobby said. "She has a car."

Silliporn worried Jenkins from her left breast to her right. He was relaxing, the sucking becoming less noisy. "Is sister?" said Silliporn. She cast her flashing eyes Bee's way.

"I'm Bobby's friend, Bee. He's told me all about you, how pretty you are, and everything." She winked at Bobby. "You just had a baby." Bee cleared her throat.

"You wink Bobby Hotwig," said Silliporn. "You girlfriend?" She kissed Jenkin's head and gave Bobby a speargun look.

Bobby pushed the button and the bed hummed down. "No, just my friend. A good friend." He wanted to call Silliporn baby or honey, say something more, but words seemed scarce at the moment.

"God, you're like something out of a picture book or one of those airline ads from Singapore. And you just had a baby." Bee had never had a baby, although she had come close when she was only twelve, thanks to her dad.

"Is it raining outside?" said Bobby. He walked to the foot of the bed and glanced around at the woman who was as big as a refrigerator. He imagined her being filled with hams and ice cream. "Jesus, what am I doing."

Bee walked past Bobby, brushed her chest against his shoulder, and took a quick peek at Silliporn's roommate. She knew the woman. "Well, Evelyn Draycart…" and disappeared behind the curtain.

Bobby took Silliporn's hand. "Bee's going to give us a ride back to my grandparents. She's as nice as can be. She's the granddaughter of the man I'm living with, taking care of. Mr. Suggs. Everything's kind of crazy, I guess."

"She wink you."

"No, no. Not like that. She's a friend, a family friend. Her name is Bee, like the bumblebee." He stopped himself from making a buzzing sound. "She wants to help." He put his hands in his pockets and pulled them out. "The doctor said you can go home now, and Bee's here with her car."

"Hey, I want y'all to meet Evelyn." The curtain between the beds flew back and there sprawled Evelyn. "Evelyn, this is Bobby, and this is Silliporn from Singapore."

"Thailand," said Bobby.

"Thailand," said Bee.

"Thailand," said Silliporn.

Evelyn grabbed both rails and twisted her neck toward them, flushing red from the exertion. "*Sawadee ka,*" said Evelyn. "*Yin-dee-ton-rob.*" She *wai'd* Silliporn as best she could and moaned.

"*Kob-kun-mak,*" said Silliporn. Her fierce gaze relaxed a bit.

"Evelyn here just had a baby and she was raised up in Thailand. Parents were missionaries," said Bee. She toyed with the red purse between her legs, a look of having passed a great crossroads on her face.

"Well, I'll be damned," said Bobby. "What're the odds?"

"Chester, a black car's in the driveway." Clara's heart tumbled up and down, in and out of rhythm, more so than usual. She took digitalis to calm the irregular beating and a blood thinner to ward off blood clots.

Chester lowered his *National Geographic* and magnifying glass. He thought about Bobby's dad having seizures when he was born. He squeezed the armrests and muttered.

"Why that's Bee," said Clara. "Lord, and there's Bobby." She looked at Chester shaking his head.

Bobby's shoulder chucked the back door open in three tries. He waved, stared for a second, and disappeared.

Bee came through the door, pushing it open with her foot. She was grinning, holding an infant car seat. Hot air rushed inside.

"Knock, knock," said Bobby.

And then in walked a tiny, brown, barefoot woman with Bobby towering behind her. She waddled with an invisible brace between her knees, her bright, wide eyes following the baby's sounds.

"Lord, just like a China doll," said Clara. She took a step to the couch and helped Silliporn ease down. "Where's your shoes, honey?"

Silliporn looked afraid, prayed her hands together in a *wai* and nodded. Strands of her dark hair, loose above her ears, floated forward in apology.

"She kicked 'em off outside," said Bobby. "House rules in Thailand." He put his hands on his hips.

She'd gone to quite a bit of trouble to get her visa and buy a plane ticket. Bobby couldn't imagine how uncomfortable she must have been on the bus. Her English was quite good, he thought, unusual for a regular Thai citizen, but she had been silent on the forty-five-minute drive from the hospital to Kuhlman. Her arms. He noticed her arms again. Just a dusting of color, pure, no blemishes, smooth, a faint trace of down just there below her elbows. The hem of her loose grass-green tube skirt lay neatly across her knees, straps hovering just above her narrow, delicate shoulders. He put his hands in his jeans pockets and noted that the tiny den held everyone. Except for the treadmill jammed in the corner, it was perfect.

"Hey, close that door, Bobby," said Chester. "Don't want them birds outside to get cold." He rocked, tried to stand, but sat back down in his blue corduroy recliner. "Gotcha a new baby, I see."

"He's a rascal," said Bee. "Look at those rosy

cheeks." She helped Bobby unbuckle Jenkins under Silliporn's worried gaze.

"This is Silliporn," said Bobby. "I told you that we met in Thailand. She's a nurse. I can't believe she's here...And you remember Bee." He looked around the room as if it were new. The red light on the VCR blinked.

"Oh, my, my," said Clara.

Frowning, Silliporn pulled back the little blanket. Jenkin's licorice eyes shined from the dough of his moist face.

"Got a thick head of hair. My, my," said Clara. "Cute as a button."

Silliporn looked at Bobby. She said nothing, but her lips moved.

Bobby sat beside her on the couch and held her hand. "She means, Wow," he said. "Like, really good."

"Yes, I mother of Bobby." Silliporn smiled and bowed her head. "He Phlai Ngam...Jenkins." Her voice plinked like a toy piano.

"Jinky?" said Clara. She touched Jenkin's soft, thick hair, wondered at his wide forehead and narrow chin. "Bobby's got thin hair."

"It's Jenkins," said Bobby.

Bee laughed.

"What's your name again darling?" Clara sat on the edge of her recliner like she did when the Braves were playing. She was thin but tall and seemed to make three of Silliporn.

"Silliporn, my name."

"Seafoam's a pretty name."

"It's Silliporn," said Bobby.

Clara nodded her head. "Seafoam."

"Whatever happened to that woman from Shreveport?" said Chester. "Does this one speak English?"

Bee laughed harder. Her breasts heaved against her fitted shirt. Silliporn's eyes were searching Bobby's. He was laughing, too. Bee leaned into the treadmill and laughed so hard that she snorted, startling Jenkins who slow-motion burst into tears. Silliporn cradled him on her knees and leaned over him like a leaf, soothing him.

Bee wiped her eyes. "I'm sorry. It's just... Where's the restroom?"

Bobby pointed. He whispered to Silliporn and put his arm around her. A charge ran through his shoulder, and his diaphragm seemed to drop away. Silliporn, the very idea and reality of her, was so complex. That dinner with her. He would never forget the green papaya salad. It had sounded strange, a salad made with green fruit. But he could still taste the sweetness, the lime, the toasted coconut, just a hint of something from the sea, cashews, and the tangy burn of dry chili against the sweet. The basil. The cilantro. That smell. How could he forget that taste?

"Bobby Hotwig. This baby eating."

Silliporn's swept-back cheeks flushed. Sweat ran between her perfect eyebrows. She wore a flesh-colored gloss on lips that rode seductively low. It was that same look of thoughtfulness and studied sympathy that he'd noticed when he first met her at Mercy Mission in Bangkok. She dealt with death on a daily basis. Her smile had made the hospice ward filled with the dying seem a beautiful place to take one's last breath.

"You poor thing," said Clara. "Is he on the teat?"

The phone clamored at full volume. Chester grabbed it and said hello into the wrong end. The tangled cord and base clattered down between the recliner and the wall. "Well, tarnation." He dragged the receiver up by the cord and with a helpless look handed it to Clara.

"Hello?" She put the phone in her armpit. "It's Nadine. She says Sammy's gave the AIDS to Harold."

On a long downhill stretch of 231, Bee passed three long-haulers in one sweep. "Walmart, Target, and Jimmy Dean Sausage," said Bobby. Half of a doublewide trailer began losing steam up the long incline ahead.

"Shit," said Bee.

Not a cloud in the sky, incoming traffic flew past. The air conditioning blew hard. Bobby's hospital-room window in Bangkok had framed mini oases of bright green amid the sprawl of buildings stretching to the horizon. The large room had contained a TV, two small plastic chairs, and a bed. The nurses had kept his door closed, but checked on him every five minutes, not just one nurse but four, one for each vital sign.

"Jesus, I hope Pawpaw's okay," said Bee.

"Sammy couldn't give AIDS to Pawpaw could he?" She hauled in the Trans Am's velocity and ran up behind the mobile home's escort vehicle. She couldn't see over the hill or around the first half of the mobile home. Flakes of pink insulation from the house on wheels streamed over the hood and up the windshield.

"No," said Bobby. "I was going to be working with HIV education and prevention. That's why I went to Thailand, what I was hired for. I'd worked the infectious disease unit and ICU at University Hospital before that."

Bee backed off the tail of the pale-blue escort vehicle "So, why did they kick you out?" She threw her purse in his lap. "Get me a cigarette, if you would."

"They said it was because I rode a motorcycle. They had this new rule about motorcycles and volunteers. They were tired of people getting killed, they said." Bobby tapped out a Camel Light. Bee gunned it. He jolted back in his seat. A brown van zoomed over the hill.

"Damn!" said Bee. She hit the brakes and jerked it back behind the escort.

Bobby sneezed. He looked at the sun and sneezed again.

"Sorry." Bee squeezed Bobby's leg. She punched past the first trailer half and pulled the Trans Am in behind the second half of the mobile home, which slowed hard to turn left at a flashing yellow light. "But why would you go and do what you did, just because of that? Was it that bad?"

The front half of the mobile home yawned across the road. No plastic covered the side. The cabinet doors in its kitchen swung back and forth. The stove door flapped up and down. A cardboard box slid to the edge. The wheels hit a pothole and the box jumped into the road. Bee accelerated into the median to pass the lagging rear of the trailer. She looked in her side mirror and slammed the brakes. The Trans Am fishtailed to a dead stop in a cloud of gray dust.

Bobby flew out the door. The open box straddled the middle of the oncoming lane. Two yellow puppies scrambled in different directions. A green pickup barreled around the sharp bend.

"Bobby!" yelled Bee. She waved at the oncoming truck like it was an airplane five miles up. The second half of the doublewide groaned to a stop. A Lexus shot from behind and skidded. Bobby dove with two hands full of puppy in front of the stalled semi. The green truck swerved and careened over the box sideways, grinding to a halt in the median.

A rubberband quiet stretched. Bobby smelled diesel and antifreeze. The puppies whimpered and struggled in his hands. Bee ran to the box. One little gray puppy. She carried the dead thing into the tall grass beyond the median.

Bobby walked to the Lexus and stood there until the passenger-side window rolled down. An elderly woman squinted at him. Bobby dropped the puppies onto the gray leather seat and said, "Thank you." He looked around. Other cars had slowed and stopped. He could hear a sad country tune. He brushed off his pants legs and walked back to the Trans Am. "Let's go," and they did.

Bee steered the bulky, black Trans Am into the Suggs' place at high noon, engine popping. Gaybert's Harley glinted in the driveway. He stood on the carport, scratching his beard. Silliporn and Jenkins were still with Clara and Chester until Bobby could get the Suggs' place in order.

"I'll handle Gaybert," said Bee.

"He have kids?" said Bobby.

"Not by me. Hey, baby!" She jogged up and gave Gaybert a big hug and kiss. "I'm sorry for not calling."

Bobby saw Nadine through the glass door. "Let me check on Mr. Harold, real quick."

"What's all this about?" said Gaybert.

"Bobby's wife from Vietnam showed up and had a baby at the bus station. You wouldn't believe it. His car got towed and there was a twin that died. He wants us to come to the funeral." She squatted and tied her shoe.

Gaybert stroked his beard. He thought about the finished jigsaw puzzle of a dinosaur on his kitchen table. He planned on framing it but worried what his buddies would think. "Listen, I need you back at the house. Jimmy down at the dealership is pissed as hell and pissed at me, too."

"Oh, him," said Bee. "I'll just go riding in his damn toy car with him. Anyway, her name is Silliporn. What a great name."

"Seafoam?" Gaybert peered into the car, opened a door, and shook his head. He looked at the tires, felt the edges of the decal on the hood. "Did you take her through a carwash?"

"Hell no," said Bee.

Gaybert made an unsatisfied face and walked over to examine the steel cable Bobby had harnessed to the leaning pine tree. A come-along dangled midair between it and another pine. He jacked it back and forth a few times until the cable hummed from the tension. He spit.

As the rumble of Gaybert's Harley faded into the distance, Harold pulled the right side of his face into a smile. "Bobby! Is it hot out there? I'm raring to go, buddy."

"Getting there," said Bobby.

"I wished I never called Sammy," said Nadine. "I just thought you'd left on us with Harold helpless and all." The corners of her mouth drew back.

"What happened exactly?" Bobby slid the glass door open to let Bee in.

"Hey, mamaw." She looked shower fresh and pecked her a kiss. "Yeah, what happened with old Sammy?"

"Bobby hadn't told us about the baby yet," said Nadine. She popped her footrest up. "But

I reckon Sammy's got the AIDS and give it to Harold." She flopped the footrest back down. "I called Sheriff Gaslight on him and he took off. You sure enough busted his nose, Bobby." She leaned to look around Bobby at the TV.

Sammy'd certainly had opportunities to acquire HIV. Drugs. Sex. Bobby had often wondered about Sammy and his dad that last night in the barn.

"So what happened?"

"Sammy was doped up." His eyes looked crazy. Said he had the AIDS and that he'd been giving it to Harold all along." She took a deep breath. "That nurse is gonna tell us what to do."

"He's full of shit," said Bobby. "You can't just pass along HIV willy-nilly."

"Itch ivy?" said Harold.

"That's the damn virus, Harold," said Nadine. "Right, Bobby? Itch ivy. It collects in your privates and such. You know Sammy did scratch himself all over."

"You're fine, Mr. Harold." Bobby shook his head.

"I told her to put my gun where I can reach it," said Harold. "I'm dead serious."

"Let's get you shaved. You're looking rough."

"Show the picture," said Bee.

Bobby pulled an envelope from a coverless paperback romance he'd found at the hospital. He handed the Polaroid to Nadine. His chest filled with helium. He felt like he had two hearts.

Nadine squinted at the picture and strained to reach it over to Harold. "Harold! Look at this cute, little colored girl. That's a brand new baby she's holding." Her uppers darted out and she sucked them back in.

Bee laughed.

"She's Thai." Bobby took the photo and held it for Harold.

"You say she's tired?" said Harold. "I need my glasses."

"You don't wear glasses," said Nadine.

"I used to." Harold craned his neck back and forth at the photo.

"Them was safety glasses. To protect your eyes from the cotton."

"Is she from China?" said Harold. "She's holding a baby."

"That's your baby. Ain't that right, Bobby?" Nadine held the remote at arm's length and towered the volume. "Lord, look at that gas station on fire."

It was breaking news on *CNN*. Security camera footage looped showing a car rolling into a gas station and knocking over a pump. The car burst into flames over and over.

Back at Bobby's grandparents', the two red oaks in the front yard dimmed the light passing through thin purple sheers into the cavernous front bedroom. Clara dusted the top of the dresser. Silliporn's suitcase lay open beside a towel on the kingsize bed. She wasn't sure where Bobby had gone, but knew he was coming back. As she floated on top of the pink carpet pile, she pulled her blouse down and adjusted the pad in her bra. She had wanted to get pregnant, and she had. Here was the proof in her arms. This was her son and she wanted Bobby to be the father. Her home life was dismal, still living with her parents, an abusive father who beat her mother. He would not allow her mom to leave their apartment. By day Silliporn bathed and fed the dying at the AIDS hospice. On weekends, she worked in her father's "store" at the Jatuchak Market selling St. Bernard puppies. He insisted that even she call him Khun Phaen, after the handsome Thai folktale character he imagined he was, although he looked more like a cunning gangster. Even though the past few days had been hell, Silliporn felt calmed by the birth, being with Bobby again in this strange place. Bee, though, worried her.

"Bee, Bobby girlfriend?" said Silliporn.

Jenkins yawned and made a milk bubble. The blush in his cheeks seemed permanent.

"Well," said Clara. "That's his friend. I'm not sure where she came from all of a sudden."

"He coming back? Bobby Hotwig being my father."

"He's getting a place ready for you, where he's staying with our old neighbors, the Suggs." She sat on the bed. "Are you religious, Seafoam? You know that Jesus is coming back."

"I coming from Thailand."

Clara sat on the bed and fluffed her hair with a pick. "Can you tell me what happened to Bobby in Taiwan? I sure do appreciate you taking care of him over there. I just thought I could ask you. He goes off into left field when I ask him about it."

Silliporn wiped the corners of Jenkins' eyes with a tissue. "Thailand. Bobby, Bobby..."

Clara frowned. "What kind of religion do they have in Taiwan? Do you think he got messed up in the religion?"

"My family...Buddha. Do know him?"

"Butter?" Clara wrinkled her brow. "I know Jesus," she said. "Jesus loves you. You know that don't you, Seafoam." She coughed. "Bobby's turned his back on Jesus."

"Jealous Lice. On this, this tree." Silliporn drew a cross in the air with her hand. Jenkins drooled in a deep sleep.

"That's right, hammered him to a cross." Clara gazed at Jenkins. "Easter Sunday's coming up and it sure would be nice to have you and Bobby and the baby at church. Maybe this baby will wake him up."

"Yes, he being my father," said Silliporn. "He not die. Bobby Hotwig falling into the river. He with the trash and peoples in small boats are like *saleng,* bringing trash from river. They come him from river."

After their single night together, she'd read about it in the *Bangkok Post* and tracked him down to Somdet Chaopraya Hospital. But, they wouldn't let her see him. Maybe Bobby fell or maybe he'd been pushed?

Clara nodded. "Mmm hmm." Clothes tumbled in the little laundry room, a zipper pecking. She put her hand to her hip, still sore from the bone they took to replace the disk in her neck two years ago. "Well, I just don't know," she said. "God never promised us more than bread and water."

The dryer buzzed.

That evening, Bee brought Bobby back to his grandparents. Since the Buick was still in the shop, Chester let Bobby drive his old, white pickup back to the Suggs with Silliporn and Jenkins. The driverside door was smashed in and wouldn't open.

Bobby pushed the clutch and shifted the lever attached to the steering column. He was never quite sure which gear was which. The whole thing seemed loose. Two bungee cords held the baby carrier to the hard bench seat. All around them, a smoky plum of dusk slid to the ground as he drove.

"This very old," said Silliporn. She watched the road going by through a hole in the floorboard, bouncing with every little bump. "Where is money?"

Bobby felt bad. "Did you think I had money in Bangkok? I had a little money but they were paying for everything. I was just a volunteer."

"I not know...But you nurse?"

"I never should have gone. I didn't deserve to be in Thailand."

The truck rattled through a red light and whined up a steep hill. Bobby wrestled the gear and the shifter wrenched off in his hand.

"Well..." He hit the brakes and the truck bucked to a stop. A horn blew. Silliporn screamed. Jenkins cried out. Bobby tried to roll the window down. He tried to open the door. "Hell!"

Silliporn covered Jenkins with her body. The cheerful blush in his cheeks faded to white. Bobby pushed in the clutch and cut the wheel deep. The car behind him flashed its lights. Another car reared up behind that one. Bobby let the truck whip back, missing the car's bumper by an inch. A horn blew long and hard.

Half in the grass and half in the road, the truck sat there, while cars took a wide berth around. An old tan Beetle passed and pulled over.

Bobby tried to finagle the gearshift back in, cursing. A tall, skinny man in dress pants, short-sleeve shirt, and thin tie walked to Silliporn's side. They stared at each other through the window for a few seconds. Bobby banged on the horn but it kept on braying like a dying donkey. Otherwise it was fairly quiet. He turned on a blinker and stepped out.

"Engine die?" said the man. A narrow peninsula of hair topped his balding head. He puffed a cigarette. "Gotcha a pretty lady?" He flipped his cigarette in the grass.

Bobby held out the gearshift like a cookie. A coal truck roared downhill, brakes steam-hissing to slow for the light below.

"You alright? You sacked groceries for me at Food Freezer. Bobby Hartwig!"

"Yeah. You still work there, I guess. Since the new Winn-Dixie came to town...Walter? Walter, I got to get out of here before we get hit."

"We got double coupons going on for North Pole week. Been working like a three-legged sled dog. Back and forth like a Japanese yo yo. What gear was she in when the knob come loose?" Walter seemed too excited for the moment.

"What the hell are you talking about?"

"Double coupons, twice the face value, even the expired ones. Brings 'em in like hungry cats from all over. Mr. Tippy, he owns the place now. He's all about the North Pole. He says it was discovered right about now. He likes to swim naked in ice water. Got him that nudie farm out in the woods." Walter lit another cigarette with a wood match, scratching it on the back of his front teeth. "What you can do, if it's in low, is start her up, let out the clutch real easy, and drive slow like Vicks Formula 44, thick and smooth. Otherwise you gotta let it whip around and take it the other way. Just got to time that light at the bottom cause you can't stop her till you get where you're going."

Walter inhaled the cigarette down to half. "We got expired formula on for half-price just so you know. Now we don't take double coupons on sale items. Just so you know." He walked away and creaked open the door of his VW. The rear engine cover was missing, and Bobby watched the engine belt spin.

Bobby turned his attention to the intersection a quarter-mile downhill. Then he gazed up the hill. He watched the evening gloom dim in tiny jerks. The sky's inner thigh looked bruised and yellow. A single fan of splayed light edged through sideways, illuminating some unseen swath over the hill. He remembered the tiny boats patrolling foamy, trash-filled eddies in the middle of the wide Chao Phraya River. He'd wanted to talk to the boaters, go home with them, see where they lived, see what they ate. Maybe he would just float down the river to the Gulf of Siam. He imagined it as deep and black and filled with shrimp striped like tigers.

"Bobby Hotwig! Bobby Hotwig!" Silliporn pushed the heavy door open and it swung right back at her. "You sleeping! Rain!"

Bobby crawled in wet. Thunder rumbled as the starter turned and died. The horn spizzled into a mouse squeak. He felt like the world was made of Legos. He pushed in the clutch and released the brake. The truck rolled backwards into the road.

"Bobby!" Silliporn covered her eyes. "Oh, dying!"

The truck gathered speed and Bobby whipped the wheel left. It slung around sideways, and he jerked it right. Rain splattered the fogged windshield. The truck rolled to a rest in the middle of the road. The light seemed red at the bottom of the hill. He beat on the steering wheel and yanked it as hard as he could. The truck crept forward an inch or two then six inches then a foot and the rest followed. A couple of cars waited on the uphill. The truck gathered speed. He wanted to turn on the lights but the battery was about gone.

"Bobby Hotwig!" Silliporn gripped Jenkins' carrier.

He popped the clutch and the truck jerked to a near stop. He floored the clutch. The rain raked in waves. The truck rolled down the hill toward the fuzzy red image of the traffic light swinging in the wind. He popped the clutch again. The truck rubberbanded and the engine caught, died, caught, stuttered, then roared. He guessed he was in second. A diesel horn bellowed. The red light passed overhead and that was that. Bobby's chest quivered and his stomach churned as the horn continued to spizzle and Jenkins wailed.

The truck rattled along, straining to reach a higher gear. "We'll make it, baby," said Bobby. He squeezed Silliporn's thigh, flipped on the lights, and wiggled the steering wheel to make sure it wasn't loose as well.

With Jenkins crying in the den, his cheeks blazing red, and his mouth rooting for a meal, Bobby worked Harold's head from side to side, stretching the tight cords in his neck. Thunder rattled the windows.

"I was asleep, Bobby," said Harold.

Nadine tapped over with her cane. "You don't wanna draw up in a ball like them old folks in the nursing home do you?" She surveyed the den and licked her teeth. "We got us a regular circus."

"Sorry, Mr. Harold, but I need to take good care of you." Bobby went from neck to arms then legs. He pushed on the balls of Harold's feet. "Hey Silliporn, I'll fix some spaghetti in a minute." She liked spicy spaghetti, Thai style.

To get her visa, she'd had to make three visits to the US Embassy located next to a tall, white complex of apartments and designer shops. Her father liked the breakfast buffet at an upscale restaurant there, piling his plate with lobster salad and dragonfruit, which Silliporn did not care for since she had learned that bats pollinated dragonfruit plants at night.

Silliporn paced back and forth in front of the TV, rocking Jenkins. A reporter embedded with the US infantry in Iraq had died. A tornado-watch alert rolled across the bottom of the screen.

"Bobby, how old is your girl?" said Nadine.

"Girl?" said Bobby.

A steady rain slapped the glass door. Wind whistled through unseen gaps. The TV flickered. The pines leaned with the wind, lit by lightning that tickled the phone's ringer with each concussive flash.

Silliporn took Jenkins into Bobby's room to feed him and get away from the sliding glass door, which she felt would burst. Jenkins' eyes

swam and his head lolled as he latched on.
After a few minutes, he blew a milk bubble
and Silliporn snuggled him on the bed. She
had never heard such loud thunder before. She
covered him with a fuzzy, yellow blanket that
Chester had bought for her at the Dollar Store.
The wind howled around the small house as
rain pelting the windows turned to gritty hail.
She lay Jenkins on the bed, away from the
window, adjusted the thin blanket, and blocked
him in with pillows. Her father's satellite
phone, which she had great difficulty using, lay
on the dresser. After the green papaya salad
that night with Bobby at the hotel, they had
shared a Thai-Indian fusion dish of prime rib in
a saffron masala.

Jittery, she returned to the living room
washed in dull lamplight that rendered an
unnatural yellowish glow. "Bobby, house shaking." Silliporn took his arm and pulled him
toward the bedroom.

After the prime rib with Silliporn, there had
been pistachio gelato with a coconut cream
reduction sauce. Even Bobby's coffee had been
fantastic. The dinner wine he'd never heard
of, super. The Johnny Walker Black, unusually
sweet and life giving. The entire dinner had
been illuminated by a silly electric candle, but
Bobby had never before been so close to such a
sincere and beautiful woman as Silliporn. After
the meal, she was coming to his room to show
him some photos of her family. She touched his
arms, his thigh. He could barely sit still.

Lightning on thunder and he drew her to his side. "It's okay. The storm'll make it nice to sleep."

"Might come a tornado," said Nadine. "There's been one up north of here the weatherman said. Killed some old folks in a trailer."

Knuckles of ice pounded the little cement porch outside the glass door.

"Hope it don't break the glass. Mr. Harold, you want to nod off?"

Harold opened his eyes.

It'd taken Bobby an hour to drive the fifteen miles in second gear with his flashers on. He'd run two stop signs and had to swing into a field and drive in circles waiting for a light to turn green. Nadine had given up and made Harold some canned salmon and eggs, bones and all.

"Let me see that girl again." Harold turned his head and widened his eyes to focus.

Bobby gave Silliporn a side hug. "She's right here, Mr. Harold."

"Ha. I could put her in my pocket."

"Bobby your nurse," said Silliporn. She glanced toward the bedroom.

"Probably in my purse," said Harold. "Ha ha. Bobby, turn that light out."

The lights flared out and Silliporn gasped. The noise of the wind rose to that of Hell's vacuum cleaner.

"Where's the damn flashlight?" said Bobby.

"Bobby Hotwig!"

The power surged for a second and the room reappeared as a photographic negative.

Nadine stumbled and fell.

"Shit on toast!"

Silliporn searched her way to the bedroom. She saw a blinking, illuminated square of orange numbers, her father's satellite phone.

Bobby bumped into the TV. He went to his knees and found Nadine. Claws of lightning pieced the scene together between three-second delays. Harold's urinal bounced on the floor. "You alright?" said Bobby. A tremendous boom and he flinched. He lifted Nadine and let her fall easy into Harold's recliner. She gripped the arms and watched the rain smear the glass door just a foot away. She thought about how Chinese people ate snakes and how Seafoam didn't like cheese. Her knees throbbed.

Bobby felt his way to the fireplace mantle. From there, he navigated his way down the bricks to a porcelain bowl filled with doodads, old batteries, pennies, hair pins, and maybe a box of matches. He pulled out a box that rattled, but in a flash of lightning, he saw that it was a box of 15-amp car fuses. His fingers felt and opened a book of matches, maybe three matches left. The noise of the storm and the darkness seemed to go hand in hand, as if they needed one another. He struck a match and watched it die. The second flared. He turned it upside down and the droplet of flame licked up the paper stem.

"Good work, Bobby," said Nadine.

Bobby lit the gray candle over the mantle. Inky shadows anchored to the floor bobbed in the orange light. He tripped. He swung his arm and knocked over the candle creating an immense velvet darkness once again. Caught in a flash of white-hot lightning, something large swung toward the house followed by the crunching noise of a tremendous fresh carrot.

The good folks at Missionary Thick Baptist Church agreed to bury Jenkins' twin in the empty grave beside Bobby's mother. The garnet-brick church leaned into the big world from a steep hill. The country graveyard wandered off to the left, nearly the length and breadth of a football field. Woods thick with oak, maple, pine, wisteria, and briars embraced the enterprise on all sides except the narrow road. Bobby followed Chester and Clara's car into the steep parking lot. Across the road, a field of green, ankle-high soybeans stared at the late morning sun.

Silliporn sneezed. For her, the hardest part of the last six months or so had been hiding her pregnancy from her father. Her mother had helped, knowing that the mighty Khun Phaen was not noble as was his namesake, but rather a brutal bastard who would most likely kill Silliporn for allowing such a thing to happen. The twin had died very early in the pregnancy, probably when she began showing and wearing loose clothing to hide her belly. But Jenkins had continued to grow, gradually pressing the tiny dead twin against Silliporn's uterus, flattening it into an almost paperlike thinness. Now he was just a tiny handful of ashes, a breath of carbon. She pulled back tears and placed her hands across her lap.

Bobby found a level spot beside the long ramp going up the side of the church. He helped Silliporn out and unbuckled Jenkins' carrier. Silliporn looked crumpled. "You okay, baby?" said Bobby. "You look beautiful."

Across the lot, Chester helped Clara out of the back seat, where she preferred to ride. In the middle of the parking lot, she stood like a bird, holding a purse as big as she was.

A gold conversion van with an airbrushed mermaid on the side and MIA stickers on the bumper swooshed up into the lot, dragging its tailpipe like a string of tin cans.

"That's old Lloyd," said Chester.

Out among the field of tombstones, Bobby saw the little mound of fresh red dirt. There were no chairs there or an awning for shade. Behind him, a man with a big belly wearing dress pants and a short, striped tie shuffled down the ramp with a cane. He squeezed a large limber Bible with iridescent gold-edged pages. Bobby knew how heavy the Bible was, how thin the pages were, how they shushed when turned with licked fingers.

"I fainting," said Silliporn. Her arms trembled. Bobby walked her to a wooden bench beneath a young dogwood in blossom and helped her onto the seat.

The split side-doors of the van creaked open, revealing a cage. The front of the cage

jerked and lowered into a platform. Lloyd
wheeled out, hanging over the parking lot.
"Hey y'all." His voice rang deep and nasal.
He coughed, phlegm smacking in his chest.
He hovered to the ground, smoking a ma-
chine-made cigar with a green wrapper. A pellet gun in a holster hung on his shooting side.
A folded pool cue named Baby swung on the
back of his chair inside a red leather case lined
with yellow velvet that had turned orange.

The preacher dabbed his face with a thin
handkerchief. "Looks like we got the hottest
part of the day." He wheezed and blew his nose.
His face looked blistered.

"You doing alright?" Chester squeezed the
preacher's arm. "I see you ain't missed any
meals."

"Show me the goods," said Lloyd. He
whirred his wheelchair into the middle of the
small group. "Hey there, Bobby. Just wanted
to pay my respects. This your war bride?" He
cracked a grin. His one remaining tooth dangled like a dirty club. He gazed at Jenkins. "All
he needs is an M-16—"

"Appreciate you coming out," said Bobby.
"Silliporn, this is Lloyd. An uncle, sort of."

"Me and Bobby's daddy was in Nam round
the same time. Never saw him over there, but
he was so damn skinny anyway. Maybe he was
turned side-a-ways." Lloyd loosed a fit of wild
laughter. Cheap candy wrappers crackled in
his lungs. "Lost my finger over there." He held
up his left hand. "What's that little fighter's

name?"

Lloyd smelled like old carpet. He'd knifed a man in a bar and then fallen off a bridge running from the police.

"He's Jenkins. This is Silliporn. She's from Thailand."

"Well, Seafoam, you're a peach." He ran his eyes up, down, and across Silliporn's tiny frame. "Bobby, I heard you lost your mind and went over there. I spent a week at Phuket. I got off that damn ship with a pocketful of rubbers and a—"

"I think the preacher is saying something," said Bobby. The hill became a sphere. He grabbed the back of the bench.

"'Bout time he said something," said Lloyd. He put the ash end of his cigar into his mouth and spit it out. "Motherduck!"

The preacher ambled over to the bench. "Bobby, it's been awhile. I wish it was better circumstances, but we better get started."

A wave of terror hammered Bobby like a chain-reaction, interstate pile-up. He watched a black Trans Am slowing on the road below: Bee and Gaybert. Gaybert took good care of Bee, giving her free reign of his apartment and his wallet. She never hesitated to appreciate his largess, but realized there were limits with his generosity.

Bee and Gaybert joined the group assembled around the gaping dirt shaft. Jenkins designed a slow and mournful sob. Bobby held a dozen yellow roses from Food Freezer, given to him by Walter. Silliporn stared into the hole beside the tiny cement vault ready to be lowered with the urn. She saw an unfamiliar wetness of red clay lining the pit, a kind of marbled, rusted fudge, which she did not like. The green St. Augustine grass soft beneath her shoes. The strange pine trees. The puffiness of the clouds. The plainness of the church with the pointed steeple. The people around her taller than she was used to. The smells of unfamiliar aftershave. The women with their strange towering hair frozen into place with hairspray. She felt dizzy.

Flying across the soybeans beyond the road, a tremendous flock of starlings scrolled in the baby blue sky. The birds split around the mourners like water, pouring overhead, then plunging into the trees, spewing raucous pops and whistles.

"We ready?" The preacher steadied his Bible and flopped it open. The supple leather cover drooped like dog ears. He slipped, tripped over the cement vault, took a high reaching step, hurled the Bible like a discus, and down went one leg into the hole and then the other. A hush greeted his disappearance.

Time did a hitch and Bobby dropped to his knees, spilling the roses. He could see the top of the preacher's head, silvery, oiled hair combed over from left to right. He drifted to Bangkok—the Chao Phraya River flowed south viperlike toward the Gulf of Siam. He was paddling one of the little *saleng* boats, wearing a wide pointed hat. The prow of his tiny vessel was pushing through thick patches of seaweed clogged with beer cans, coconuts, and chunks of marine-grade Styrofoam. There was the dog's head, eyes like cloudy plums.

Clara dropped her fan, staggered, and caught her mother's headstone behind her. Her eyes zoomed to Bobby. She could never leave this Earth until she knew that Bobby would be okay. It was just too much, watching him stumble through life. She often awoke at night, worrying that she and Chester would die and that Bobby would wind up like his dad.

"Tarnation," said Chester. He'd seen this very thing happen once before, at the funeral of his baby sister. It had been a deacon and he'd broken his leg, falling in the grave.

"Jiminy Cricket," said Lloyd. Life had been hell since he snapped his spine, but life goes on. Just another day in the crazy life of Lloyd. Preacher in the hole. Birds screaming. A log truck flying by every five minutes.

Silliporn lowered herself to the ground on invisible puppet strings and fainted at the feet of an elderly woman who came to all the funerals. Chester grunted and tried to squat to raise Silliporn's head. He saw her silent tears and felt his own rising behind his eyes. "Bobby!" he said. Chester pitched back and sat on the ground, cradling Silliporn as best he could.

Bobby's tears dripped into the grave and onto the preacher. His head felt like a gush of warm water. The ground spun. He plunged into

the yellow river doing ninety. The force tore
his shirt off and ripped his pants. Yellow turned
black and the current dragged him upside down
into a ball. He receded deep inside himself. He
listened to his heart beat slower and slower.
His mother had asked the same questions over
and over after his father disappeared. What
time is it? Where have you been? Where's
Robert? Is that a spider on the wall? No, mama,
that's an old nail hole, and he finally put a
piece of tape over it. All was cool in the deep
river, yet hotter and hotter. His eyes opened
to choking brown. A sledgehammer pounded
his chest. A crinkled water bottle, plain as day,
spun atop foot-high river meringue. Something
jerked his hair. His head banged wood. He vomited.

The hole in the ground, red dirt. Starlings
marking time in the trees. The sound of a baby
crying, his baby.

"Bobby! You're choking the preacher!" said
Bee.

Bobby saw a clip-on necktie in his hands
and the top of a sweaty head. He tasted grass
and rolled on his back to examine the sky.

When the leaning pine tree fell toward the
Suggs' house, the cable Bobby had rigged held
just long enough to swing it right on top of his
grandparents' old cabin next door. Sister Haylie, the retired Benedictine nun who'd bought
the cabin from Chester and Clara, wasn't killed
like everyone thought, although she did see

God, Mary, their son Jesus, and a host of angels.

The Price is Right wheel bleeped around. "Stella's still looking very, very good with seventy cents," said Bob Barker. The microphone stayed an even six inches from his mouth as he helped Stella, a dwarflike woman, spin again.

Harold stared out the glass door watching Sister Haylie snag pinecones using a broom handle with a nail in the end. She was staying with the Suggs for a couple of weeks until the crevasse in her house was remedied. He noted she wasn't bad looking for seventy-five and looked over to Nadine on the phone with Claudette.

"She's a hard worker, Claudette. She's cleaned this house top to bottom. A man just can't keep a house. A real nice lady. Did a lot of work at the nursing home in town when she was one of them nuns...I think maybe that's where I seen her." Nadine wiggled her toes.

Silliporn spread rice on a brown plate and picked out the broken grains. The funeral had been on Thursday. Now it was Saturday, and she'd been able to gather her wits somewhat. "*Ma-gruud,* some limes?" she said to Bobby.

"Bobby?" said Harold. He worked his mouth, trying to make the left side move.

Bobby fished some concentrated lemon juice from the refrigerator. "This okay?"

Silliporn smelled it. "I want scrape." She pantomimed grating a lime and kissed his arm.

"Hey there, Mr. Harold," said Bobby. "Look, it's Kathleen." He pointed at the TV. Harold's favorite used to be Dian with the long, dirty-blonde hair but now it was Kathleen, the curvy, African-American model.

"She's a pretty black girl," said Harold. Kathleen was wearing a red bikini. She ran her hands across the prow of a bright yellow speed-boat. "I need a cigarette, Bobby."

"A cigarette? What for?"

"I'm just craving a cigarette." He looked out at Sister Haylie. "She's a fish eater." He coughed. A commercial for hair replacement played.

Bobby smiled. "I tell you what. Let's get outside. You take two steps on your own today and I'll slip you a Camel."

Chainsaws from next door started up again. Sister Haylie tapped on the glass and Bobby slid it open.

"Have they got it off the house yet?" said Bobby. *The Price is Right* Showcase moved on to a safari in Africa.

"Buh buh bout got it," said Sister Haylie. She stood six inches below Bobby's chin. In her youth, she'd been petite, but had gradually filled out, the flesh on her arms hiding the points of her elbows. She had a plain, smooth face, and used bobbypins to keep her short gray hair in check. She picked a crumb off Harold's shirt and turned down the TV. "Mmm, is that ruh ruh rice, I smuh, smell a cooking?" She gazed at Silliporn in the kitchen.

"Yep," said Bobby.

"Your muh muh mother would buh be

proud."

Bobby looked at her. "My mother?"

"I nuh nuh knew everyone at the nuh nursing home." Part of her sisterhood's community mission was visiting the sick and making clothes for the needy, usually knit hats and scarves for the elderly. She looked down at Jenkins perched in a bouncy seat.

Bobby's mind raced, trying to remember if he recognized Sister Haylie as one of the nuns he'd occasionally seen at the County Manor for the Aged. He'd never paid much attention, too distracted by the sight of his mother refusing to eat.

"I bet that sailor don't even want them trips, Claudette," said Nadine. "The other lady looks jealous. What you think?" She gazed around the clean room and felt happy-dizzy. To make up for lost time, Bobby had agreed to skip his Saturday night back with his grandparents. Sister Haylie had rubbed her sore hip and doctored it with antibiotic ointment. She'd even helped her get a bath and scrubbed her back. She felt so relaxed she dropped the phone and then knocked over her water.

Silliporn told her mother goodbye and powered down the satellite phone. It was 9 p.m. in Bangkok. Her father was not home as usual, hanging out at the neighborhood brothel where he carried on affairs with a series of young women with names like Lustra, Star, and Gemini. She thought about how heavy he was, about how he pressed her into the bed.

The hottest part of the day was passing and she listened for Bobby. She heard the riding mower and realized he was still cutting the grass. The mower passed the side of the house and a volley of chewed-up pinecones thumped the brick. Jenkins twitched. He lay napping on the bed, his mouth open wide, a serene look on his face. Silliporn pulled back the blinds and watched Bobby pass into the front yard. He was shirtless, sweating, wearing a ballcap. He looked healthy, but his shoulders slumped over the steering wheel as if he held a great burden.

"Bobby?" she heard Harold calling.

She went into the tiny living room. "You need?"

Nadine grinned at her, on the phone with her daughter Debbie.

"Well hey there, Seafoam." Harold cocked his head toward her.

A ladybug landed on her arm. She blew on it until it took flight into the kitchen.

"I need Bobby."

Nadine paused. "He's mowing the grass, Harold. Let him be…Just like a child, Debbie…"

"Honey, I'd like for somebody to cut my toenails. They're getting awful long." He wiggled his toes.

"Oh, I fix," said Silliporn. She found the wash pan and a bottle of Jergen's lotion. She ran warm water, pulled a clean rag from a laundry basket, and pushed a chair to the recliner. She wore snug jeans and a Harley t-shirt that

Gaybert had given her, "as a welcome to Amer-ica."

"Well, she's in here right now, Debbie. Cute little thing."

Harold's bad leg jerked and quivered as Silliporn took his paralyzed foot and washed it. "Lord almighty," he said. He looked at Sil-liporn's thin arms coming through the large arm openings of the t-shirt and then gazed out across the front lawn as Bobby passed by.

Silliporn washed his feet with liquid soap, scrubbing each toe. She thought about her pa-tients back at Mercy Mission. Would Bobby ask to marry her? Bee seemed to be very fond of Bobby, but they acted like sister and brother.

"Well, Debbie, I think all the rice we been eating since she got here's got me constipat-ed," said Nadine.

The rag caught on the littlest toenail and it nearly came off. Silliporn worked it loose and held it up.

"Looks like a damn tooth," said Harold. He took the toenail from Silliporn and examined it, dropped it to the floor.

Next she lotioned each foot, massaging the soles, heel, and toes. "You like?"

Harold's eyes swooned. He was silent. Na-dine watched Silliporn's hands from the corner of her eye.

Jenkins started to cry from the bedroom. Silliporn thought of her father grunting and puffing on top of her, the smell of dogs and alcohol. She stood to check on Jenkins.

"Well, Debbie, if you ask me, I think Bobby's sweet on Bee," said Nadine. She shifted her hips and coughed.

Sister Haylie tidied up the canned goods and relegated the salmon to the laundry room. "Buh, Bobby, have you buh been drinking the milk?" The shopping channel droned. The camera panned a Hummel figurine with blushing cheeks.

Bobby broke back the legs of the wheelchair. "Mr. Harold likes his milk, not me. Never did."

She finished laying out her French-toast assembly line and knocked a wad of whipped margarine off a case knife into a skillet. A fresh pinecone arrangement with young cattail heads choked the tiny kitchen table. She kept her eyes glued to the figurines. Whenever the camera closed in tight on a finely glazed ankle or hand-tinted udder, she steadied her hands on her hips and nudged her head out like a turtle.

"Oh, I juh just luh love the Kuh Kitty Kisses."

Bobby looked. A little porcelain boy in red pants held a gray kitten over a basket. "They misspelled collectible."

"What's that, boss man?" said Harold. "What the hell are we watching?"

Sister Haylie sprinkled cinnamon in a bowl of milk and egg yolks. She saved the whites for a lemon icebox pie, Nadine's favorite.

"Some piss-ant statues is what I'm watching, Claudette," Nadine whispered. "I'd change it but she's big on it. Got some Catholic connections. Bunch of her dolls got busted when the tree fell on her house. She said that's why she retired from being a nun. They wouldn't let her bring that crap in there. Kept it at her sister's house...That's right, she ain't got no kids I know of."

"Nuh Nadine, tuh turn that up when thu they show the One-Five-One. Thuh thuh that's the muh Madonna figure I was tuh telling you about." She dredged a piece of white bread through the egg slick and laid it in the skillet. Cinnamon smells sifted through the house.

"Let's wash your hair today, Mr. Harold. You got a serious cowlick."

"I don't want to, Bobby. Rochelle washes my hair." He sat shirtless in the wheelchair, scratched his ribs, and coughed. "We having pancakes for breakfast?"

"French toast. I can get you in and out of the shower in a hurry. Let's eat first. Debbie sent you some maple syrup."

"I don't need a shower. We having bacon? That's real good with maple syrup."

"Miss Haylie, you don't eat meat do you?" said Bobby.

"Buh buh bad for your teeth."

"She's a fish eater." Harold laughed. "Are you paying rent?"

Sister Haylie coughed and passed a cloud of noisy gas.

Claudette gave *The Price is Right* blow-by-blow to Nadine. "What's that contestant's face look like, Claudette…Kind of like Old Man Simms' wife? Lord, she was big as a schoolbus. Used to wear that damn yellow raincoat everywhere. Nadine wrinkled her nose at the TV. "Here's another one of them damn statues."

"Mmm mmm, maple syrup," said Harold.

"The insurance muh man said thuh that cable Buh Bobby puh put on the tree made it swuh swing and hit my house." She turned to the stove and busied herself with the French toast.

Bobby slid a t-shirt on Harold.

"He muh might've saved *your* house, muh mister." Sister Haylie waved a spatula. "Don't help that buh barn out back, though."

Bobby cut his eyes her way. "Why are you bringing that up?" He washed Harold's face with a warm rag. The damn barn.

"Hell, man. That's hot."

"Your muh mom used to talk about it in fits. How you buh burned the barn down, how your duh daddy disappeared. I nuh know more than you muh might think."

Bobby took a deep breath and tapped his teeth together. His mother had seemed so comfortable in the nursing home, too comfortable. It had just swallowed her up and made her vanish. At least he knew she was dead.

"She wuh was awful luh lonely in there. When your duh daddy left, shuh shuh she sort of left, too."

"I don't think that's news to anybody," said Bobby. He wanted to tell her to shut the hell up.

Silliporn appeared with Jenkins pressed to her chest, patting him on the back. "Bobby Hotwig, what wrong?"

"She guh gonna eat? Duh do you like French toast, duh duh dear?"

"Fishes toast?" Silliporn's white teeth dazzled Sister Haylie.

"This." Bobby pointed at the golden-brown slices stacking on a plate on the table.

Silliporn put her hand to her mouth and handed Jenkins to Bobby, who took him in the crook of his arm.

"One-Five-One! The Madonna!" said Sister Haylie. "Mine guh got knocked over in the tornado and didn't break." She crossed herself and mumbled. "Nadine, I cuh can't hear!"

Glued to the phone, Nadine listened to *The Price is Right* yodel-guy game as narrated by Claudette. She heard the yodel guy tumble off the mountain and visualized it.

After breakfast, which was a bust as soon as Harold accused Nadine of swapping the maple syrup for Aunt Jemima, which was a lie, because she'd swapped it for a generic brand Bobby'd never heard of. Silliporn took Jenkins outside for a short, bumpy stroller ride, and Bobby worked on getting Harold into the shower.

"Hell no!" said Harold.

"Look, you need a good scrub." Bobby examined the walk-in shower. The entry was too small for the wheelchair. He decided to use the Hoyer lift, jack him out of the wheelchair and swing him onto the shower chair. Bobby hadn't slept well all week and the bones in his skull felt loose. His heart throbbed in his eyes.

"Let's stand you up real quick and get this harness under…He reached in and turned on the shower." Bobby reached in and turned on the shower.

"Honey! Nadine!"

Nadine sat in the other bathroom with the door closed, thinking about how her daddy would never share his chewing gum. "What!"

Next door, Sister Haylie supervised two men with chainsaws. Here and there, a crack of wood and a thump interrupted the rev and whine. The day had turned sunny with puffy clouds chasing along to the northeast.

Something didn't feel quite right and Bobby realized the TV was off.

"What's funny?" said Harold. Steam poured from the running shower and fogged the mirror over the sink.

Bobby covered Harold with a towel and laughed. He laughed harder. "Oh God." He bent over with hands to knees. Tears flooded his eyes. The pressure in his head tripled.

"You gone crazy?" Harold looked like he wanted to laugh. His lip curled and dropped.

"Oh, oh." Bobby collected himself. He wiped his face on a hand towel and took a few deep breaths. A jolt of electricity ran through his chest. He started laughing again, but wanted to yell *No!* as loud as he could over and over. With sweat draining off his face, he lowered the hydraulic arm and hooked the canvas sling beneath Harold.

"Nadine!" Harold pushed against Bobby's chest. "Please don't, Bobby."

Bobby pumped the lift handle. The sling jerked Harold up and swung him out of the chair. The lift wheels scooted back and forth.

"Don't you drop me, boy." Like a two-legged cat, Harold blocked himself from going into the shower.

"I have got to get you clean." Bobby looked determined, his face drained of all comedy. "Put your haynes down."

"No," said Harold.

Bobby pushed the lift. He pulled Harold's hand off the tile and bumped the rig in with his shoulder.

"Aw hell, man! Honey!" Harold gasped as the warm water hit his legs and stomach.

A wave of despair ran through Bobby. With his tennis shoes on, he stepped in behind Harold, and thrust his arms into the spray. He couldn't tell if it was hot or cold.

"Help!" Water scoured Harold's face. He groped the wet tile.

"Bobby Hotwig!" said Silliporn, holding Jenkins.

Soaked, Bobby hovered Harold onto the shower chair. There was hardly any room to maneuver. He gathered his wits, unfastened the hooks, and kicked the lift back into the bathroom, slipped, and fell.

Harold gasped like a goldfish. He hadn't felt running water on his skin in over two months. Slumped in the shower chair and leaning against the wall, the spray caught the side of his face. He spluttered and kept his eyes glued on Bobby.

"Lord God Almighty," said Nadine. "That's good work, Bobby. Just don't drown yourself. Scrub him good. Seafoam, don't pay no attention to his hollering." She shuffled out with toilet paper stuck to her house shoe.

"Baby!" said Harold.

Nadine looked at her recliner like an old friend, backed up to it, and lowered with a heavy but happy "Oof!" She picked up the remote and waved it at the TV. The phone rang.

Sister Haylie grabbed Bobby's wrist. He moved his arm side to side, hoping she'd let go. The barrel end of the .45 wandered around the living room like a telescope looking for UFOs. Silliporn ran with Jenkins into Harold's shower. Nadine and a spic-and-span Harold sat in their recliners like a pair of Abraham Lincolns. Nadine was on the phone with Clara, mesmerized as the steel barrel waved back and forth in slow motion. A squirrel that Bobby had been feeding hopped onto the stoop in front of the glass door and looked in. Bobby saw the squirrel from a million miles away.

"That's a squirrel viewed through the wrong end of a telescope." His hands felt numb. He'd just talked to Sammy on the phone and was going to find him. He envisioned the road to Sammy as a coiled rat's intestine. He thought about *Candyland* and then *Hi Ho! Cherry-O.*

"Bobby's got the gun," said Harold. "He's gonna hurt somebody."

"Buh Bobby, puh puh please," said Sister Haylie.

"Sammy called and said a bunch of stuff that upset Bobby," Nadine whispered to Clara. "He won't say what it was. His eyes look funny. Sister Haylie's tangling with him right now. Let me see if he'll talk to you." She held the phone out toward Bobby. "Bobby! Bobby! Clara's on the phone. Come here. Put that gun down."

Sister Haylie held Bobby's wrist with two strong hands, hands that could knit a yarn hat in less than thirty minutes. The tendons rose from the backs of her hands like taut ropes. She could have been modern dancing with Bobby, except for the gun. He didn't want to hurt her, but was having a hard time making sense. It occurred to him that he needed to go for a long run. He relaxed his grip and the gun fell, spun, and pointed at the TV where Dick Cheney had a hurt look on his face.

Bobby found one running shoe in the bedroom. He jerked out a dresser drawer looking for socks and it fell on his foot. He opened and closed the blinds. He lay on the unmade bed, pulled the thin, stretchy blanket over his head, and slept for two days dreaming wild dreams. The colorful walls in the hospital in Bangkok. How everyone was shorter than he was, wearing precise smocks and skirts. One nurse took his blood pressure. Another came in to take his pulse. He realized that they all looked alike, that it was Silliporn in a white uniform, with multiple versions coming into his room. One Silliporn was counting his respirations. Another was taking his temperature. They kept filing into the bright room, wearing the same outfit, with the same pleasant smile. The one taking his blood pressure pulled off the cuff and reached into her pocket, pulling out a syringe with a long capped needle. One by one capped needles came out of pockets. The first needle slid into his deltoid muscle, the second into his thigh. He couldn't move. He heard that damn ice-cream truck song...

The racing thoughts had urged him, pushed him, compelled him to do it. Screamed at him until he had to at least try to get the voices to shut the fuck up. The sad thing was that he really didn't want to kill himself. Those damn thoughts, like snakes inside his head, fighting to get out. The thoughts had begun when he was ten years old, but now they plagued him. On that endless night, he hadn't been able to find his cat Merk in the dark apartment, the night reversing on itself thousands of times as pill after pill dipped in ketchup went crazy straight to his brain and then to his heart beating wildly. And then he drove in circles on roads of pliable wood. Cars moved without proceeding. He couldn't feel his foot pressing the gas or the brake. The on-ramp moved away as fast as he approached. He needed help. He drove ninety, a hundred miles an hour, passing everyone on the freeway, which became other roads in other countries, blurs, and then a parking lot. He swung sideways across three spaces, two reserved for hospital employees. He imagined walking on stilts into the calm waiting room and kept his head low.

"Hey Debbie Dee, your cold sores look better," said Bobby. "I wrote a story about you finding that poor old woman sprawled like a cantaloupe sideways in her nursing home bed." Bursting with serotonin, his voice bled in a high squeal. "Wah, wah. Read the waffle iron."

The receptionist pushed away from the counter and motioned a nurse over.

"You want me to mop the toilets, Debbie Dee? You know I don't mind. Hell, I'll mop the whole damn store, the parking lot, and maybe the interstate. Anybody around here know how to work the microwave?" He felt empty. He felt full. He wanted to hike the Appalachian Trail. He looked around the waiting room and put his hands to the wall, waiting for it to crush him.

"Bobby," said Dr. Hallway. "Can you hear me? It's Dr. Hallway." He fingered the key in his pocket used to operate the secure elevator.

"Are you a Christian, Dr. Hallway?" Bobby slammed his head into the wall.

Hallway flinched. "Bobby, let's go upstairs and get you signed in." He nodded to the nurse and whispered, "Code five."

"Put your life in Jesus' nail-scarred hands!" Bobby sang loud and soulful. "Put your life in Jesus' nail-scarred hands! Code six, seven, and eight." Tears streamed down his cheeks.

"Bobby?" Hallway kept his distance. "Bobby?"

Bobby remembered Merk. He felt that someone had opened his apartment door in the night and let Merk out. "What do you use, Debbie Dee? Carmex? You ever get a cold sore in your nose? God, that's the fucking..."

Hallway looked at his watch. He thought about throwing a handful of change on the floor to distract Bobby.

Bobby burst out of the waiting room door

and charged his car. The door was still open
and the keys in the ignition. It was that no
good cocksucker who'd said his name was
Thomas Jefferson, the one who'd "helped" him
carry in the couch and then wanted to use the
goddamn phone every five minutes. Bobby tore
up the parking lot and whomped over a curb
with a part-time security officer dancing after
him.

"Four hundred and fifty horsepower of
maximum destruction!" His face went blank.
"There was this guy Weedy at the corner store
who came in and stood by the cash register
with one sock on his hand, a gray sock. Weedy
was alright. Didn't bother anybody. Every now
and then he'd say, 'Where's my other sock?'
Then I'd say, 'Check your foot, Weedy.'"

Dr. Hallway was needy. He was Weedy.

"I'm invisible," said Bobby. "Put your life
in Jesus nail-scarred hands!" He saw an apos-
trophe hit the windshield. Then green grapes
of water splattered the world. He saw people
standing in line for oxygen. "Too much televi-
sion," he said…and drove in circles.

While Bobby slept it off, Sister Haylie prayed, cooked, and watched the shopping channel. Silliporn helped Harold back and forth on the toilet. She was tiny but well versed in body mechanics. She wanted to talk with Bobby about her plans for Jenkins. She had called her mother on the satellite phone, crying.

"Seafoam, you sure are pretty," said Harold.

"Oh, your wife very pretty." She swung his legs sideways, raised the head of the bed, and maneuvered him into a secure sitting position. She brushed his hair. The TV made a crowd noise in the background. She heard a knock on the screen door.

Sister Haylie looked surprised. "Hello? Cuh cuh can I help you, honey?"

Rochelle hefted herself into the kitchen, carrying her giant black purse and key ring. "Got some new help I see."

Nadine craned her neck around. "It's a red letter day. Hey there, Rochelle." She pummeled the lever on the side of her chair and shifted her weight back and forth.

"Are yuh you here tuh tuh help with Muh Mr. Suggs?" She rolled up her thin white sleeves and massaged her red fists.

"Hey there, baby! Why the whole world come to see you," said Rochelle.

"I'm Sister Haylie Buh Buh Bannister, muh muh maiden name."

"Sister?"

"Anybody seen Bobby?" Harold coughed.

Rochelle looked around the clutter. She admired Silliporn's snappy yellow dress and loafers. "Where is that boy?"

"He's suh suh sleeping." Sister Haylie looked disgusted.

Rochelle raised her eyebrows at Nadine. "Well anyhow, bath time, babydoll." She moved into the bathroom, turned on the hot water, and rummaged for the bath pan.

"Are yuh you a nuh nurse?"

"Yes," said Silliporn.

"Nuh no, I mean the buh black girl."

Rochelle glared. "Girl? Don't I look like a full grown woman to you?"

"Wuh, wuh, wuh, well…"

Silliporn disappeared into the back bedroom. She still tired easily and was glad Rochelle was on duty. Jenkins slept on his back in a white crib jammed in the corner by the window. Through the blinds, thin lines of sunshine crossed his body. She looked at Bobby's outline beneath the sheet on the bed. The blanket lay in a wad against the wall. She saw the top of Bobby's head and listened to his slow breathing. His legs twitched. Before she'd come here, she'd fantasized about marrying Bobby and escaping from her father. That didn't seem like such a sure bet now.

An hour later, Bobby lay still, putting things together in his head. Sammy'd said on the phone that he knew where his father was. Said he was

sucking dicks at the monastery. He'd wrestled with Sister Haylie. Where was the gun? It
couldn't be true, though, at least the part about
the monastery, or could it? Bobby couldn't get
that damn game *Candyland* out of his head.
The striped path. The Peppermint Forest. He
imagined blue ponies. He thought about that
little girl Jon Benet Ramsey. There was a photo of her in a pink sweater with straight bangs
that he couldn't shake. The disco song *You
Can Ring My Bell* played in his head. Silliporn
leaned over him. He rolled onto his stomach,
and she drew her nails down his back. She
kneaded the muscles at the base of his neck. He
sighed and sank deeper into the mattress.

"Bobby Hotwig. Two days sleeping. I worry
you, Bobby Hotwig. You wake now?" The clank
and rattle of an aluminum ladder wafted from
next door. A power saw whined, ripping plywood for Sister Haylie's new roof.

"I'm sorry, Silliporn. Or do you like Seafoam
better?"

Silliporn smiled a worried smile.

"One day I'll have to explain my dad to you.
How he and Sammy got tangled up with each
other. I just get so bent out of shape, thinking
about it. But when I look at you..." His voice
cracked.

"Bobby Hotwig is live now." She took Jenkins from his crib and lay down beside Bobby.
Bobby felt like his breath was being vacuumed
from his chest as Jenkins grabbed his finger
and held on tight.

"Phlai Ngam," she said in her quiet voice, Jenkins' Thai name. "You see father?"

Bobby relaxed. He kissed Jenkins's tiny hand, then he heard Bob Barker's voice, the rattle of Nadine's cane, and a vague kitchen noise. A wave of panic sat him up. "Mr. Harold!" His heart raced. His vision faded to black as he stood for the first time in forty-eight hours and struggled with his jeans. "Oh, hell."

A hammer on wood from next door pounded the air.

Bobby shivered and pulled Silliporn close. Her hair smelled like baby powder. Electrons swirled in his adrenal glands.

"Ssh!" said Silliporn. Jenkins was drifting off to sleep.

Bobby pulled on a yellow t-shirt, hurried into the bathroom, and became lost in washing his face.

His heart pounded as he gazed into the mirror. His eyes seemed perfectly round. He drifted to the night he'd had Indian food with Bee and chased her through the grassy park before she'd let him catch her, squirming and giggling. She'd struggled out of her pants and ran. He tore his shirt off and lost a shoe. He cornered her at the edge of a ten-foot-deep ravine. She didn't run this time and half naked they did it slick with sweat on the lip of the embankment. The sky black and clear. His glasses flew off into the creek below. Then she'd punched him in the chest, raked him hard on the shoulders with her nails, and rolled. She'd pushed between his legs and knocked him down. The chase was on again. For three days he'd found grass and other little bits of nature in his underwear, socks, and shoes.

"Bobby?" said Nadine.

"Huh."

"Harold needs you, Bobby. You still sick?"

"No." Bobby burst into the living room. The brightness lit a fire of joy in his soul. Within half a second he made a detailed mental list of what needed to be done. "Hey!" he said to Harold. "It's, it's 9:30. Let's get you cleaned up and stretched out this morning."

"Hell, Bobby, you alright?" He watched Bobby grab the urinal, empty it, pick up a pile of dirty towels, disappear, come back with an armload of clean laundry, crank the head of his bed down, rush in the bathroom, get a warm rag, and wash his face. "Hey!" Bobby left the hot water running and ran back and forth with the rag, giving Harold a speed bath. He rubbed his tailbone with A&D ointment, powdered his privates, sprayed his armpits and feet with Right Guard, and then took a wet hand towel to his head.

"We'll wash your hair proper tomorrow," said Bobby, then he got to work stretching Harold's legs.

"Hey!"

Bobby flinched and backed off the pressure. Hammers continued to bang from next door. *The Price Is Right* theme song played. Nadine still hadn't gotten it through her head that

Rod Roddy wasn't Johnny Olson, the original announcer. Bobby re-focused and put Harold through a steady workout. He felt alive.

"Yeah, Claudette, he's woke up. Sister's keeping an eye on them roofers next door. Harold says it's the tar in the shingles that makes roofers drink so much. In the Army, he seen one fall off a roof, catch his neck on a T-square, and cut clean through. Died right there before anybody could say pass the salt." She shifted her hips. "Here comes a whopper." The camera flashed from a lily-white woman in a black muumuu to Rod wearing a brilliant silk jacket with a green dragon on it. He laughed, rubbed his own big belly, and made google eyes. Back to Dian, modeling the next item up for bid. "What's that stuff? Smell-good spray? Ha, Dian done sprayed it on old Bob. Lord, I can see her front crack in them pants." A serious look crossed her face. "I reckon we're too old, Claudette, to make the trip. What you reckon a plane ticket costs out there? Two hundred dollars?"

Silliporn came from the bedroom with Jenkins. She was desperate for Thai food. Sister Haylie put butter and cheese in everything, which made her nauseous. Silliporn's nipples, especially the left one, the one Jenkins pre-ferred, were chapped and sore. The bedroom smelled like poop and they were out of diapers.

Bobby didn't notice that Silliporn had walked out the back until a wasp slipped through the open door. He pushed on the ball of Harold's foot, stretching his hamstrings millimeter by millimeter. A cramp grabbed the back of Harold's good thigh and he shot up. "Hoo!" Bobby slacked off, one eye following the wasp.

"Harold! Quit your hollering." Nadine craned her neck and lost her uppers onto the floor.

Bobby straightened Harold's leg, sat him up, and leaned him forward to limber his lower back. The wasp settled on Nadine's dentures, and she dropped the phone. Bobby caught the wasp in a jar and released it out the back door where Silliporn lingered in a small pool of sunshine. On TV, Kathleen caressed the air over a brand of crackers he'd never heard of. It was the Check-Out game. "Hi ho the cherrio," he said. He tried to whistle. The floors needed mopping. He washed off Nadine's teeth and handed them to her in a tissue along with the phone.

"Bless you, Bobby. Can you get me a glass of water?" She squinted at him, the lenses of her glasses thick with dust and dandruff.

"Sure thing." He began singing. "Surely goodness and mercy shall follow me! All the days, all the days, of my li *ah ah ah* ife." He pinched Harold and did a deep voice, "Thank you, thank you very much." A heavy hook speared his heart and yanked down. He almost fell. He imagined his pills laid out on the center stripe of a busy road. He needed to take something else. Not lithium, though. Lithium turned him into a robot, puckered his lips, and made him crave lemonade. He thought about his dad, the Army, and how they'd moved just about every year until high school when they settled in Kuhlman to be nearer Chester and Clara. He'd been euphoric to be off the military bases and living where he considered home was. He'd never had friends and leaving Fort Hood, Texas, had stirred no emotion in him whatsoever except quiet ecstasy. It'd taken him some time to get used to the new high school in Kuhlman, though. Sammy Dushane had called him a faggot in the locker room the very first day. Bobby had ignored him, but when Sammy put a jock strap over his head, Bobby struck him sixteen times with his right fist, one for each year of his life. Sammy was dirt poor and the oldest kid at the orphanage, Child Heaven.

He noticed water running out of the glass in his hand.

After Harold's bath and stretching routine, Bobby swept and mopped. Outside, with Silliporn watching, he vacuumed the Buick and cut the lawn between the house and the road with Harold's riding mower, chewing up one hundred and fifty-three pinecones. He studied the pine stumps and planned to burn them out one by one. The upended stump of the tree that fell on Sister Haylie's house waved a crazy wig of roots high in the air, but he was able to winch most of the root ball back into the massive hole with the come-along. Harold took five consecutive steps on the shuffleboard court and then stood for a full thirty seconds by himself on his walker down by the pond. Bobby wanted to go for a run, but Sister Haylie had lunch on the table, tomato soup and tuna salad sandwiches caked with mayonnaise. Silliporn ate her last packet of Ramen noodles and begged Bobby to go to the store.

The roof fabric sagged on the back of Bobby's head as he cinched down Jenkins' carrier with the seat belt. He hadn't showered in three days and his hair lay flat and bent.

"We fix?" Silliporn pointed to the roof felt. "Some nails?" She plucked at a spaghetti strap on her sundress. Her hair bounced. Her lips glistened red. A thin gold bracelet decorated her brown wrist.

"Pins might work." An urge to hold Jenkins overpowered Bobby. He choked up and walked to the mailbox to recover. The sun blazed, silencing the cicadas into a stupor. A mocking-bird trilled an endless song, flitting along the boundaries of its territory.

Silliporn sat in the back seat with Jenkins. From the side and rear, Bobby really looked like a skinny Robin Williams. Her father had loved his movies and became obsessed with him after the filming of *Good Morning Vietnam* in Bangkok and Phuket. It was the first thing she'd noticed about Bobby when he visited the AIDS hospice in Bangkok.

"Do you like catfish?" Bobby gazed in the

rearview mirror as much as he watched the road. "That's what's good around here." He felt the sun's nuclear oven on his arm. Baked wind whipped through open windows. The drive to Food Freezer took about fifteen minutes.

Food Freezer sat between the interstate and Kuhlman. Over the past thirty years tornadic episodes had rearranged the metal siding. The original building was baby blue but had acquired yellow and red panels over time. Only the ZER remained of the big red letters over the entrance. Bobby pulled into the crumbling asphalt lot and saw Walter's VW. A vinyl banner stretched between two metal poles at the head of the parking lot announced: "NORTH POLE DISCOVERY WEEK! DOUBLE COUPONS!" Beneath the sign simmered a small, plastic igloo with a plastic penguin on top. A shirtless man with one arm and an American flag mounted to his pushmower cut the grass growing in the cracks of the pavement. He kind of looked like Bobby's dad Robert.

Bobby noticed Silliporn's sandals. Her toes looked brand new. He hefted Jenkins' car seat into one rusty buggy and got another for groceries.

Silliporn pushed Jenkins and stuck close to Bobby. The coldness of the store shocked her. Goosebumps sledded across her arms and shoulders. "So cold!

"Well, it is North Pole Week," said Bobby. He spotted Walter in his tiny glassed office and waved. Giant paper snowflakes dangled from the steel beams of the high ceiling, rocking in the AC's breeze.

Walter wore deerskin pants with his dress shirt and skinny tie, a cigarette cocked behind each ear. "You bring coupons? As long as they're in English, we'll take 'em. How are you ma'am?" He nodded and smiled at Silliporn. "How do you like our fine country?" He adjusted a cardboard figure of Admiral Peary flanked by two of his Eskimo companions, Ootah and Seegloo.

The two sackers stared at Silliporn. The owner, Mr. Tippy, had a younger brother with the 'Mongoloid ailment' and felt the grocery business was a kind of God's mercy for others with the condition.

"Tom and Tom?" said Walter.

They looked at him and went back to sacking for about five seconds.

"Yes," said Silliporn. "So cold here."

"Is it frostbite week?" said Bobby. Boxes of baked beans and ketchup flanked an artificial Christmas tree with a sheet draped over it. The store smelled like dirty mop water.

"Mr. Tippy likes it cold," said Walter. "Says it makes people spend more money." He stared at Silliporn and peeked at Jenkins.

"Okay, cowboy." Bobby pushed the buggy back and forth, raring to go.

"Here." Walter winked, handed Bobby a small wad of coupons then stepped over to help the Toms move things along.

Bobby and Silliporn wandered into the vegetables. All of the shoppers tagged them with side glances. Jenkins woke, pumped his fists in slow motion, and gurgled. A stuffed polar bear reared by a display of apples. Its fur was yellow. Its shoulders slumped. A few teeth were missing and the eyes were different colors. Bobby focused on the list then thumbed through coupons for scouring pads, canned chili, and frozen pizza. Silliporn picked out a cabbage, onions, and garlic. He tossed in potatoes and a bag of raw peanuts. The aisle ran alongside a dairy display to a seafood counter in back. In an empty freezer case filled with foam beads lay the "Unknown Polar Traveler" in his icy grave. A smiling mannequin's face wrapped in a furry hat protruded above the fake snow. Static drew thousands of the weightless white dots to Bobby's arms and shirt. He wiped at them without result and cursed. Other than the buggy squeaking, the roar of air conditioning, and the pre-recorded narrative of Mr. Tippy describing the discovery of the North Pole, the store echoed quiet.

Loaf bread, cornmeal, rice, cream of celery soup, sprinkle cheese, a block of margarine, buttermilk, 2% milk, Eight O'clock coffee, pork chops, hamburger, sugar, Red Diamond tea quart bags—Bobby mentally crossed the items off the list. He could hardly read Nadine's handwriting. "Fuzzy cock?" Then there were the diapers and things Silliporn needed. He saw a box of one thousand straightpins and put it in the buggy. She lingered over the seafood and picked out a bag of frozen shrimp.

The only thing fresh was catfish. Bobby rang the bell, gazing at the piles of yellowish fillets set into crushed ice. A short lady with a hairnet bursting with red curls emerged from a shadow behind the case. She had bruised eyes and wore brown lipstick. She laid her open Bible on a small steel table. "May I serve you?" She shifted a homemade snuff packet from one side of her mouth to the other, licked her index finger, and turned the page.

Bobby said, "Ten fillets, please." He imagined she used to make peach baskets as a little girl.

She took a minute to wash her hands, humming the refrain from "Bringing in the Sheaves." "You want to pick 'em?" She glanced at her Bible. "That little lady speak American?"

Silliporn looked at Bobby. Jenkins examined the vast empty spaces above him, the snowflakes rocking at the end of twenty-pound fishing line.

"To keep the weight on their bones, Peary and his men ate one stick of butter each and every day." The old speakers made Mr. Tippy's soothing voice sound tinny.

"She holds her own," said Bobby. "Just the ones there on top are fine."

"Does she know Jesus Christ?" said the lady. A bright smile pushed against her dark eyes.

"Jealous Lice?" said Silliporn. She recalled her discussion with Clara. "Yes, he has salivation."

"Praise God," said the lady. She laid the bag of fish on the counter and wiped her mouth.

The checkout lines had diminished with the whirlwind sacking of Walter. He put Tom and Tom together on one aisle, while he worked the other. After restoring order, he stepped outside to smoke, clacking the floor with old tennis rackets strapped to his shoes.

Passing through the frozen food to the register, Bobby decided he loved Silliporn more than anything in the world. A skinny man wearing a red apron shook from the cold as he punched in the prices with one finger, which was an angry-looking transplanted toe. He glanced at Silliporn after each item and grimaced. She nodded each time. Bobby put his hand on her back and whispered in her ear. She slapped his arm. Jenkins blubbered and escalated to a wail. Bobby asked one of the Toms what the hell he was looking at.

"I am, I am, I am looking at you," said Tom. His lower lip quivered.

Bobby turned red and looked through the coupons for one that made sense. He wanted to hug Tom and bake him a rice pudding with raisins, take him to Six Flags and ride the roller coasters with him. He found a coupon for frozen apple pie. The cash value was one-twentieth of one cent. Twenty made a penny. Two thousand made a dollar. How much were pillow tags worth?

"Sixty-two dollars and forty-six cents," said

the cashier. He wasn't much taller than Silliporn.

A woman who looked like Greg Allman put a liter of Tab and a pack of salt pork on the belt. The cashier frowned at the woman.

"Mama, I wish I could have some bubble gum," said her little girl.

"Well, wish in one hand and spit in the other," she said.

"And see which one fills up first?" said the little girl.

Her mother broke into a maniacal laugh. "Her little baby ain't getting what he wants." She pointed at Silliporn. "Why should you?" She ran her index finger around the rim of her ear.

Silliporn cringed. She gripped the metal grid of the buggy.

"Sixty-two dollars and forty-six cents," said the cashier.

"Spare me the changeling," said Bobby. He couldn't find the check Nadine gave him. He swatted at the foam balls clinging to his shirt and pants. He looked at Silliporn on the verge of tears, the cashier frowning, Greg Allman with football breasts coughing, her daughter sulking, and then at Jenkins wailing.

"The mate was a mighty sailing man," Bobby sang.

"Thuh skippuh bwave and sure," said Tom.

"Damn straight," said Bobby.

Back inside after making a full lap around the shuffleboard court with Bobby, Harold faced the TV, standing with his walker that was fitted with bright-yellow tennis balls on the leg ends.

"Who wants to play Pyramid!" The game show host smacked his hands together.

"That's Dick Clark," said Harold.

"Hell, Harold, that's Donny Osmond," said Nadine. She looked fresh as a daisy. She wiggled her toes, freshly powdered by Sister Haylie.

"That's Dick Clark," said Harold. "Them Osmonds all died out. Spaceship got 'em. Them Mormons copied the Masons." He remembered a film on cults he'd seen at the Baptist church. Mormons, Mahomedans, fish eaters, statue worshippers, Presbyterians. He shifted his weight.

"You ready to sit down, Mr. Harold?" said Bobby.

Harold flopped into his recliner. He grinned and grunted.

"We need to celebrate," said Bobby. "If you can walk around that shuffleboard court again in the morning, I think we ought to go out."

Nadine perked up. "There's that new Red Lobster in Kuhlman." She licked her lips and pushed her dentures in and out.

"Red Lobster? You sure? Hmm, Silliporn can get some shrimp," said Bobby. "You like shrimp, Mr. Harold?"

"I used to," said Harold. He looked out through the glass door at Sister Haylie walking back from the garden.

There was a brief silence as thoughts of who would be paying for the celebration crossed everyone's mind. Bobby had managed to get a credit card, noting that he was an explorer on the application and that he made $32,000 annually. A commercial for dishwashing detergent ended and a camera on the strobing set of *Pyramid* zoomed back and forth. Donny explained everything that had happened in case new viewers had joined. The phone rang.

"Hey, baby," said Nadine. She squinted at Bobby. "It's Bee."

A flash passed through Bobby. "Tell her we're having a party tomorrow." He said it before he could pull the words back into his mouth.

"We're doing alright," said Nadine. "The grass is getting awful high below the road...No it's awful quiet today. You know them construction people can't work Mondays, just like hairdressers...That's right, drunk as Cooter Brown from the weekend."

"The category is hot sticky buns," said Donnie. "Hot...Sticky...Buns..." The audience laughed.

"Bobby Hotwig?" Silliporn called from the bedroom.

"Here's Bobby, and he'll tell you how Harold's doing." She held the phone in Bobby's direction.

The screen door slammed and Haylie came

in with a basket of green tomatoes. Bobby gave her a what-the-hell look.

"Hey, Bee," said Bobby. Bee's voice threaded through him. "I think we're going to Red Lobster tomorrow...I guess it's brand new...Probably do an early dinner...Yeah, he just might get up and walk to China."

"Is Silliporn coming?" said Bee. She liked Silliporn, was attracted to her, and she felt a real connection with Bobby. Watching him take care of her grandpa Harold and hold little Jenkins made her heart melt into her stomach.

"Yeah, she'll be there. It'll give her a chance to get some seafood, something besides salmon patties." He imagined Bee's blonde hair in tight pigtails, the ones that just touched her shoulders. Most women who wore tube tops looked trashy, but Bee came off looking good, classy even, healthy good. Paired with her serious eyes and easy laugh, Bee was a deadly combination of looks and smarts.

"Okay, good. I really like her," said Bee. "It's like she just wandered onto a movie set. She's gorgeous. I still can't believe she had your baby."

Harold's eyes followed a young rabbit from a stump to a clump of monkeygrass. The rabbit stood on its hind legs and looked skyward. Harold made a gun with his thumb and index finger. "Pow...Bobby, who you talking to?"

"Hey, Bee. Mr. Harold's got his supervisor eye on me. Better get back to work." He placed the cordless phone back in the charger.

"Seafoam, let muh me show you something." Sister Haylie motioned Silliporn into the kitchen.

Bobby watched Silliporn's perfect rump. She was wearing the t-shirt with a big sparkly heart on it. Nothing much was going on at night except waking up to feed Jenkins and then coaxing his fierce eyes back to sleep. But that was okay. Like Bee said, he still found it hard to believe that she was even here, let alone having had a baby. Bobby focused on the green tomatoes in Sister Haylie's hands. "Why the heck did you pick them green?"

Sister Haylie looked surprised. "Tuh tuh to cook 'em, of course. Fuh fry 'em."

Bobby looked disgusted. "Mr. Harold likes tomato and mayonnaise sandwiches. Those would've been ripe in a few days."

Sister Haylie waved him off and held out a tomato for Silliporn to look at.

"Yes?" Silliporn didn't care for tomatoes, not even in a salad.

Bee, wearing a short, pale red, sleeveless dress with white piping that edged fake lapels, had downed two margaritas by the time Bobby and the whole gang arrived. She sat at the bar, legs crossed, smoking Marlboro Lights. Squirrel, the bartender, was all over her, lighting her cigarettes and giving her free drinks.

The Suggs' handicap-parking pass was expired but Nadine directed Bobby into the blue-lined space by the front door. The vast and faded parking lot left over from a truck stop hosted fifteen cars, two semis, and a garbage truck. The steel skin of the Suggs' old Sedan DeVille popped and shimmered in the heat. The leather seats were still in good shape, but the car was filthy inside, strewn with yellowed church bulletins and wadded tissues. Nadine had worried Harold into buying it when he retired from the cotton gin.

Just a slight breeze whiffed here and there. The big sign on top of the windowless square building said, "Red Lester's." Another said, "Seafood, Suds, and Lingerie."

"What the hell place is this?" said Bobby. He opened the trunk to fetch the wheelchair. Fried food smells hung heavy like wet laundry. A man with a big belly and part of his jaw and neck missing walked out, belched, and crawled into the garbage truck.

Nadine tried to get out, but the door was locked. Wearing a soft jean skirt with a frilly lavender top, Silliporn sat still, with hands on knees. She had been to a Red Lobster in Toronto with her father when she was fourteen, and this place seemed very wrong to her. That was after he'd gotten her pregnant the first time. A chill swept her moist shoulders.

Bobby opened everyone's door, turning the car into a four-winged jumbo jet. The engine fan continued to whir. AC units on top of the building whined. A thin pipe spurted a stream of water down the side of the metal facade, creating a shimmery delta on the crumbly brown macadam. The heat hovered at eye level.

Inside Red Lester's was dim and tepid. Yellow shag carpet covered an unlevel cement floor. Nadine snagged her toe on a petrified French fry and pitched into the wall. Bobby caught her by the arm.

"Ha," said Harold. "She's already drunk."

"Harold!"

"Hey y'all!" Bee hugged everyone except Bobby who was lugging Jenkins in his carrier. "Gaybert wanted to come, but couldn't make it," said Bee in a loud voice. She tried to kiss Silliporn on the cheek and missed.

Bobby moved closer to Silliporn and looked around. Glasses clinked. Dishes rattled. No lobster tank and they had to walk through a roomful of lingerie on racks to be seated. Squirrel walked up and handed Bee another margarita. "On the house," he said and winked.

What's that smell?

"Honey, where the hell are we?" Harold fingered a red, see-through teddy on a hanger. "I want lobster not underwear."

A woman in white scrubs with pink hearts pushed through a double-door. According to the letters on her behind, her name was Baby Doll. Bobby glimpsed a bald man with a spatula and a bottle of beer in the back standing next to an IV pole.

"Five of you'uns with the little teeny tiny baby?" said Baby Doll. She'd spent a small fortune on her hair, but her skin looked thin and sallow in the dim light. "Y'all foller me."

"I need to go to the restroom, Bobby."

Bobby nodded as they maneuvered through the nighties, a display of edible underwear that looked to be ancient, air fresheners, flavored cigars, and throwing stars.

"Bobby, where are we?"

"I think it's a Cracker Barrel for crack-heads."

"Harold," said Nadine. "This is Red Lobster, a new one, right here close to town." She took her time with her cane as her knees popped and squished.

Bee sat beside Silliporn and helped her situate Jenkins on an upside-down barstool. The dark brown table tilted toward the pocked sheetrock wall decorated with old framed photos of Nascar drivers and a variety of musicians with long beards. Bobby wheeled Harold to the men's room feeling like he was in a crowded aquarium floored with dirty yellow gravel. Nadine sat on the end beside Silliporn. She picked up a peeling laminated menu. "Bailey's Truck Heaven" had been taped over.

"Seafoam, did you learn English in Taiwan?" said Nadine.

"Y'all know what y'all want to drink?" said Baby Doll. She looked at her watch wrapped around a wristband.

Nadine ordered water for Harold and Bobby. Squirrel brought out three margaritas for the ladies. He was about to wet his pants over Bee, and now Silliporn.

Silliporn tasted hers. "Is sweet drink."

Bee swayed into Silliporn, spilling blonde hair onto her brown shoulder. "You are just the hottest thing ever," said Bee. "And this baby is just the cutie pie from hell." She leaned over Silliporn and tickled Jenkins' toes. "Damn, you smell good."

"Careful, Bee, don't knock the baby over." Nadine wrinkled her eyebrows and squinted. "I don't see lobster on this menu. Bee, do you see lobster on this menu?"

Bobby wheeled Harold back to the table.

"There they are," said Bee. She knocked over a bottle of hot sauce.

Bobby unhooked the footrests and pushed Harold's legs under the table to hide the wet spots on his pants.

"This ain't Red Lobster," said Harold.

"Harold, yes it is," said Nadine. "Ain't it, Bobby?"

Bobby sat on the end opposite Nadine and sunk a straw into Harold's brown tumbler of ice water. Sensitive to alcohol, Silliporn's cheeks and forehead flushed red. Bee was whispering in her ear. When Sammy Dushane walked in dressed as The King wearing a nose splint, the table went quiet, except for Silliporn. "Oh, Elvis the Presley!" she said and knocked over the ketchup.

Bobby choked on his water. Calls of "Elvis!" popped up from the other diners. Squirrel turned on a row of colored spotlights that lit up a small, black stage. He plugged the microphone into a fifty-watt amp. A long, tortured squeal scraped the walls. Sammy walked right on over to the table like they were one big happy family.

"Big strippers!" said Sammy. "High lollers!" He was soaring. He wore a one-piece white jumpsuit made from paper-thin polyester, and his underwear shouted through even more than Baby Doll's. An awful Elvis wig, a thin blue scarf with gold stars sewn onto it, and a pair of black dress shoes rounded out his costume.

"Who the hell are you?" said Harold.

"Honey, this here's Elvis." Nadine's eyes shone.

Silliporn laughed.

"The hell it is," said Harold.

Bobby stared at Sammy. It was the summer when Bobby's dad vanished that Sammy had started hanging out with them. Everybody had felt sorry for Sammy because he was an orphan.

"This ain't Red Lobster, and you ain't Elvis," said Harold. "Let's get the hell out of here, Bobby."

"Pawpaw, it's alright," said Bee. "Less pretend it's Elvis." She kissed Silliporn on the mouth.

Silliporn pulled back. She felt dizzy and her elbow struck the carrier. The upside-down barstool holding Jenkin's carrier rocked. Jenkins startled with a whimper. Bobby leaped up, banged his knees, dumped his water, which spread across the waxy table, and caught the carrier just in time. Sammy staggered away to the bathroom.

For ten minutes, a tape of warm-up music played a steady electronic beat, faster and faster, louder and louder. A woman in her sixties, wearing an oversized, red t-shirt with two big zeros on the back—a horseshoe champion back in the day—got up and dirty danced in front of the plywood stage. A group of church bikers in leather waltzed in and took up quarters in the back, rearranging the furniture to suit their purposes. Squirrel sat a jug of cheap red and a stack of paper cups on the bar for them. Baby-doll brought two frosty drafts for Bobby and Harold. The lights blinked and the pale breeze from the vents petered out as Sammy "Elvis" Dushane took the stage.

"Can we order?" said Bobby.

"Hold on," said Baby Doll. "I can't be in two places at one time." She disappeared into the lingerie.

"How about one place twice?" Bobby frowned. Nadine stirred her margarita. Her face registered bliss. Harold drank his beer with a straw.

"Silliporn," Bee whispered into Silliporn's ear. She laughed. "Silliporn, Seafoam, Silliporn, Shreveport, Silliporn."

Silliporn brought her elbows onto the table. Her glass was empty. Her pulled-back hair looked wonky and a wisp of luxurious black spilled across her eye. She felt sick and pushed at Bee with a stray arm as Jenkins sucked madly on a pacifier.

The bikers forgot the paper cups, partaking from the jug as Double Zeros teased Sammy, inching her t-shirt up to the bottom of her pendulous bosom, which descended to the waist of her black knit pants swarmed with cat hair. Two bald bikers flanked her, cheering her on. In the excitement, a lit grape-flavored cigar fell to the greasy shag carpet and began to smoke. Drums thumped. Sammy was "all shook up," and out of the blue sailed a can of Coors Light across the room, missing Sammy by inches, and glancing Harold's forehead.

All hell broke loose. Bobby leaped, charged toward the stage, and went for Sammy, who crashed into the biggest biker. Bobby kicked Sammy on the floor. Elvis kept on singing but Sammy didn't. Bobby jacked Sammy's arm behind his back and choked him. A small fire on the carpet jumped into action. Squirrel screamed.

"You motherfucker!" yelled Bobby. He dragged Sammy to the table. "Tell him you're sorry! Tell everybody you're sorry!" Bobby shook him by the back of his head.

Bee and Silliporn rushed out the door with Jenkins.

"Bobby!" Nadine lost her dentures and went to all fours.

Sammy spit over his shoulder and Bobby slammed his head into the table. Sammy bounced and grabbed a heavy black wooden chair. Bobby smelled smoke. Double Zeros ran weeping between them, her hands spread

across her ungainly breasts. Bobby yelled like a
Russian weightlifter. He panicked and grabbed
Harold's wheelchair. He heard lug nuts drop-
ping into a hot iron skillet.

Squirrel yelled, "Far! Far! Far!"

The next day dawned gray, promising an afternoon thunderclap. Bobby made sausage and
toast for breakfast. He put the maple syrup
on the table, which Nadine had poured into a
Mason jar and hid behind the toaster. Silliporn
had twelve days to make a decision before her
visa expired. Since arriving, she had located
Bobby, given birth, buried a child, and been im-
mersed in a culture so different from her own
that she felt dizzy.

As each new day arrived, the passing of
time lay heavy on Bobby. Is that what would
happen? Silliporn would just get on a plane
and leave with Jenkins? He wanted something
magical, a scenario where everyone got what
they needed, what they wanted. *The substance
of things hoped for, the evidence of things not
seen.*

Chewing slow, Harold's head drooped over
his plate. A room-temperature breeze blew
in the open glass door, pushing through the
house. He lifted his dead arm with his good
arm and laid it in his lap. "Bobby, I been thinking."

"Yes, sir," said Bobby. He stood by the cof-
feepot with his back to the table, reading an
old copy of the *Thrifty Nickel*. He was pondering

what Sister Haylie had said about Harold and her husband's death at the cotton gin and that when it came to young widows, Harold could only think with his little head and not his big one.

"I need to get on the tractor and get that grass mowed down below the road. I don't want rats in there eating my tomatoes."

"Hell, you can't ride the tractor." Nadine ran her finger across the plate and licked the syrup. "Bobby, don't you listen to him."

"Tell you what, Mr. Harold. Let's get your exercise in first, maybe go around the shuffleboard court twice, and then see what the grass looks like." He heard Silliporn singing to Jenkins. She was sitting on the shower chair that he had pulled into the den beside Harold's bed. His breath caught. She was so good looking and even-keeled. And she was the mother of his child.

After a glass of water, a bathroom break, loading the washing machine, and walking Harold, Bobby parked Harold beneath the black walnut tree by the garden and rode the mower down. It was old but ran like new. White clouds in a hurry tracked overhead from southwest to northeast. Shadows lumbered across the ground, gliding over every imperfection like a soft hand.

Bobby struggled with Harold. "Grab the wheel." Harold stood with his good leg on the mowing deck and arched backward. Bobby stumbled and cursed. Harold cursed. Bobby shoved him onto the seat. "Christ, man."

Harold sat cockeyed on the mower with the wind vibrating his thick hair. "Ha!" He took on a serious practical look. The grass had to be mowed so that he could move on with his busy day.

Bobby fine-tuned Harold's perch. "We're gonna mow. Just hold onto the wheel, alright?" He cranked the mower, put the throttle on turtle, flipped the blade toggle, and popped the parking brake. The mower jerked then barely moved, throwing a plume of murdered grass to the side. Harold's shoulders lifted. He looked straight ahead. Bobby let go and walked beside him as the mower cut a weaving path. When he crossed onto Sister Haylie's property, Bobby just let him keep going. A fire-ant hill exploded in a cloud of red smoke. Bobby let the dust blow away and yanked the wheel around.

Halfway back, meandering toward the pond, Harold yelled, "Bobby!" Bobby cut the engine. The wind shushed around them into a brilliant silence. "Stick a fork in me, Bobby."

"You sure, Mr. Harold?" Bobby surveyed the snakelike path Harold had cut. "Did a nice job."

"I'm done. Get me in the chair, Bobby, and let's look at the pond. I want to tell you something."

Adjoining Sister Haylie's former convent, just above it on a low hill crowded with hardwoods, sat pristine Kuhlman Abbey, a Benedictine monastery established in the early nineteenth century. Harold told Bobby that his father Robert had been holed up there all these years.

"He turned into a fish eater," said Harold. "He was sure different." He looked at Bobby sideways with a serious look.

Bobby knew better than anyone that his father had wanted to join the monastery, to discover the wonders of the craziness he called "Sprinkle Cheese"— only Jesus could have created the delicious shakeable cheese—but Bobby found it hard to believe that his dad had actually made it in and made a secret life there. A part of him wanted to believe that he was still alive, that he was atoning for his sins, waiting for salvation and face, face enough to come back and tell his son he was sorry and that he loved him. Bobby could then do the same and be done with it, move on with his life. His mother was gone forever, but his dad, his dad might just be out there, just down the road, thinking about Bobby, perhaps uttering those three simple words.

The wind eased. The pond lay flat. Bobby sat in the webbed chair next to Harold, pulling up clovers and flipping the white heads in the water. A small bream lazed up and poked at one. "Well, Mr. Harold, dad was different all right. One day, after we moved to Kuhlman, a tractor-trailer pulled up to the house. An hour later, five hundred cases of carbonated water with a catfish logo sat in our driveway, blocking in that damn Mercury Bobcat that would never go away. I guess he thought he'd won the dingdang lottery, been named an exclusive distributor for Catfresh Beverages out of Sarasota, Florida. He'd managed to save up a thousand dollars in savings bonds, but then he blew it on the water. Was supposed to have been for my college."

Harold laughed.

"I cleaned out the garage and basement and that's where those damn boxes stayed for two years until mom made me drag 'em to the curb. Who the hell wants to drink water named after a catfish? There's just no way he's out there with scary Jesus. He's not that smart. He had seizures when he was born. Turned black." He put his hands over his face.

The sky glowered yellow. Cut grass fattened the air. Crickets chirred slow motion in a row of blackberry brambles. Pushing Harold back to the house, Bobby parked the chair, stepped off to get a fat, red tomato, and pulled out a few morning glory vines taking root. The dirt beneath his flipflops scratched like chalk. A cold drip splattered on his neck and ran down his spine. He could smell the electricity of rain in the air.

"That's gonna make a fine sandwich, Bobby. We got any good mayonnaise?"

"You like Bama, don't you?"

"Course I do," said Harold. "You don't take me for a fool do you?"

"Hell no. There's mayonnaise and then there's *mayonnaise.*"

"Damn straight," said Harold.

"Damn straight," said Bobby.

Jenkins' dark, flashing eyes followed Bobby's face. In the kitchen, Silliporn talked to her mother on the satellite phone. Sister Haylie had taken Nadine to the community college beauty shop for the five-dollar special by young beauticians in training.

Bobby had a bright idea and carried an old recliner out of the garage. It smelled musty, but not too bad.

Bee held Jenkins out like a T. "You's a boo boo. You's a boo boo," she said. Jenkin's tin-can smile disappeared, reappeared. "Well, here's some news," she said to everybody. She wore black jeans and a blood-drive t-shirt.

Harold purred in the wonky recliner. Bright pokes of sun danced on his face. A single cicada cranked a slow electric noise. A squirrel gnawed a pinecone high above, sending a steady rain of cone dust and frayed scales onto Harold's maroon socks. Silliporn sat cross-legged in the thick grass on an old blue spread. She wore sunglasses and a yellow halter top. All she needed was a big red sucker. The radio in the Regal finished out "Mr. Blue Sky."

"Hadn't heard that since high school," said Bobby. He opened the box of one thousand straight pins. "What's your news? You know Silliporn's only got eleven days left."

A caller requested some Chili Peppers.

"Mother angry me," said Silliporn. "She say come now."

"How do you sit with your legs crossed like that?" said Bobby.

"I guess I'm having a little Jenkins, too," said Bee. She squeezed Jenkins and pressed him to her chest.

A pinecone's ravaged core sailed down. A couple of cars passed, bumper to bumper.

"Yes, you having Jenkins." Silliporn smiled. "Bee, being mother now." She nibbled a cracker and adjusted her bra.

"What do you mean?" said Bobby. He put some pins in his mouth. The inside of the Regal was warm, the seats worn and soft. He poked at the sagging ceiling cloth.

"I'm pregnant," said Bee. "Gaybert's baby." She coughed and nodded to Silliporn on the blanket.

Silliporn thought for a second. "Yes, he your sweet father. He long hair." She made hand motions suggestive of long hair. "He rich." Her eyes sparkled.

"I guess." Bee looked at Bobby's legs hanging out of the car.

"That's big news," said Bobby. He leaned his head back and threaded the first pin and then another. A silvery row took shape. He looked at Bee from toe to crown, blinked, and drew his lips together. "I've never been to Wisconsin."

"What?" She moved to the blanket with Jenkins between her and Silliporn. Jenkins wiggled and pumped his fists.

Harold coughed and looked around. He heard music. "Am I dead?" A warm breeze laid his head back down.

"I wonder if breastfeeding is a form of cannibalism?" Bobby dropped a pin. "Dammit, where the hell is Mrs. Nadine?"

"Cannibalism?" said Bee.

"The baby eats its momma. Right?"

"Yes, Jenkins eating me," said Silliporn. "He hunger me."

Bee laughed. "Bunch of psychos."

Silliporn laughed. "Yes, like circus," she said. "You learning Thai language, *wa?*"

Bobby laughed and went back to pinning. The Chili Peppers jumped around inside the radio.

"I really am pregnant, y'all. Give me some pins."

"What's Gaybert think?" said Bobby.

"I haven't told him yet."

Bobby helped Silliporn open the door while Jenkins rooted under her shirt.

"Look at him go," said Bobby. "Little flesh eater." He squeezed Silliporn's thigh, and she slapped his hand.

Sister Haylie's spotless Civic crept up the driveway. Nadine's fresh globe of shellacked hair hit the doorframe with a crunch. "Sorry we's late, Bobby...What in blue blazes?" Nadine pointed her cane at Harold in the old recliner. He looked like he was in a coma.

"He loves it. I'll get him back inside before we leave." He waved at Sister Haylie and walked Nadine inside the house.

Silliporn watched Bee keep at the pins.

"This car old car."

Bee stared at Silliporn's exposed milky nipple. "Think maybe I could try?" she said. "Practice?"

Five minutes later, Bee pulled Jenkins off her slobbered breast and caught her breath. Silliporn giggled and fixed Bee's shirt. Jenkins looked dreamy and turned his head side to side hunting for the real thing.

"Oh my god. He really doesn't have teeth."

"Your god is old man?" Silliporn jiggled Jenkins on her knees. A dozen rows of pins glittered overhead. All four doors stood wide open and a warm breeze crawled through.

"My old man thinks he's a god," said Bee. "What about your dad?"

Silliporn frowned. "He bad man. He sex to me and shame."

Bee whistled. "My dad raped me, too." She tickled Jenkins big toe. "Small world."

"Oh." She touched Bee's face. "We like us too much. I touch your hair?"

"Fuck men." Bee leaned over Jenkins and let her hair fall across Silliporn's lap.

"Oh, your hair like cigarette?" Silliporn made a face and pushed Bee's head away.

"Hey." Bee looked hurt and worked another pin into the roof. "Can I come visit you in Thailand?"

A pinecone thunked the car hood.

"I may dying soon," said Silliporn. "Father think he sexy Khun Phaen but he *mao sut*." Tears spurted onto Jenkins' onesie.

"What?" said Bee. "King pin?" She held Silliporn's moist hand. "He wears a mole suit?" She nuzzled beside Silliporn and held her close.

Within a couple hours, the Buick's ceiling sparkled with a thousand straight pins in weaving rows. A light rain peppered the windshield. Silliporn sat in back with Jenkins, headed to Food Freezer.

"Heck, I don't even know what kind of music you like." Bobby adjusted the rearview and it fell off.

"Jealous Lice!" Silliporn flinched and looked to make sure the steering wheel hadn't come loose. "I am his name say many times."

"Well, don't get too friendly with him." Drips of rain wiggled in through the open windows.

"He is good god for you?"

"I once did CPR on a twelve-year-old girl run over by an eighteen wheeler in a parking lot. A really big truck. Her friends said her dress got caught under the wheel and it pulled her under. Her lungs were coming out of her mouth..."

"Oh, Bobby Hotwig."

"I swallowed her blood and it didn't taste like grape juice." Bobby gripped the steering wheel with stiff arms. His eyes hurt. He looked on the seat for Nadine's grocery list and it wasn't there. "You don't think maybe the baby is your dad's do you?"

Silliporn looked out the window. She saw

a trailer. A little boy in a diaper, drinking milk from a fruit jar, waved and fell over like his feet were nailed to the dirt.

"I am terrifying for A's." She frowned. She'd had access to free HIV screening working at the Mercy Centre, but was too afraid. She'd never really had symptoms, but her father…She leaned over and kissed Jenkins broad forehead.

Bobby relaxed his grip on the wheel and stared into the rearview. He forgot about driving for a full five seconds. He cleared his throat. "Bee's gonna go and get tested with us next week. One big happy family." He saw a Low Shoulder sign and lowered his shoulder. The tires bit into gravel, spanking the undercarriage with grit and rocks.

Jenkins sputtered in alarm.

"*Cha-cha!*" said Silliporn. "Bobby Hotwig!"

"Never kill a mockingbird," said Bobby. "They sing all the songs."

"I very love music." Silliporn relaxed and tickled Jenkins' face.

"Sad songs?" He took a deep breath and felt lost.

"I like Turtle. Happy song."

Bobby pushed in his Atlanta Rhythm Section cassette. He'd made a copy for Bee. "This is pretty happy, overall, I'd say." The tape player made a racket. Bobby hit eject and a wad of slippery, knotted tape slithered out. "Well, damn."

The Buick bucked over the speed bumps in the

Food Freezer parking lot. A mossy steam spirited from the pavement. The plastic igloo baked in the sun but the North Pole Discovery Week banner was gone. The cooling units on top of Food Freezer churned the mashed potato silence.

"Eggs, milk, coffee, corn meal," said Bobby. He couldn't remember the other stuff he needed. He pushed the buggy with Jenkins' car seat perched on top. The front wheel chattered like a killdeer. The automatic door swooshed open.

"Oh, so chirry!" Silliporn rubbed her arms.

"Y'all care for a sale paper today?" said a wiry woman in yellow polyester pants and a sweatshirt thick with sequins and acrylic paint. She examined Silliporn from head to toe, peered at Jenkins, and then at Bobby. "They's free and they's a Bible verse with each special." Her eyebrows nearly circled her eyes.

"What we be a needin' is wool coats," said Bobby. He laughed, but it didn't come off right. He took a paper. "Pork chops, family pack, two ninety-nine a pound. The man and his wife were both naked, and they felt no shame. *Genesis* 2:25."

The wiry woman giggled. Mr. Tippy ran a nudist colony somewhere deep within his extensive land holdings. Bobby looked at the tile floor, worn but clean. Back in high school, he'd mopped the whole store by hand dozens of times, front to back. He saw a bit of mop string caught on the base of the banana display. He saluted Silliporn and bagged four Granny

Smith apples for a pie.

Silliporn turned a coconut over in her hands and shook it. "Is dry."

"Cabbage, three for a dollar... Naked I came from my mother's womb, and naked I will depart." Bobby pushed the cart into a man's behind. "Sorry about that." The man's massive bottom tapered up to a slender chest. Bobby smelled unwashed hair.

"Why, I thought from the sound of yer voice that it was old Walter trying to knock me down," said the man. "Got you some apples?" He examined Silliporn like she was for sale. "How de do, ma'am."

"You're a centaur," said Bobby. He pinched his leg and looked at the sale paper.

"No, I'm a Hodges. Travelbob Hodges." He put his hands in his pockets.

Bobby snapped the sale paper. "'He said to him, Take off the sackcloth from your body and the sandals from your feet. And he did so, going around stripped and barefoot. Frozen pizzas on sale."

"You sure do favor Walter. You know, the manager. Are you kin with the Coggins?" He raised on his toes.

"Not that I know of. I'm a Hotwig. My gorgeous lady friend here is a Wongmalasith. Her father is named after a character in an epic Thai poem."

Silliporn's mouth made an O and then an upside-down U.

"Well she sure is a pretty thing. Do you

speak American young lady?" Travelbob's eyes sparkled. "Wel-come to Mur-ica."

"*Sawadee krap,*" said Silliporn. She wai'd him.

"Nice to meet you, centaur, sir," said Bobby.

"Hodges," said Travelbob. "Well, very nice to meet you, too, and your wife and child."

Bobby turned the cart around convinced the conversation was over.

"Do you have a church home?" said Travelbob.

"Your breasts were formed and your hair grew, you who were naked and bare. Sauerkraut." Bobby kept walking.

Travelbob followed. "If you take the Holy Ghost Seekers bulletin to the hamburger place in White Curd after church, the waitress'll give you ten percent off. You even look like a Coggins from behind."

Bobby pulled away, headed for the bread.

"It's on the bypass. Next to the *Mexican Restaurant Coming Soon* sign!"

"Everybody's coming soon," said Bobby to the apples.

Travelbob spied a bag of dried apricots and wondered if it was pork of some nature.

At the back of the store, the fish lady with the hairnet sorted out a dozen plump frog legs. "Taste just like chicken, don't they, honey?" She handed the bag to Silliporn. "Ain't fishy a'tall." She thumbed a page in her Bible with her ungloved hand.

Silliporn held the bag. "Is chicken?" she said.

"That's right honey. Tastes like chicken. I heard your name was Seabreeze. That's sure a pretty name."

"It's Seafoam," said Bobby.

Barreling down the Food Freezer parking lot and smoking a Hav-a-Tampa, Lefevre Tippy's last earthly image as his heart leapt into a frenzied confusion of electrical pulsations was a close-up of a dildo machine hard at work. A nudist client from Atlanta had sent him a video of the Golden Thruster 5000. The Thruster 5000 had more attachments than a Kirby vacuum cleaner. His silver LTD punched through the metal siding just this side of the automatic doors and screeched inward, ripping off the side mirrors between two steel beam uprights.

Jenkins blinked and jumped in the buggy.

"What the hell? Seabreeze, stay here." Bobby ran to produce and saw the LTD smoking from the hood, covered with corn. The horn made a weak, bleepy noise. Tom and Tom remained at their stations sacking groceries with alarmed looks, waiting for something worse to happen. Bobby scanned the area and saw Walter pinned at the waist to the potato display and a slumped body inside the car. A cashier, the one with a toe thumb, ran up waving a fire extinguisher, and slipped on a tomato. Folks outside rushed in. Folks inside rushed out.

"Walter!" Bobby yelled.

Bent back over the potatoes, Walter sucked air like a bad windshield wiper.

Bobby peered into the LTD and saw Mr. Tippy's ashy face. He opened the door, felt the dead man's carotids, and moved back to Walter. Gasoline soaked Bobby's tennis shoes. "Get out! Y'all get out!" he yelled. He told the cashier with the fire extinguisher to get on the intercom and tell everybody to get out A.S.A. fucking peanut butter P. A little twirl of smoke curled inside the LTD. Bobby slammed the car door.

"Silliporn!" He ran back down the aisle, and she was gone. The fish lady licked her thumb and turned a page. "Seafoam!" He ran the full length of the store from produce to frozen food. "Seabreeze! Jenkins!" He raced back to Walter. A clot of people clogged the doors. "Shreveport, Tylenol, Bossier City, Louisiana!"

Mr. Tippy's lap crackled inside the car.

"Help me push!" said Bobby to the cashier with the toe thumb.

The car didn't budge. Mr. Tippy's polyester suit blazed into yellow flames. Thick, black smoke leaked through the broken windows. They pushed the display instead and it moved a sixteenth of an inch.

"Push, push!" Bobby yelled.

Tom and Tom joined and pushed the display sideways.

"No!"

The display moved about a foot.

"Yes!"

Tom and Tom gave a mighty heave. Bobby and the cashier gave a mighty heave. Walter crumpled to the floor in the gasoline. The inside of the car burst into a polyester inferno.

Bobby grabbed Walter by the shoulders. Tom and Tom each hugged a leg. With his eyes closed, the cashier sprayed the car with foam. Walter's eyes rolled open, then closed. He tried to speak. The sprinklers kicked in and Tom screamed, dropping Walter's leg. A fireball whumped into a league of leaping orange flames as they hurtled through the door.

Three days later, the Food Freezer conflagration still swirled in Bobby's head. Walter was in intensive care after hip surgery. Bee had spent the night at the Suggs and made a scorpion bowl with a liter of vodka from Kansas City and a big can of fruit punch from Hawaii.

Around midnight, Bobby unearthed himself from the floor. Bee and Silliporn snored lightly on the bed. Jenkins' crib was empty. "Holy Toledo." He stumbled into the doorframe and shivered. The house felt like a furnace. His throat felt cold and his head throbbed.

Bobby glanced in Nadine's dark bedroom, raucous with her jagged breathing, and tripped into the living room. A halo fuzzed around the ceiling light, reaching into the old den and bathing Harold in a queer light with Jenkins cradled in his good arm.

"Cut the damn light off, Bobby," said Harold. "I got this baby."

"Crap, you okay?" said Bobby. He touched Jenkins. "Holy cow."

"I'm cold, but he's warm."

"I'm sorry." He peeled Jenkins from Harold's ribcage and pulled up the blanket.

Harold dropped off into a humming snore with a peaceful look.

"Hey," said Bee in her underwear. "Pawpaw saved the day." She took Jenkins, tiptoed, and laid him in the crib. He yawned and dug his little fists at his closed eyes.

"Bobby's putting his shoes on," said Bobby. He put his tennis shoes on. He admired Bee's unpierced earlobes. "I'm going out to the barn. I don't know if I heard something or if I dreamed it."

Bee nodded. She slipped on her shorts and shoes and grabbed two PBRs from the fridge.

It'd only been a week since the full moon. The polished sky gleamed and sparkled. Shadows draped down the pine trunks, gathering at the bottoms. The sounds of an endless night played in loops—tree frogs chorused in the dogwoods floating beneath the night screams of restless cicadas. Bobby smelled green things and a faint char in the stillness. The beer chilled his hand.

"Silliporn says it's a rabbit we see in the moon," said Bobby.

"I like that better than an old man," said Bee.

"To be honest, I can't see the old man there.

She says that I'm a goat by birth, but that I should be a rabbit."

"Why?"

"She says that all rabbits want to go to the moon, to play with the big rabbit."

"Why?"

"I don't know, just that they want to be with the big rabbit."

As they walked to the edge of the scorched barn, which seemed to take forever, Bobby eyed Bee's hand dangling by her side. He picked his way through brambles. A sound of claws scrambling on metal broke the spell. A possum wobbled backwards across sheet metal, its red eyes aglow in the light of Bobby's keychain flashlight.

"Looks like the devil," said Bee.

The possum hissed long and hard, turned, and rushed into the tangle below.

Bobby pulled himself up and tiptoed across the shifting metal. His heel sank through rust and he fell.

"Bobby!"

He'd dropped into the hole the possum found. His leg felt wet and burned. Through the trees, he saw the moon fading from right to left. "I can see the rabbit."

Bee crept on hands and knees. She heard the possum hiss from below and a deliberate sound of movement through tight places.

"Holy cow," said Bobby.

"What?"

"Look."

Bobby reached up and showed her a silvery pocketknife marked US on the side. "That's Army issue."

"I'm coming down." The sheet metal popped and groaned. She gazed into the black over Bobby's hunched shoulders. "Smells bad."

Bobby's tiny flashlight yellowed the nooks broken with charred beams. His breath struggled to reach the deep part of his lungs. To see left he had to turn sideways and duckwalk on charcoaled wood and chunks of cement block. He felt Bee's hand on his neck.

"If I worked at a convenience store, I'd want to make sure the coffee pot stayed full," said Bobby. "If the coffee's hot and fresh, nobody misses a few dollars from the till here and there." He saw the warped deck of an old bushhog, still with a flake of red paint. The grease fitting had exploded.

"It's the same way with the service people at the Chevy dealership. But, Bobby, what are you looking for in here?"

His knees ached. He banged his head. "Ow. Let me come back your way."

Bee screamed.

"What the hell?" Bobby turned and smacked his face on a board.

"Black widow!"

Bobby rolled onto his knees and found the spider tap dancing across a dirt-covered rock, the shell of a moth stuck to the surface. "She's just looking at the magazines," said Bobby. "Ma'am would you like a chair or do you think you might scratch up a dollar for that periodical?" The bright red hourglass lifted and disappeared beneath the stone.

"What is wrong with you, Bobby?" She stood in the hole, ready to scramble out.

Bobby faced her knees and lit her face with the flashlight from below. Strands of hair stuck to her eyebrows. She scrunched back down.

"To God be the glory," said Bobby.

"Great things He hath done," said Bee.

A whippoorwill called out, "*Quick over here, quick over here.*"

"Let's get back in the house," said Bee.

Bobby squeezed around and slipped sideways to look left.

"Damn, Bobby, your leg's bloody as hell." She looked up at the breathy black sky, speckled with stars, clarified by the moon.

"Bobby Hotwig!"

Bobby froze at the sound of Silliporn's voice and the sight before him. On a piece of burned burlap sack lay a long bone. He fell backwards and landed in Bee's lap. Cobwebs clung to her illuminated hair.

"O perfect redemption, the purchase of blood," said Bobby.

"To every believer the promise of God," said Bee.

"Bobby Hotwig!"

"*Quick over here, quick over here...*"

Sunday bloomed pink then bright blue then purple then boiling gray. Finding the leg bone in the barn and slicing open his own calf had saved Bobby's skin, but Silliporn made him quit the Suggs and Bee for the day and attend the Easter worship service at Missionary Thick Baptist where they had buried Jenkins' twin. Sister Haylie stayed behind with Harold, a pleasant day of the shopping channel awaiting her.

The church came into view and Bobby felt like he was five. When he was a kid, he used to run through the cemetery with his cousins, tagging tombstones as he turned tight corners. There used to be an outhouse full of spiders and flies. Chester and Clara's car shimmered in the packed parking lot. The orange of the dirt over the twin's grave still winked from among the headstones, stands of flowers, and green grass going crispy tan from the heat. Rain threatened to pour and a low rumble of thunder vibrated the sky.

Bobby parked across the road in a pullout next to a field of soybeans heavy with pods. "Jesus escaped this morning. He's on the loose, so watch out," he said to the soybeans. He felt light, but imagined he looked heavy. Silliporn looked otherworldly, spotless in her white sundress. The yellow sash around her waist made her look like Easter.

She wiped sweat from her face. "Door open!"

Bobby helped her out and grabbed Jenkins' carrier. "Jinky, if you see a man with a beard, a funny hat made out of briars, and bloody hands, call out. You hear me?"

Jenkins looked puzzled but happy in his tiny blue short pants. An empty log truck blew by and jumped his eyes.

"Bobby Hotwig!"

"What?"

They scooted across the road and up old cement stairs embedded in the hillside. The still air revealed the history of the world. The quiet and humid lobby revealed that the service was about to start. Bobby gave Jenkins to Silliporn and pushed the carrier beneath an empty coat rack.

"My hands are in my pockets and she is grasping a baby of Asian descent," said Bobby.

The deacon minding the sanctuary door withdrew the light yellow bulletin and held it to his thigh like a ping-pong paddle. He volunteered as a crossing guard at the elementary school on Tuesdays. His father had lost an arm at Guadalcanal. He cut his eyes at Silliporn and examined the bulletin ink on his fingers. In the sanctuary, an organist covered in age spots played "Close to Thee."

Inside, bright squared tunnels of light bored through frosted arched windows. Many heads turned and Bobby scoured the packed pews. Lloyd in his wheelchair stuck out like a sore thumb. He waved them over to the crowded pew beside him. Bobby saw Clara and Chester. Chester slipped a peppermint in his mouth and started to stand but Bobby motioned him to stay. The windows rattled lightly to louder thunder.

Bobby noticed Silliporn moving toward Lloyd and followed. Bottoms shifted, a child wearing suspenders moved to a lap, shoulders squeezed, and a gap opened at the end of the pew. Jenkins stirred and made a baby sound. Bobby lingered over a stain on Lloyd's dress shirt. He smelled past his sell-by date. Lloyd licked his chapped lips and, as Silliporn squeezed by, took a deep breath.

Most everyone knew the story of the burial mishap and gazed from Bobby to the preacher with crinkled eyes. Two or three hearing aids squealed at the ruffled silence. "It wasn't so long ago that I came out of the grave," said the preacher. He got the appreciative laughs he needed. A few in the audience had come just to see if he would say it.

Lloyd punched Bobby in the arm pretty hard and made a sound like a tire going flat. "Just like yer daddy," he said.

An empty log truck rattled by on the empty country road, windshield wipers scraping the glass. In homes all around the county, mounds of green beans and collards cooked to death lingered warm on stoves. Nearly-done skillet chicken waited in ovens ready to bake up hot. Dinner rolls itching to be eaten. Motley collections of plastic pitchers marked "sweet" and "unsweet" sweated on dish towels. Bobby rubbed his arm and watched a tiny, flat tick crawl up the neck of the man in front of him. His hand found Silliporn's knee, and she pushed it away.

A fat black fly lazed in erratic circles around the congregation. Bobby realized he was singing page 48, "Fairest Lord Jesus." He pondered "woeful heart." The tick settled at the man's hairline and dug in. "Foul weather," he said to the tick. "I'm hungry," said the tick. "Soups on," said Bobby.

Silliporn poked his ribs. She switched Jenkins from lap to shoulder. Jenkins and his chubby red cheeks stared at the blue and brown eyes fixed on his own. The fly's green iridescent belly matched the choir's robe sashes.

"I won't be needing my Bible for this one," said the preacher and he didn't.

Lloyd pushed his chair back and forth with his foot. His eyes wandered to Silliporn's legs and stayed there. When he'd landed in Phuket, he'd stolen a ship's radio and sold it for enough cash to drown in pussy and Johnny Walker Red for two weeks. He wondered if she liked to be choked.

The preacher went through the scourges and wounds from top to bottom. Bobby had never heard the part about the fishhook in Jesus's tongue. The light faded from white to a kind of yellow. Lloyd handed Bobby a twenty-dollar bill. Andrew Jackson looked like a woman, a crude spurting cock aimed at his mouth. Lloyd nodded, pointed at Silliporn, and slid his hand in his pants for a quick game of pocket pool.

"It wasn't just sour wine that they held

up to his mouth to mock him with," said the preacher. "It was the worst kind of rotten vinegar soaked in hot peppers from…Africa…Imagine the burning. Imagine how thirsty he was and seeing that cup come up…" A crack of lightning sent the image home.

Lloyd licked his lips. He remembered walking into the Phuket bar to play some eight ball. One table was open and, on the other, six sailors in white bellbottoms took turns at a barmaid.

"And they leaned the cross out just a bit so the nails would tear the flesh even more…"

Jenkins rooted at Silliporn's chest.

An old lady sneezed.

The light inside took on an amber cast.

Jenkins made a tearful plea.

"Well, I fry mine in bacon grease," someone whispered from behind.

Bobby held the pornolized twenty and watched Lloyd assemble his cuestick in his lap.

The owner of the bar was shouting and demanding money for the girl. The sailors were laughing, drunk off their ass, and broke to boot. Lloyd had been raised Christian and if there was one rule he took to heart, it was that you owed nobody nothing. If the sailors wouldn't pay up one way, he'd make sure they paid in another.

Bobby grabbed the cuestick.

Lloyd shifted from Thailand to Vietnam. The heat. *Boom!* went a clap of thunder. He heard choppers and went for his pellet gun. A tracer shell of lightning burst and charged the particles in the room from negative to positive. Thunder exploded. Glass rattled.

Bobby's favorite part of Easter was the boisterous singing of "Up from the Grave He Arose," but that wasn't going to happen this year.

Men in polyester coats swarmed. Women in long dresses cowered. Children screamed. Tongues of red pew cushion rose up in confusion. Wind and oceans of rain poured from the sky onto the perplexed House of God. It began to hail, and the sun began to shine.

The County Health Department in Birmingham looked like a pyramid with the top cut off. Bobby and Silliporn followed Bee into the crowded waiting room, ready for their HIV tests. Most everyone was African American, except for an albino man with brittle rusty hair drinking a carton of strawberry milk. A banner over the reception desk asked, "Did you know there is a syphilis epidemic in Jefferson County?"

"I did not know that," said Bobby.

On the counter, a sign asked people to report dog fighting. A TV mounted next to the high ceiling ran an infomercial about gonorrhea.

"I'd like to report a dog fight," said Bobby.

"It doesn't feel safe without a condom," said the young woman in the video.

A muscular man licked her neck. "But I want to feel you for real," he said. "From the inside."

"That shit's getting me hard," said an old man in a shabby blue quilted overcoat. He scratched his pimply throat. The men around him laughed.

A door slammed opened. "Forty-eight!"

A young woman with a toddler stood.

Bobby, Silliporn, and Bee filled out consent forms and took their numbers. Jenkins squirmed in Silliporn's arms, mouthing at her shirt.

Bee looked worried. "I feel like I'm in church."

"Did you bring your cue stick?" said Bobby. He felt bad about Lloyd losing his tooth and going to jail, but Lloyd liked jail food.

The TV shifted to the muscular guy looking scared in a doctor's office, dropping his pants, and shaking his head. All the men looked away. A young woman with her hair bound back with a red piece of cloth nodded her approval.

"Forty-nine!"

"Y'all look away about now," said the old man. He said it loud enough for the whole room to hear.

Everyone looked at the TV and then looked away.

"Gross," said Bee.

There was some shifting in the room and Bobby led them to a corner under the TV. The scene moved to a happy gay couple having drinks on a patio. Chairs scraped in the waiting room.

"I heard on the news that the old lady in back of Food Freezer never left her spot during the explosion," said Bee.

Silliporn maneuvered Jenkins to her breast and did her best to cover up with a cloth diaper. A round of throats clearing was followed by a curious silence.

"The smoke knocked her out but she's okay. Had her face planted right on her Bible," said Bobby.

"What about that other guy who died?" said Bee.

"He was spraying the car with an extinguisher, when it blew. Me and the Toms barely got Walter out. It was awful. I heard him scream. I looked back and he was pounding on the window with his toe hand. Then it exploded. Five hundred firetrucks showed up in less than ten seconds. I swear to God."

"Fifty!"

"Five hundred," said Bobby.

The nurse looked tired. "Fifty!" The old man in the blue quilted coat stood and sighed.

"Bobby danger himself," said Silliporn. She punched his arm.

"Hell, I was looking for you. She got out of there faster than, faster than a..." He caught himself and tried to be less country. "Faster than you know what."

"Good for her," said Bee. "She had to."

"Yeah, I'm glad she did, but I didn't know what the hell was going on. And there was Walter dying on top of the potatoes and poor old

Mr. Tippy being cremated and then that poor fella with his toe thumb. If the Toms hadn't been there..."

"Don't tell me you're too big, that they don't make your size." The TV couple argued. "But I want to feel you for real, from the inside."

Bobby listened in on a conversation to his left about a used Cadillac with Dan Tanna hubcaps. He felt cold. The light in the room entered through the slanted windows and hit the floor at a right angle. The light crept across the floor and then rose vertically in a room-wide shaft to the ceiling. He looked at his ticket, 63.

"This nice place," said Silliporn.

"Can I burp him?" said Bee. She laid Jenkins against her shoulder and patted.

"I talked to Walter in the hospital," said Bobby.

Jenkins belched.

"Did he break his back?"

"Busted his hip and bruised his kidney. He wants me to go in business with him and redo Food Freezer. He broke down and cried. Said he was sorry about a bunch of stuff." Bobby felt his heart pounding in his face.

"He sure enough owes you for saving his life."

"Nobody owes me anything," said Bobby. He picked up a collection of ads disguised as a magazine and the cover fell off.

The day was warm, cloudy, and sticky like a

honey bun. Gaybert drove with one hand on the wheel and the other in his lap. He was taking 278 to 431, a day trip to the outlet malls in Boaz. Bee sat in back with Jenkins, blowing into his eyes and making them cross. She laughed and felt her own belly, her own child. Gaybert slid in a Turtles cassette.

"So happy!" said Silliporn. She tried to say *together* but it came out with a *zer* at the end. She sat up front, her tiny frame resting in the center of the black leather seat. She could barely see over the dashboard, but she liked the way the engine machinegunned through her body.

"This tape sucks," said Bee. "Put in some real music. Jenkins needs some manly music. Don't you Jinky?"

Gaybert ignored her and glanced at Silliporn's smooth brown knees below the neat hem of her linen dress. He had withdrawn five hundred dollars in fifties from the bank that morning. He glanced at her face, her black hair held back from her eyes with bobbypins.

"I'm a little nauseated back here," said Bee. "Turn up the air or roll down the damn windows."

Gaybert downshifted the Nash 5-speed to slow for an uneven pavement sign. The Koni racing shocks exaggerated the bump. Jenkin's eyes blinked wide. Gaybert nodded and turned up the air.

"Oh, so cold," said Silliporn. She hugged herself.

"Well, dang," said Gaybert. He backed the air down a notch and cracked his window.

Jenkins began to whimper and scowl. He kicked his feet, arching his back, smacking his lips.

"He hunger me," said Silliporn.

"You got that right," said Bee. She kneed the back of Gaybert's seat.

"Hey," said Gaybert. "Knock it off."

"I'll knock it off."

Gaybert looked in the rearview at her. "There's something I never told you."

"We might need to change seats," said Bee. "Jinky's getting fussy."

"I come into back," said Silliporn. "No problem."

"I've been fixed," said Gaybert. "Ever since my first wife miscarried and we got divorced." The Turtles moved on and Gaybert sang along: "And you know she'd rather be with me."

Silliporn was unbuckled and climbing into the back seat. Gaybert twisted to try and help. Bee reached around and pinched his side through his shirt. The Trans Am veered into the passing lane. A ship's horn bellowed. A Peterbilt big-rig bore down on the Trans Am, air brakes exploding. Gaybert floored it and the five-liter V8 cannoned them forward, throwing Silliporn into Bee's lap.

"Gay-bot!"

"Gaybert!"

The eighteen-wheeler headed into a jack-knife, swerved three times, horn bellowing, regained speed, and straightened. Gaybert cruised at ninety for a couple of minutes and then slowed back to sixty-five.

"Shit." Gaybert popped out the cassette and turned down the volume. A scratchy, staticky Jemson Handloser relayed the day's funeral announcements. "Hobart Witherspoon died in his sleep last night, reading his Bible," said Jemson.

"How could he sleep and read at the same time?" said Bee.

With Jenkins fed, Gaybert rolled into a sprawling fashion outlet center. He hated shopping, but was eager to impress Silliporn. He drove into a vast, flat parking lot surrounded on three sides by strip malls. He slowed for an old woman with bright bluish hair in a wheelchair. She had her hands folded in her lap like two freshly killed birds. The man pushing her seemed tired and angry or maybe it was just his red irritated skin.

"Bootsy Boot Boutique has some killer deals," said Bee. She led the way, followed by Silliporn pushing the little, red stroller with Jenkins.

The blue sky reached from horizon to horizon forming a flat bubble over Boaz. A lone black fly buzzed Gaybert's long, red hair. Gaybert was nearly twice as tall as Silliporn. At the curb he insisted on lifting the stroller and Jenkins onto the sidewalk. Then he stepped on a piece of pink chewing gum. "Dammit to hell."

Silliporn laughed as he scraped his shoe. His face turned red.

"Come on y'all," said Bee. She opened the glass door, *ding dong,* into the busy shop piled with shoeboxes everywhere, floor to ceiling.

"Smells like feet," said Bee.

"Smells like the trunk of an old car," said Gaybert.

Jenkins kicked his feet and punched his little fists, yawning.

"Smell like Taro," said Silliporn. She craved the squid-flavored fish snacks from home.

"Silliporn, look at these boots," said Bee. Black patent leather boots that came up to her knee. She hunted for her size among the boxes.

Silliporn was busy parking Jenkins and watching Gaybert thumb through the fifty-dollar bills in his wallet. She liked how tall he was, his long hair, how his face was neatly shaved. Bobby only shaved every few days and the stubble was rough against her face.

A woman named Thoralene with a towel around her head asked if they needed any help. As if expecting the question, she explained. "I take a shower here every morning. This used to be a health spa. You like them boots? Everything in this area, see the red tape on the floor? Everything inside the red tape is eighty percent off."

"I hope so," said Bee. "These boots are two hundred dollars." She noticed Thoralene's large biceps.

"Them are special made in China," said

Thoralene. She winked at Silliporn. "Imported and all."

"Try'em on, babydoll," said Gaybert. He spoke to Bee but was watching Silliporn, looking at her perfect feet in sandals

Silliporn stepped over the red line.

"Seventy percent off!" said Thoralene, pointing to the adjoining blue tape. "Ask me about the free socks."

Bee walked around with one boot on. She crossed the tape. "What about the free socks?"

"Seventy percent off!" said Thoralene. "Free pair with a church bulletin."

"I guess we'll pass then," said Bee. "This boot squeaks."

"Sound like toy," said Silliporn. She tried on a pair of loafers.

Thoralene saw a woman with six children come through the front door and hurried their way, toweling her hair and checking her dress pocket for peppermint candies.

They walked from store to store, Gaybert's stack of fifty-dollar bills growing thinner. Silliporn selected jeans with rhinestone eyelashes on the back pockets. Bee wound up with two short-sleeve tops, one black and the other silver. She looked at some long-sleeve button ups that she thought would look good on Bobby. Gaybert threw in a Dale Earnhardt t-shirt for himself. They decided to have lunch at Pasquales.

"Whoo, I'm already beat," said Bee. She slid

in the booth, and Silliporn sat next to her.

Silliporn had never had pizza before. "Oh, is cheese." She nibbled the crust and picked out a sausage ball with her fork. "Is meat?"

Bee laughed. "Sausage, from the pig." She made an *oink oink*.

"Oh, moo," said Silliporn.

"No, oink oink," said Bee.

"I think she means pork is called moo in her language," said Gaybert. He blushed. "Course, I don't speak Chinese."

"Yes," said Silliporn. She ate the sausage ball shaped like a jellybean and made an it's-okay face.

Gaybert went over to the jukebox and put in fifty cents. The opening guitars of "Black Betty" blasted the restaurant.

Silliporn put her fingers in her ears and smiled at Gaybert. Jenkins threatened to cry but settled once she lifted him from the stroller.

"Hey, baby, me and Silliporn want to get our nails done. Don't we?" Bee pantomimed a manicure.

Silliporn poked at a tomato in her salad and nodded her approval. The whites of her nails were brilliant.

"I reckon," said Gaybert. He twisted his hair into a rope and let it fall.

After they finished lunch, on their way to Nail Shine Express, Bee hauled them into a store that sold only toy pianos. She'd always wanted to play the piano. The pianos were on the floor and she had to bend over to play one. She plinked a simple tune.

"My what a pretty colored girl," said the shopkeeper. She was an older lady wearing a brown wig with little circlets for bangs. Her name was Rainette. "Warms my heart to see y'all out and about. We just all got to get along, don't we?"

"What?" said Bee.

Gaybert frowned. "Colored girl?"

"Times is a changing. We got us a black comes to our church on Sunday. Real nice lady, quiet and all. What's yer name, honey? Colored folks always got such pretty names."

"Silliporn." She pushed Jenkins back and forth in the stroller. He was getting restless.

"Seafoam? Why I never heard that one. What did I tell you all?" She put her hands on her hips like she had won the jackpot.

The bells on the door jingled and in walked the man with the irritated face pushing his mother in a wheelchair.

"That's the judge from Kuhlman County," said Bee. "His nephew is Sheriff Gaslight."

"Is sick?" said Silliporn. She noticed a bluish pallor around his lips, and his face was pinched. He was breathing or rather panting and wincing. His mother in the wheelchair looked decomposed, her lips slightly parted as if about to speak.

"Dammit, I need a chair if any of y'all could stop staring and help a fellow." He tried to lean down and brace himself on a tiny black piano. He wound up sitting on a child-size piano bench with his hand going to his chest.

"Son," said his mother. "I want to look somewhere's else."

Gaybert's left eye began to twitch.

Rainette got on the intercom and asked if there was a doctor in the house. She dialed 911, and then ran outside wringing her hands.

Silliporn rushed to the judge's side. "You go down. Head down. Come, come." She looked back to Bee and Gaybert for help.

The judge locked eyes with Silliporn and slipped onto the floor. Silliporn grabbed his neck and lowered his head to the hard, cheap carpet.

"Son, why are you a laying in the floor?" said his mother. "Is he sick?" She kept her hands folded, a tissue with lipstick on it gathered in her lap.

Silliporn checked his carotids and felt a bounding, irregular pulse. The judge was sweating. His eyes looked funny. "You rest now. Doctor come."

"Good work, Silliporn," said Bee.

In the heat of the moment, Gaybert had gathered Jenkins to his chest and was rocking him up and down.

Vexed and with an elephant sitting on his chest, *"Anh yeu em,"* the judge told Silliporn that he loved her in Vietnamese. His breathing became deeper. His eyes relaxed and even twinkled. Sirens bellowed in the parking lot, and the toy piano store was soon awash in flashing lights.

A scrap truck backed up the Suggs' driveway to the barn for the final load of charred metal. In the front yard a dozen stumps that Bobby had stoked with pinecones and motor oil spumed smoked. Bee, Silliporn, and Gaybert were off on another shopping trip.

"Ought to clear two hundred dollars," said Nadine. She gripped the TV remote and put her finger into a burn hole on the recliner's arm-rest.

Sister Haylie sat in Harold's wheelchair, pinching the knot of her apron. Harold gazed around the room testing his left eye. It'd gone blind in the night, but he hadn't told anyone. Bobby came in the back door.

"Mr. Harold, let's get outside."

"I don't feel right, Bobby."

"Aw, get outside, Harold," said Nadine. She wanted Sister Haylie to look at the sore on her backside, which was getting worse.

"How about an Ensure? You didn't eat much breakfast."

The Price is Right trumpeted into the room.

"I don't think so, Bobby." Harold looked Sister Haylie in the eye. "You took that money for the operation but you kept it, didn't you?" His right hand trembled.

"Whu whu whu whu," said Sister Haylie. She went for the rosary beads in her apron pocket.

"If I roll over, maybe you can look at my

hip," said Nadine. "I hate to ask Bobby." She breached on her side with her eyes glued to the TV. "Lord look how dark skinned that lady is."

Harold stared out the glass door through the chimneys of stump smoke, past the garden, and to the pond. He shuddered.

"Yuh you tuh took uh uh advantage," said Sister Haylie. She gazed around the room and visualized the stations of the cross.

"What?" said Nadine. "Bobby, can you help?" She lay sideways in the recliner, grunting.

Harold had let wet cotton be loaded into the gin. Bobby knew the story. The resulting friction had caused a fire between the roller and the saws. The fire extinguisher was busted and Haylie's husband—what was his name, Doug?—had jammed his arm in there with a hose. He'd been drinking on the job and Harold had allowed it.

"Look what my beauties have for you to bid on," said Bob Barker. The audience went wild over a brown crockpot.

There was a knock on the screen door.

"About done out here." The scrap-metal man wore an old sweater, thick rough pants, and heavy oiled boots. His ears looked yellow and his eyebrows were clogged with dandruff. He showed Bobby a skeleton scrambled on top of charred plywood and burlap. A leg bone was missing as well as the skull. The scrap man's son, about twelve with a thick mustache, poked around in the soot.

"Looks like a deer," said the scrap man.

"Looks like a deer," said Bobby.

"What you got, boy?" said the scrap man. "Get on over here."

His son simpered over and handed off a warped and smoky *Hustler* from 1976.

"Some things keep for a reason," said the scrap man. He put the magazine inside his sweater, reached out and touched Bobby's face as if it were his own, then turned with his son and walked away.

"Hey. Why don't you let him have the magazine? I remember when I was his age…"

The boy pulled a thick stack of water-damaged *Playboys* from the back of his loose pants and waved them at Bobby.

"Oh," said Bobby.

The scrap man winked.

Silliporn wore her new pair of jeans and a pink plaid shirt from Dress Barn, courtesy of the trip to the outlet malls in Boaz organized by Bee and funded by Gaybert. She sank into the worn backseat of the Buick and toyed with Jenkins' hair.

"Damn, you look better than fried chicken with a cup of hot coffee," said Bobby to the rearview. He pulled into the new parking deck at Kuhlman County Hospital. He had the little knife from the barn in his pocket.

"This hospital?" said Silliporn.

"Yep."

They walked to the end of a corridor.

"Is so quiet."

The elevator opened onto the bright step-down unit. Sharla, a hefty nurse with big-rig arms, showed them Walter's room.

"You drive a big-rig?" said Bobby. He bit the inside of his cheek.

"That's right," said the nurse. "How'd you know?"

"Seen you," said Bobby. "On the highway." He coughed.

Walter's thin scattered hair looked greasy. "Hey, Bobby." His eyes brightened. He moved and winced. An IV dripped saline into the crook of his arm.

Bobby turned off the overhead exam light and shifted the overbed table. He moved a folding walker into the corner and straightened the sheets on the bed. He pulled the curtain out just a bit and peeked at Walter's neighbor. "Hey there."

"Hey yourself," said a man with a terrible rash on his face. It was the county judge from the toy piano store.

"You like honey buns?" said Bobby.

"Now they're sending in street people to harass me," said the judge. He'd had a mild heart attack and wanted a private room. He squeezed his nurse call light and touched his face as if it were a rock.

"Bobby...Leave him alone," said Walter. He made a cuckoo motion with his hand. "What's this lovely girl's name again? Seabreeze?"

"Yes," said the nurse through the speaker.

Silliporn tidied up the wide reclining chair and sat Jenkins' carrier in it. "You happy, better some?" she said.

Walter smiled.

"When are you gonna get me a goddamn private room!" the judge yelled. "I've got a good mind to call the Sheriff up here and clear one out for me. He's my nephew you know!"

Bobby took a deep breath. The judge had silver hair and big teeth. He peeked at the judge. "Sir, if you don't mind, you're disturbing the other customers. I might have to ask you to take it outside."

"Who the hell *are* you?" said the judge. "Nurse!"

"I see you have a catheter," said Bobby. "Looks a little dark in the bag. Maybe you ought to run it through one more time. You need a straw?"

"Boy, what's your business?" said the judge.

"Bobby Hotwig!" said Silliporn. She recognized the judge.

Bobby threw back the curtain. "Did you have your E.G.G. today?"

"My what?" The judge saw Silliporn and froze. There was a young woman in Vietnam who had been sending him letters and pictures since 1978.

"How about your T.O.A.S.T.?" Bobby yelled.

"Get out of my room!" said the judge.

"You're looking for the face you had before the world was made," said Bobby. "You stole Weedy's sock. Your face is red and irritated."

Silliporn tugged Bobby backwards by his starfish t-shirt.

The judge stood, yelled, and grabbed his chest. He gasped and fell back on the bed.

Jenkins blinked and cried toward Silliporn.

"Two for a dollar," said Bobby. "How about a private room in hell, cocksucker!" He growled like a dog. "Bare not false teeth against thy neighbor. Joshua, Judges, Ruth, and Song of Solomon!"

Sharla blasted into the room, saw the judge akimbo on the bed, and called a Code Blue. The room swelled with scrubs and white coats and stethoscopes and needles. Bobby, Silliporn, and a puzzled Jenkins drifted down the hallway to the elevator. Walter pretended to doodle in a word-search book.

In Bangkok, Silliporn's father stepped off the bus. He wore a muscle shirt and baggy Bali pants with a bright orange and yellow dragon design. He'd managed to obtain an expedited visa to the United States based on his emergency medical claim that his daughter had given birth to twins and that one child had died. While at the embassy, he'd made a day of it, eating dragonfruit at his favorite buffet, and buying himself slacks and button-up shirts. At the airport, he stood in line for ninety minutes with his passport and bought a roundtrip ticket to Atlanta, Georgia. The airline agent had a good laugh with him trying to pronounce Alabama. Khun Phaen thought about flying through Toronto, where he had first tried to sell Silliporn when she was fourteen. The deal had gone sour at the Red Lobster when a PETA group burst in, smashed the restaurant aquarium, and made off with thirty lobsters. There could still be warrants. Ticket in hand, he hopped a *tuk-tuk* into the Khlong Toey slum and checked off on the latest batch of St. Bernard puppies headed to Lithuania with pure white heroin sewn into their bellies. He bought another battery for his new satellite phone. He couldn't wait to find Silliporn and smash the one she stole from him over her head. It had taken great willpower not to call her on the phone. But she had been foolish enough to call her mother. He went home, drank a glass of water, and beat his wife for not packing his bag like he said. He swallowed ten condoms of black tar heroin just for the hell of it and went to bed.

Silliporn convinced Bobby to drive to his grandparents' house and talk with them. Bee had told Silliporn about Bobby's dad, explained the barn incident, and told her that his dad Robert was living at Kuhlman Abbey. Again, the story of his dad at the monastery, and again the half hopes that he was really there, instead of dead.

Bobby lay on the couch in the back den with his eyes closed. He heard the *whump* of his dad hitting the ground. The crackle of flames from the hay in the loft. Snake bites of fire flitting through knotholes in the barn walls. Their last night together.

Chester and Clara gazed at him from their recliners as if they knew his thoughts. Silliporn breastfed Jenkins beneath a large beach towel on the floor. A Billy Graham crusade from Gothenburg, Sweden, circa 1955, played without sound on the TV.

"Bobby, you've got to let your daddy go," said Clara. "Robert didn't want you to find out."

Chester squirmed and tapped his fingers on the armrest.

"Find out what?" said Bobby. He kept his eyes closed. The judge's red, scaly face raced through his head.

"He never did really come back from over there in Vietnam," said Chester.

"Lost his mind," said Clara. She put her Sunday School book down.

"I know," said Bobby. A fly attacked the window. Ice clanked in the icemaker. "Private room my ass." He clenched his jaw.

"He lived a good long life in there," said Clara. She put her hand to her mouth. Tears slicked her eyes.

"In where?" Bobby felt a piece of dry twine being pulled from his nose.

Silliporn watched the TV. Billy Graham raised his Bible toward heaven like a plate heavy with savory meats.

"Same place that dang doctor wanted to cart you off to after your... your troubles," said Chester. He coughed.

"The State Hospital?" said Bobby.

"Robert lived there for twelve years. Sometimes he knew us, most times not," said Clara. "He painted angels with a toothpick and food coloring onto dried lima beans."

Bobby felt his nose. He wanted to sleep forever and pushed his head into the cushion. "Lima beans?"

"Held his breath," said Chester.

"Did what?" said Bobby. He opened his eyes.

"Died when you was in Taiwan," said Clara. She fluffed her hair with the pick. "Held his breath and died. Had his body buried right there. You know he never got along with your mama."

Bobby wanted to go to sleep.

"Taught himself to hold his breath for fifteen minutes," said Chester. "Nobody could stop him. After y'all moved back from Texas, and he bought all that damn sparkle water, he told me he was going to hold his breath for sixteen minutes and die when he was forty seven."

"On his birthday," said Bobby. Bobby had jumped from the bridge on his father's birthday. He slammed his fist hard on the carpet and held his breath.

Jenkins pulled off Silliporn's breast and stared with a bewildered look.

"Bobby Hotwig." Silliporn scooted to him and held his hand.

"Walter Coggins down at Food Freezer says he's my dad," said Bobby. He rubbed his face.

He smiled at Jenkins and Silliporn.

"Oh Lord," said Clara. She knew it was possible.

Chester coughed. He knew it was possible, too. Bobby favored his mother but not Robert. He didn't have Robert's tan or his narrow shoulders. Chester had suspected it, ever since Robert had left for Vietnam. So many young women without their men, easy prey for grown men with good jobs and an eye for opportunity. Men like Walter Coggins and Harold Suggs. A fly buzzed a long slow arc into the kitchen and disappeared into the gloom.

The visiting nurse confirmed that Harold's left eye had gone blind. She recommended an outpatient visit for a full physical at the hospital. She thought he was losing weight, too.

Bobby sat him up in the bed and swung his legs over the side. "Come on. Silliporn's outside in her polkadot bikini. Don't want to miss it. Tomorrow's her last day here." His throat lumped into a hard knot.

"She's a pretty girl," said Harold. "Even with my one eye."

Nadine held the phone to her face. "Hell, Claudette, one eye, two eyes. He don't know the difference..." *The Pyramid* was on. Donny Osmond traded jokes with Howard from Spearfish, South Dakota. Nadine squinted at Bobby as he helped Harold into the wheelchair. Harold hung his head and scratched his thigh through his thin pajama bottom.

"Mr. Harold, we need to get you in for a checkup. You might need some vitamins or maybe a good old fashioned..." Bobby choked back a sudden pang of sorrow in his chest.

Harold tried to grin. "Yeah."

A bowl of ripe tomatoes that Silliporn had picked glared red on the counter. Harold's salmon and eggs sat cold on the table.

"So what do folks do in Spearfish?" said Donny.

"We have a college," said Howard.

The audience oohed a collective sigh of relief.

"Let's burn some more stumps." Bobby felt wasted. "You want to mow the grass again? Go see the pond? Smoke a cigarette?"

"Hey, Bobby." Nadine covered the phone. "Claudette's husband is getting his chemo today and she wants us to meet her in the hospital cafeteria. Food's real good."

"I don't think Mr. Harold's up to it. He needs to get outside and walk, though. It's been three days." Plus, Bobby was worried that the judge might be coming out of his coma. Better to stay away from the hospital.

Nadine looked stymied. "Claudette, let me call on Sister Haylie. She can drive us. We don't need old men dragging us down anyhow." She guffawed.

Outside, after a single bite of egg, Harold stared into the trees. Silliporn's farewell dinner was that night, and she sat on a blanket with

Jenkins. The Buick's radio wafted through the open doors. "Oh, Gay-bot like this music."

"Gaybert likes George Michael?" Bobby watched Harold's head nod. A piece of pine straw fell on Jenkin's onesie.

"Gay-bot rich."

Bobby walked to the other side of the yard with a can of lighter fluid. He piled pinecones on a stump, squirted, and threw a match on it. Orange flames boiled, devilling smoke into the stacked air.

"Bobby Hotwig! Too many smoke!"

Bobby turned back. "Just this one. I promise." He wondered if Gaybert was his father or maybe the scrap-metal man or maybe Mr. Tippy.

Two squirrels trotted down the power line and leaped on the house. Bobby rolled Harold onto the shuffleboard court. "Watch your foot, Mr. Harold." He swung the leg rests back. "Ready?"

"I reckon I killed that man," said Harold. "I never should of loaded that cotton wet."

"Sounds like it was an accident."

"Tore his arm clean off."

"It was an accident, Mr. Harold. Not your fault at all. He'd been drinking somebody told me."

"Don't matter now." Harold looked up the dull blue sky. "What's life worth, Bobby?"

Bobby looked at a vein running across Harold's hand. The cicadas lulled and roared, lulled and roared. "Not much if you're dead."

"I reckon the ground catches everything," said Harold. Bobby nodded.

"Bee come tonight?" said Silliporn. "Gaybot?"

"Yep, but later," said Bobby. "You gonna cook some shrimp?"

"We go store?"

"Let's get Mr. Harold some exercise and we can go. Come on Mr. Harold. How about it?" Bobby grabbed his armpits.

Harold sat there, unmoving.

"On three. Got to stay active."

"Can we sit by the garden, Bobby?"

"We're losing ground, Mr. Harold. You have to help me out here."

Silliporn came over and shook her finger at Harold. "You walk. I help."

"Like a China doll." Harold squinted with his good eye. "I'm gonna miss you, Seafoam."

Robert Hartwig smoked a joint in the barn loft. He'd told Bobby and Sammy to go on and fish and stayed behind. His belly was full of fried squash and porkchops. Nadine had dragged Harold to Red Lobster in Birmingham with Claudette, her husband Ike, and Chester and Clara. The dim loft seemed to hold the entire universe. Robert drained his doobie, making little fires with his lighter in the loose hay. His mind raced. He got naked without realizing it. He coiled and uncoiled a thin, husky rope, put it around his neck. He examined the rafters and drifted back to Vietnam, crawling through tunnels with a Colt .45. They threw dice to see who would go in. The officer always rolled the dice for the enlisted men...

Bong Son...the last man dragged in on a bloody blanket and gushing blood from a shoulder stump fell from the transport door. PFC Robert Hartwig grabbed air and fell twenty feet on top of him. The helicopter, tail up and hovering a crop circle into the tall wet grass, lifted for two seconds, spun, and caught a bazooka round through the open nose window. Time did a curlicue. A lone machinegun sprayed the entire world. The UH-1 Iroquois with crossed Cavalry swords jerked, did a half gainer, and slammed into the ground. PFC Hartwig surveyed the inferno. The soldier at his feet wanted a cold bottle of sparkling water. Robert said no problem and went to the refrigerator but the handle was broken. The soldier, a kid from St. Ansgar, Iowa, died without getting his cool, fizzy drink. Robert squatted, pulled out a canister of sprinkle cheese mailed from home, and ate some from his bloody hand...

...fiddled with his dog tags beneath the slack rope around his neck. Robert opened his eyes. A tendril of smoke twined into the hot, barn air flecked with magnetic dust.

Down at the pond, Bobby tossed a deck of rubberbanded cards on the grass. In distinct passes, the blued pewter sky absorbed shade after shade of night. Bream and bluegill rippled the water, sucking at the evening revival of Jesus bugs. He looked across the road for Sammy, who was supposed to be finding some hooks. Fireflies strung themselves between the trees. Bobby threw a rock. The bottom muck poofed an invisible lazy silt mushroom. Bubbles colonized the surface and cattails rattled in the breeze. He jogged up to the house in a mild panic.

Sammy could see the silhouette of Robert in the open loft door. A shaft of green-yellow light enveloped him. He climbed the stairs one at a time until he saw Robert standing on two hay bales with a rope around his neck and fire at his feet. The overhead beam gave a little screech.

Bobby walked up to the barn. He saw two silhouettes struggling in the loft and spat.

Mr. Tippy's will directed his body be cremated and the ashes spread across the magnetic North Pole. Food Freezer re-opened, leaving the burned-out Cadillac in the vegetable section as a memorial. The parking lot was so crammed that the vehicles were killing the grass in the cracks.

"Nebraska, Georgia," said Bobby. He read another license plate. "Rhode Island...Damn."

Expecting the cold inside, Silliporn was wearing one of Harold's flannel shirts.

The heat rushed them when the door swung open.

"Whoo. Hot as Hades," said Bobby.

The elderly woman who passed out sale papers stood there just about naked. "May I take your coverings?"

Walter rolled over in a wheelchair with his leg extended. He wore a necktie. "As long as we don't serve alcohol, ain't nothing nobody can do. Why don't you get comfortable and grab a buggy?" A long red scar ran the length of his right thigh.

Bobby took the sale paper from the old lady. Masking tape covered the little knots on her pancake breasts. "What the hell?"

Silliporn waved at the Toms in their generic Speedos. "Is for Easter party?" The atmosphere made her think of Songkron, the annual water festival in Thailand, where one's main concern became throwing water on others. It was crazy but fun.

"So it's all yours? The store?" said Bobby. He tried to imagine he was at a cat food factory filled with chicken guts. "Catfish, naked people, and all?"

"Well, everything went to the Toms, but Mr. Tippy named me the operator as long as I made it a nude grocery store."

"That's neat," said Bobby. He couldn't remember why he was there.

"I want you to go in with me, Bobby. Father and son." He struggled to keep an even keel. "In the will, I get to choose a partner. I'll be needing some help running the store and the colony out in the woods." He pointed to where Robert Peary and the Eskimos used to stand; in their place was a new sign advertising Tippy's Sunluvver Nudist Colony.

Bobby stared at Walter's ears. They had the same creases his had. Walter had told him that when his dad Robert went off to Vietnam, his mom had called him over to fix her TV. She didn't have anyone to haul it in for her so he went to her place.

A couple wearing brown robes walked in. "Y'all from out of town?" said the salepaper lady.

"All the way from California," said the man. He pulled off his robe, but left his slippers on.

"Praise to God," said Silliporn.

"Holy cow," said Bobby.

"Amen," said the salepaper lady.

"This is crazy in Alabama," said the woman.

"He is rising," said Silliporn.

"Up from the grave he arose," said Bobby.

"Yes, dear Jesus," said the salepaper lady.

She lifted her hand toward Heaven and Bobby saw a mole in her armpit that looked like a maroon brain.

"He lives forever with the saints to reign."

Jenkins gurgled and made a spit bubble.

Silliporn started to pull her dress over her head and Bobby said, "Whoa." He looked around. Warm air worked its way between his t-shirt and his skin. Eight cashiers on duty. One of Sheriff Gaslight's deputies patrolled the front in full uniform and helped one of the Toms sack a birthday cake. Lines backed into the aisles. A recording of Mr. Tippy reading from Apsley Cherry-Girrard's *Worst Journey in the World* played over the sound system. A row of saggy bottoms, a couple flossed with thongs, gathered around the blackened LTD cordoned off with velveteen rope. Bobby's father had died in an insane asylum. His father was naked in a wheelchair with a busted hip, talking to him. His father was made of deer bones. His father lived in a monastery. His father had been locked away and held his breath until he died the very day Bobby had jumped into the Chao Phraya River. His father was an old man who'd had a stroke and just lost the sight in one eye.

"Just to our underwear," said Bobby.

Bee burst through the automatic doors, already down to her bra. "Hey guys!"

"One more scab and the jar will be full,"

said Bobby. He tried to imagine cleaning pig intestines for a church picnic. Nothing was working. He handed his pants to the salepaper lady, who winked, put them in a wire basket, and gave him a plastic number.

Jenkins pumped his fists and drooled.

"The trouble is sweat and breath," read Mr. Tippy from the beyond. "I never knew before how much of the body's waste comes out through the pores of the skin…"

"Double coupons are a thing of the past," said Walter. "We've sold more groceries this week than a month of Sundays." He moved a paper bag into his lap at Bee's approach. "And naked people don't steal."

"We need to buy some shrimp, Walter, dad, sir," said Bobby. He saluted a naked woman with a red kerchief around her neck. "Seafoam leaves tomorrow and we're having a party at the Suggs' tonight."

"Hell, Walter, you should come," said Bee. She let her hair loose from a clip.

"I'll do that," said Walter. "That alright, Bobby?"

"Sure. You need a ride?"

"Your old buddy Sammy's carting me around in his minivan. I'm thinking about hiring him back on at the store."

"Oh, Elvis the Presley," said Silliporn. She laughed.

Bobby clenched his teeth, bit his tongue, and pinched his thigh.

"Oh, look," said Silliporn. She pointed at

Bobby.

"The more the merrier," said Bobby.

Mr. Tippy smiled as he read from the grave. "So all night long our breath froze into the skins, and our respirations became quicker and quicker as the air in our bags got fouler and fouler…"

Sammy shoved Robert through the barn loft door, jumped, rolled, and ran like hell. Bobby stared at his buck-naked father on the ground with a rope around his neck. "Sammy," Robert whispered. He raised a broken hand toward Bobby, fingers askew.

Bobby limped him to the beat-up Bobcat wagon. Fire danced in the windshield. Dry planks popped and cracked like roasting bone marrow. He could hear the sound of a fire engine in the distance, coming up the back roads. He lifted the hood, unscrewed the air filter cover, and fumbled for the spare key. The engine dragon-roared. The radio popped and cracked as Jemson Handloser read funeral announcements.

"Edith McGlawn, ninety-two, passed on to be with our Lord yesterday at the County Manor for the Aged." Jemson paused and recounted an anecdote about Edith involving a rabbit and Vacation Bible School. "Needless to say, I spilled my orangeade, but Miss Edith was right there with more…"

Robert choked. "Take me…home to Sprinkle Cheese, Sammy."

Bobby ran over a rock and swung the back end of the Bobcat onto the road.

"I'm taking you to the hospital," said Bobby. He turned off the radio. The engine screamed without the air filter. Mayflies splattered the windshield.

"Please don't, son. Do like your daddy says and take him to see Sprinkle Cheese."

A thrill of hot water shot from Bobby's feet to his eyes. The Bobcat leaned to the inside curve and stuttered the pavement.

"I know what you want to know, son. Your mama is Haylie Bannister," said Robert. "She went into hiding with them nuns." He coughed and spit blood. "I hate you spent them years in the orphanage, boy."

The Bobcat flew by the cotton gin, just condemned and ready to be razed. Fluff from the seed house swirled into the road. Bobby felt hot and cold. He felt like throwing up. His chest and thighs quivered.

"Her husband was killed right before I went to Nam. She was a mess. I was a mess. Ever'body was a mess…"

Bobby played back Sammy's life at Child Heaven, the beatings, the awful clothes, a new daddy every six months to share with twenty other throwaways. It all seemed so real. It was real.

"Right up here, Sammy," said Robert. "I'm going to be with Sprinkle Cheese." He'd been talking to death the idea of becoming a monk. None of the medications helped. Bobby took Sprinkle Cheese to be a manifestation of Jesus.

"Life and death is just a flimsy bookmark…" Robert gagged and spit. He rubbed his throat. "Sammy, without Sprinkle Cheese, I'm telling you, boy…Hell's bells, boy…" He rolled his window down a bit and cool wet air rushed in.

Bobby saw the scary Jesus and slid the Bobcat to a crooked stop. "You and your goddamn Sprinkle Cheese," said Bobby. "And by fucking God, I'm sick and tired of you calling me Sammy. I'm Bobby, you motherfucker. Sprinkle Cheese be damned and you with it."

"Sammy!" said Robert.

"Sprinkle cheese!" Bobby screamed over the engine.

"Sammy!" Robert opened the car door and jumped. The seatbelt jerked him sideways. His head hovered above the pavement as Bobby drove like a maniac down the monastery road.

Bobby slammed on the brakes in front of the gate to Kuhlman Abbey. The engine burned and popped like a hot oven with nothing cooking.

"Sammy?" Robert hung out of the door with his head on the ground, a cheek bleeding dark red in the light. "Save yourself and come with me." He reached out his hand toward the shadows beyond the gate.

Bobby unbuckled him and pulled him to a small patch of grass bright green in the headlights. A mist rose from the ground around them. The wind soughed through the pines to a tremendous chorus of cicadas, millions celebrating the end of something, the beginning of something else.

"Sammy, you've taken His name in vain."

"Sprinkle cheese, seventy times seven," said Bobby. He blew the horn a few times to wake the elves or whatever the hell they were and drove.

In the kitchen, choked with an extra card table and two TV trays, Bobby chopped cabbage. Silliporn, in a red apron over her white Easter dress, butterflied shrimp. In a bikini with a towel around her waist, Bee cut tomatoes. A horn blew *beep beep* and Bobby took a deep breath.

"A horn blowed," said Harold. He looked out the glass door. He toyed with the blanket on his legs and drifted back to the TV commercial for dog food. A puppy froze in mid-air and an X-ray of its bones appeared. Harold scratched his chest and thought about his mother wearing a bonnet to church.

Nadine wiggled her toes in the recliner and squinted, happy at the bustle around her.

"Get out there and help them old folks," said Bee.

Bobby went to the carport. A tall skinny man with a serious toupee was helping a woman shaped like a stack of tires. Bobby poked his head back in the kitchen. Claudette and Ike. "The Turnipseeds are here!"

Nadine banged on her recliner shift and popped up like burned toast.

"Hey there, Mr. Ike, Mrs. Claudette," said Bobby. "It's been awhile."

"Well, lookie here, honey," said Ike. "Son, it's good to see you." He jostled his catheter bag and winked. "You win some, you lose some." He let go of Claudette and pulled a pack of Dorals from his pressed shirt pocket.

"Hey, Bobby," said Claudette. She wobbled and Bobby grabbed her.

"Let me walk you in." His grandparents' car slowed in front of the house and he waved. "Watch out for this anthill, Mrs. Claudette."

Behind them all, a tiny cloud like an eye pinned itself to the warm, dimming sky. The pond frogs barumped in expectation of a perfect summer night. A few lightning bugs blinked in slow motion, drugged in the stillness. Bobby released Claudette into the maelstrom and trotted back outside as Chester eased the car into the grass. A family of swallows swooped and darted batlike toward the pond. Bobby poked Chester in the belly. "Hope you got room," he said.

Then Bobby saw Sammy's ragtag minivan coming down the road. Next door, he noticed Sister Haylie step through the screened porch of the little cabin. Too many thoughts crowded his head. He tasted the yellow water of the Chao Phraya River, felt his clothes ripping off, saw Jenkins' black eyes, the wooden box used to cart out the dead at Mercy Mission in Bangkok, a bottle of Catfresh carbonated water draining into the street, his glasses flying into the creek with Bee's hands around his neck, Mr. Tippy on fire.

The green papaya salad, prime rib masala, pistachio ice cream. There had been candied dried shrimp with the ice cream, crunchy and sweet and hot. The walk around the hotel, past walls behind which there was a palace, he couldn't remember. It had been a series of frames advancing within the dark interior of a camera, his existence caught on film. The young man who sat behind a little gilded desk at the end of the hotel hall had been asleep, head on his folded hands. Bobby's roommate had fled that afternoon, and the room was theirs.

He felt sure now that his heart had actually stopped when his bare chest touched hers. And the condom. He had used a condom. Yes, he had used a condom. She had wanted him to, right? It had been all too fluid, too dreamlike, too much pleasure to have been real at all. *Poof...*

The party din drowned out *Wheel of Fortune* as Randy from Willamette, Oregon, spun with vigor. Nadine and Claudette sat side by side in the matching recliners. "Look at them big ears," said Claudette. "Like two car doors," said Nadine. She wore a Golden Thruster 5000 t-shirt that Bee had given her. Nadine thought it was a machine that cured cancer. She beamed and mumbled the letters. "It's a person," said Claudette. *"Big money,"* said Randy from Willamette. "Pat's standing on a step stool," said Nadine. *"There is an N,"* said Pat. "Wind come along with them ears, Randy'll be on a direct flight back to Willamette," said Claudette. Nadine laughed and caught her dentures.

Silliporn imagined she smelled lemongrass.

It was Ike's cologne. She stirred a brown sauce to pour over the shrimp. "Oh, somebody missing," she said. She spooned the sauce into a green bowl and ran to the bathroom to check her lipstick.

Bobby hustled, brushing past Chester then Ike. "You okay, Mr. Harold? Feel some better?" He slid a dish of baked beans from the oven.

"I think so, Bobby." He looked lost in his wheelchair, his mind on faraway places. "How about a beer, Bobby?"

"Heck yeah," said Bobby. "Sammy?" He stared hard at Sammy. "Can you grab one?"

Sammy hopped into action, fished a can of PBR from the cooler, popped the top, and handed it to Bobby who gave it to Harold.

"Thank you, Bobby." He sipped the foam.

"Granny, you okay?" said Bobby.

Clara cradled Jenkins. "Precious baby," she said.

"Walter, need another beer?" said Bobby. He slid the macaroni and cheese in the oven.

"Not a thing, Bobby." Walter rolled himself away from the stove. Bee knocked his leg.

"Oops, you okay?" Bee wiped sweat from her eyebrows and kissed Walter's bald spot.

"All better," said Walter. "You're gonna love running the colony." He grinned. "I don't know if I'll be able to stay at the grocery store, though." He blushed. "With your beautiful self on the premises."

"Hey, you'll have my ass to stare at," said Bobby. He watched Silliporn lingering by the glass door.

Bee pulled a fifth of vodka from a bag and there was a *knock knock* on the door.

"Gay-bot!" said Silliporn. She curled a loose lock of hair behind her perfect ear.

Khun Phaen liked the new smell of his little rental car. Hell, he'd realized right away that Bobby wasn't Robin Williams. He sipped a bottle of magnesium citrate to flush the condoms of heroin cramping his gut. The long interstate seemed terrible and lonely. He turned on the radio and sang along. "Bone to be wiiiii iii lll d!" He checked his unfolded paper map every fifteen seconds. He belched. He felt he needed to buy a gun or trade for one with the heroin, but there wasn't time, plus it was too risky. A contact in Atlanta had given him a driver's license and put him in touch with a small-time dealer in Kuhlman County, where he was headed based on his wife's information. Some guy named Sami Dooshane.

Welcome to Alabama the Beautiful. His Atlanta contact had told him about rest stops at state lines. He pulled in and parked between two big-rigs with engines idling. The hot evening air felt cool compared to Bangkok. The trees made him feel small, and the bug sounds sent chills up his arms. He wasn't sure where the bathroom was. His innards griped. A state trooper pulled into the parking lot, noting the car parked among the semis.

"Howdy dowdy," said Khun Phaen to the

evening attendant on duty. His English was terrible.

The attendant looked at Khun Phaen's tight black slacks and white shirt. "Hidee doo." His cloudy eyes grew and shrank behind his thick lenses. He tapped a "Do you believe in the old rugged cross?" pamphlet on the counter.

"Okey dokey," said Khun Phaen, rattled for the first time in a long time. He took the pamphlet and examined the strange letters, the picture of a man with a drooping head on a cross.

"Jesus," said the attendant. He pointed at the pamphlet, then toward the ceiling and smiled.

"Jealous?" said Khun Phaen.

"God's son," said the attendant.

"Velly velly," said Khun Phaen. His gut bubbled. He searched for words. "Shit come out."

The attendant's face went blank. He sucked his cough drop and pointed to the men's room.

Khun Phaen waddled that way and pushed into the handicap stall, groaning and cursing under his breath.

The trooper came in to pee and grimaced. A toilet flushed. It flushed again. It flushed again. The trooper zipped, washed his hands, thought about mad cow disease, and hurried back to his cruiser.

In the party hubbub, Bobby rolled Harold's wheelchair over a loop of Ike Turnipseed's catheter tube. When Ike stood, he hollered and his second plumbing job in a week was free. He'd bled like a stuck hog but the paramedics assured everyone that he would be okay. Clara and Chester volunteered to take Claudette to the hospital and Sister Haylie left right after that. It was quite the unexpected end to a sad but lively evening.

Bobby admired Bee curled on the bed with Jenkins. He closed Nadine's door to block out her heavy snores and went to the open glass door in the living room. A warm breeze fluttered the thin curtain.

"Close it, Bobby," said Harold. He lay in bed with his head cranked up. "Mosquitoes'll get in."

Bobby stepped aside and Silliporn passed into the house with wet eyes as Gaybert's Harley grumbled into the night. Bobby touched her arm as if saying goodbye.

"We need to get up early, to get to Atlanta," said Bobby. "Plane leaves at 4:30 in the afternoon." He stepped onto the little porch and stared into the shadows. He listened. High above, a jet scratched across the sky. The rain gutters were clogged with pine straw and a hollow *drip drip* sounded in a downspout.

Bee shimmied out in her underwear and rubbed her eyes. "I laid the little one down. Y'all want to go skinny dipping in the pond?" She glanced over at Silliporn.

Bobby laughed.

"I'm just excited about my new job at the

nudist colony, I guess." She pulled a folding chair beside Silliporn. "You sad, honey? I'm sure gonna miss you."

Silliporn parted her lips and tried to speak. Tears somersaulted down her nose.

"Let's get some sleep." Bobby put his hand on Silliporn's. Bee took Silliporn's other hand, kissed it, and led her to the bedroom.

Harold stared from his bed. "Bobby, can you empty the urinal?"

"I'll pour it outside so I don't wake Jenkins." He opened the back door and tiptoed on the pine straw to an iron kettle boiling with purple phlox in the moonlight. The wind picked up and died, picked up and died. A log truck's chains clanked from far far away. The scrabble of rocks and wood left from the salvaged barn glowed like fool's gold in the moonlight. He smelled pond. He smelled tomato vines. A shadow slipped between trees and a hand slid across his mouth.

"Holy…" Bobby leaped and hit a pine tree.

Bee laughed. "Jesus, Bobby, you nearly jumped over the moon. You okay?" She pulled him close. "Settle down."

She smelled like vodka and sunscreen. Bobby's insides melted. "The devil's in the details."

"What do you mean?"

"Hell, I don't know."

"I'm pregnant, you know."

"Yeah, I know."

"I think Silliporn's in love with Gaybert."

"Yeah, I know."

"I don't mind, though."

"Yeah. I know."

"You're about the weirdest damn psycho ever to draw a breath."

"If you can't get rid of the tapeworm, at least try to work with him."

"Prozac, because Zoloft is for pussies." Bee laughed.

"Damn straight." Bobby sighed at the clarity of his situation.

After a half hour "suck" on the bed as Clara called it, Jenkins fell into a milky stupor. Bee and Silliporn spooned on the bed, snoring like little girls at a sleepover. Bobby pulled the .45 from the dresser and emptied the chambers. He tiptoed from the room.

"Hey Bobby," said Harold. "Can you turn this light off?"

"I brought the gun. Like you wanted," said Bobby. The words tugged the pit of his stomach. He slipped the cold metal under the sheet, next to Harold's good thigh.

"Is that bastard loaded?" Harold pulled it out from under the sheet. "Heavy as a rock."

"Be careful." A wealth of joy piled high on Bobby's shoulders. He slid the gun back under the sheets, turned off the lamp, and plugged in the seashell nightlight. "Good night, Mr. Harold."

"Good night, Bobby. You're like a son to me, Bobby. Just wanted to tell you that."

Bobby adjusted Harold's pillow. He swallowed, picked up a piece of popcorn, crumbled it, walked a thousand miles to the bedroom, and lay on the floor beside those he loved most.

Khun Phaen had never seen a turtle in the wild and slid his rental car thirty feet off the road into a boggy low place. He jumped out, slipped in mud, and ran toward the beast as it scooped its way across the double yellow stripe. Monstrous with a long whipping tail, tangles of algae fringed its shell. A set of headlights blazed, coming up fast. Khun Phaen didn't much care for dogs or people, but his grandfather had survived and escaped the prison camp of a rich Cambodian prince because of a turtle like this. He was captivated and grunted with its weight. The turtle reared a fat head on a long neck. Khun Phaen screamed and ran in a long circle. A pickup slowed and pulled over.

Travelbob Hodges turned up the radio. Top of the hour and Jemson Handloser waded through the funeral announcements. Travelbob adjusted his thermos of coffee and switched his emergency blinkers on. He rolled down the window. He had an ax in the back of the truck. He knew the only way a snapping turtle would ever let go was if it thundered or if a blade came down across its neck. He brushed cheese-cracker crumbs off his shirt.

Khun Phaen danced with the turtle clamped onto the base of his thumb. He was just getting over the panic and beginning to feel the pain, which sobered him somewhat. The last condom of black tar had torn at the rest stop and he felt woozy. He saw a man with a body shaped like a centaur holding an ax.

"Why you're the second Chinese I've seen in two weeks," said Travelbob. "I'm a Hodges. People call me Travelbob 'cause I drive around all night drinking coffee."

"Help to me!" said Khun Phaen. The sky seemed terrible and big. Sow bugs chucked through the air like Milk Duds and hammered away at Travelbob's headlights. The turtle continued to thrash its dinosaur legs. Khun Phaen moaned. A tiny glow of light bulbed on the jet-black horizon.

"Simmer down. You got yourself in a pickle," said Travelbob. He poured a cup of coffee.

"We extend our condolences to the family of Ezra Stumpwater, who lost his mother of ninety-eight years yesterday morning in the parking lot of Food Freezer. We just praise God that she had the bright sunshine of creation on her face when she passed onto the farther shore…"

Khun Phaen struggled to keep the turtle still. A long vein of white-hot lightning snaked into the beyond followed by a low rumble.

"Hold her steady, brother, and I'll send him to the stew pot." Travelbob waved his ax back and forth, eyeballing the neck. "Kneel down and hold that bastard in front." He raised the ax and motioned for Khun Phaen to kneel.

A log truck flew by and air-braked to a stop

a quarter-mile ahead.

"We'd like to thank our sponsor this week," said Jemson. "Hodges' Scrap Metal…"

"That's my baby brother's outfit," said Travelbob. "Wife got caught in a hay baler about thirty years ago, real tragic and suddenlike, but his son's pitching in and learning the business." He put down his ax and thought. "Married him a Portugal woman this time around. Hairy as an ape but got a pretty face. That boy of his looks just like her. Reckon what language it is they talk over there?"

Khun Phaen cursed.

"Looked to me like Travelbob was executing a Jap," said the logger into his CB. "Had him knelt down and all…" He breathed fast. Just last week, his life had come to a standstill after a truckstop flirt acquired his wallet. He'd made the mistake of calling the law and they'd arrested him for soliciting a prostitute. The whole thing had been captured live on *Truck Stop Hidden Camera*. He hurried back onto the road.

"There will be a singing this Sunday at Missionary Thick Baptist Church," said Jemson in his calm, soothing voice. "If you like old-time gospel…"

A burst of lightning dropped every sowbug and mosquito within half a mile. A thunder bomb riding the flash knocked Travelbob on his overlarge behind. The flat end of the ax swung onto Khun Phaen's foot. He leaped south and the snapper pulled tight inside its shell going due north.

Radio static.

"Dearest Lord Jesus! Heaven popped a porchlight!" said Jemson. "And now, we'll move on to the sick. Barbara Braswell reports that her son Gil was X-rayed and found to have an Army issue pocket knife in his stomach…"

Mỹ Lai...PFC Robert Hartwig has so many leaves in his helmet band that his head looks like a giant aloe plant. He fires his M-16 into the neck of an old man, one bullet at a time until the swollen head rolls away. He steps on the chest and a gush of black-flecked air sprays his jungle boot...drags a knife across the old man's tummy...stuffs a hand grenade in there...He helps a little girl whose clothes are on fire...

Bobby sat on the floor, doodling on his arm with the needle and shoe polish. By the light of a tiny flashlight, a map of the universe as revealed to him that day in Bangkok vomiting river water was slowly emerging. He imagined an engine idling somewhere close. A fraction of light swept the bedroom. A single cricket chirped in the closet. Bee snored. Silliporn sighed. Nadine roared, choked, went silent for fifteen seconds, and roared again. A tingle crept along ancient pathways in Bobby's skin, the same breathlessness of childhood in the darkest hours of night.

He put the needle away. A drop of blood slid down his bicep. He listened through the open window. He had to pee and tiptoed past Harold through the back door into the crisp of midnight. He thought about how twelve times an hour five minutes go by. Pee foam slithered down the trunk and sieved into the pine straw. He looked sideways and tried to say something. He brought his elbow around and caught a man's nose. A stolen steak knife downshifted into the base of Bobby's neck.

"Nanu na…" Bobby fell on his face and stared. He saw the larva of a pincer beetle and counted his blessings up to forty-five, including the hiking boots that had lasted so long. He tumbled deep within the yellow blackness of the Chao Phraya River. He held his breath for centuries. A pressure withdrew from his neck, replaced by a blowtorch. A blow to his temple. Bobby receded to a tiny dot and ascended to rain gutter level, watching as Khun Phaen wiped his nose with a bloody hand.

Sprayed with mud from Travelbob's truck, Khun Phaen circled Bobby doing a drunk pagan dance, then went through the open back door. Bobby noticed the light at Sister Haylie's. He slipped inside the Suggs with Khun Phaen and, without wanting to, floated through the ceiling into the attic where he saw a wooden chest. Inside it were Masonic manuals and a fancy hat. A squirrel exploded from the insulation and clung to the rafters upside down. Bobby heard Harold yell, "Hold up boy!"

Bobby opened his eyes. He sucked in. Hot wax spurted into his chest and he collapsed. He reached for his neck, breathing now like a sleeping cat. He pulled himself up and saw the rectangle of light that was an open door and then a thick Asian man with a knife facing Harold. Harold held the cocked .45 dead center on the man's chest.

"I'll blow you to kingdom come, boy," said Harold. "Drop that cutter."

"Velly velly," said Khun Phaen. He grimaced, swayed, and widened his eyes.

Bobby leaned in the doorframe. He tried to speak but only a squishy noise came out.

Harold couldn't see Bobby with his blind eye but could hear his lungs sucking. "Bobby, you okay?"

Khun Phaen swiveled. He was exhausted

and seeing double. He needed some menthol powder on his chest to perk him up.

"Steady, old man," said Harold to himself. He coughed and the gun wavered in his good hand.

Bobby stared. From his punctured lung, air crackled like bubblewrap under the skin around his shoulder. He fell toward Khun Phaen. Khun Phaen caught his neck and turned him into a shield. Bobby sprayed blood-streaked phlegm from his nose and mouth and stared at the gun barrel doing little circles in Harold's hand.

With Bobby in a chokehold, Khun Phaen revived his spark and called out. "Silliporn! *Ma!*" Sweat steamed his face and wet his ruined white shirt. *"Gah-ree!"* he said, calling her a whore. His cheeks were bright red and looked swollen. His hand throbbed from the turtle bite. "Silliporn! *Ma!*" Then he called Silliporn a slut. "Oh, you are old old man," he said to Harold in Thai. He sneered and maneuvered Bobby sideways past him.

"Bobby, hold on," said Harold. "I've got a bead on his head." The gun dipped up and down. "I said hold it, Chinaman!"

Khun Phaen watched him and walked backward, dragging Bobby with him. Bubbles of blood foamed from Bobby's mouth. "Silliporn! *Ma!*" He laughed and scooted past the fireplace to the bathroom with a bedroom door to either side. Bobby bit his arm. Khun Phaen yelled, pounded Bobby's head from behind, and regained his harness grip.

Nadine woke up on her back and gazed around the dark room. She heard godawful noises. The door pushed open. She struggled to cover her bare thighs with her flimsy gown. She smelled lightning and blood and threw an alarm clock at the thing coming toward her. "Harold!"

On his side, Harold fumbled to release the rail catch and it fell with a clang. He struggled to sit up and slid his legs to the floor.

Khun Phaen swept his hand across the wall, hit the switch, and light flooded the bedroom. He saw a flabby old woman flat on her back, cursed, and struggled to turn with Bobby clutched against his chest. Bee rushed with a lamp and crashed it across Khun Phaen's head and shoulder. He staggered and dropped the knife. Bobby pitched onto the bed across Nadine's lap.

"Oh Lord! Bobby!"

Hands on knees, Khun Phaen blocked the doorway. From the hallway, Bee saw the knife, and kicked him hard from behind. Khun Phaen stumbled over the knife. She dove for it.

Harold gripped the edge of the bed, sweating. He saw his walker on the other side of the room next to his bathroom door. He slipped the gun into the band of his pajama bottoms, lost his balance, and fell backwards. The gun slid into his underwear.

"Silliporn!" Khun Phaen growled. Bent over, he kicked his leg backward and trapped Bee's hand with the knife. She lurched and stumbled back to Silliporn, squatting, rocking Jenkins beneath a thin blanket and whispering to him madly. The sound of her father's voice calling her name had drained the color from her face and the soul from her body.

"Oh, Bobby Hotwig," she said in a small voice, thinking he was dead.

Bee slammed the door, twisted the flimsy lock, and shoved the dresser in front of it. She ran to the window. The crib blocked her way and she jerked it into the middle of the room. "Silliporn!" Bee motioned for her.

Khun Phaen tried to stand and staggered. He vomited and groaned, but the sight of Bobby sprawled on top of Nadine brought a tiny smile to his face. Bobby's respirations sounded like an icepick going in and out of Styrofoam. Nadine wept like a baby, stroking Bobby's head, mouthing "Harold" over and over.

Harold gripped the sheet and pulled himself up. He breathed hard. Three solid steps separated him from the walker. He heard Bee scream, a door slam. He heard Nadine babbling and moaning. He stood, bracing himself against the bed. Pain shot through his leg and then his chest. He shuffled a step forward. He heard sounds of wood smashing and took another step.

Khun Phaen put his shoulder into the door, crashed it from a hinge, and broke the lock. The door pressed against the dresser. The light from Nadine's bedroom lit the room in a wash of dull orange and gray. "Silliporn," he called in a voice sweet and childlike. She wasn't even his child, but he knew who the father was, knew exactly where he was buried minus head, feet, and hands. He kicked at the mess of shattered wood in front of him.

With the window open, Bee yanked on Silliporn's shirt. "Quick, quick," she whispered. Silliporn remained frozen. She wondered if Jenkins would grow up to be like her father. Maybe it would be best that she die with Jenkins in her arms. Maybe he would spare Jenkins if he saw her dead. Gaybert on his Harley drifted through her mind. She saw her mother cutting a pineapple for dinner. She watched as Bee took a struggling Jenkins from her arms and passed him through the window to a waiting pair of urgent hands.

Sister Haylie hurried Jenkins to her house and locked the door. Without thinking, she pulled a Madonna figurine from a shelf and proceeded to act out the manger scene for him on her bed. She looked around for a Joseph but all she could find was a wooden spoon.

Harold staggered from the end of his bed to the corner of the den that bled into the tiny living room. Facing the fireplace he groped his way sideways toward the commotion, holding to the rough wooden mantle. He grunted with each move. His leg cramped. He stumbled and swept the mantle, knocking off the candle and a framed photo of dead relatives.

Khun Phaen hit the light switch. "Oh, my little baby," he said in Thai. The sight of Silli-

porn cringing on the floor carved a big pump-
kin grin on his face. He chuckled as Bee backed
away toward the open window. She looked
tasty in her underwear and t-shirt. He bran-
dished the knife at her then Silliporn. "We have
some fun, how about it?" he said in Thai. "Such
beautiful ladies."

Bee yelled, "Bobby!" and tried to scramble through the open window as Khun Phaen
lunged her way.

Bobby struggled off Nadine's bed and fell
to the floor, gasping. He clutched his bleeding
neck, making tiny squealing sounds. Nadine sat
up, thought she saw Harold standing outside
her door, and fainted.

Harold struggled for breath. He braced himself in the doorway and felt for the .45 tugging
his underwear down. Khun Phaen had Bee's
legs, pulling her back through the window. She
screamed and kicked and saw a shadow moving
from tree to tree. With fistfuls of pine straw she
turned on Khun Phaen and struck his head. He
laughed and wrestled her to the ground, cutting her arm with the knife.

"Bee!" Harold shouted.

Khun Phaen turned, shocked to see the old
man.

"Pawpaw!" Elbows flying, Bee bit Khun
Phaen in the Adam's apple and threw herself
toward Silliporn. He dropped the knife between
his legs, unsteady on his knees in front of the
open window. He gagged. The room swam
away.

"Prepare to meet your maker," said Harold. He pulled the trigger. The gun clicked. He pulled it again. The gun clicked.

Khun Phaen sat dumbfounded, counting the clicks. One, two, three, four, five... He wanted to laugh but couldn't. He watched as the gun slipped from Harold's hand, the hand going to Harold's chest as he crumpled to the floor.

"Ai farang," said Khun Phaen with disgust.

"Pawpaw!" screamed Bee. She hovered over Silliporn.

Khun Phaen's laughter flooded the room. *"Ee hee-ah!"* He grinned, traced the knife across his neck, and put hands to knees to catch his breath. Silliporn cowered behind Bee just a few feet away. She had that terrified look on her face that he hated. He wanted to fuck her one last time, infect her before he killed her. He turned and grabbed the windowsill to raise himself and an ax smashed through glass and wood, catching him on his shoulderblade. His face hit the sash, splitting his cheek. The ax swung again and crashed more window and skull. Khun Phaen fell back, groaning. Sammy scrambled through and dove for the gun shining in the floor. In the other bedroom, Bobby lay silent as Nadine screamed for Harold from her bed. In the distance, a siren called out long and sorrowful. Hidden within a sparse stand of poison ivy in the woods behind the barn, a whippoorwill stood over a single brown egg lying on the naked ground. "*Quick over here, quick over here… Quick over here, quick over here,"* she called.

Harold's sudden darkness rushed to a point of burning white light. He could hear sounds of scuffling and a sorrowful, "No, no, no…" He ascended into the attic and saw a confused squirrel pressed flat to a beam, its tail flicking. Bobby joined him and they spoke for years and years as paramedics and deputies swarmed the rooms below. Harold told him about feeling the plow blade tear through the red dirt as a child, about eating cold sweet potatoes in the field, about watching the gin rip the seeds from the cotton, about jawing with Chester under the black walnut tree all those summers gone by.

Harold read Bobby's mind. He said the man who had raised Bobby, Robert Hartwig, was nuts for sure, that he'd lost his marbles in Vietnam. Harold said that you had to take your afflictions and lay them out, study them, and decide how to put them to work for yourself. The bad doctor covers his mistakes with six feet of dirt, he said, and the bad cook smothers his with gravy. But you can't afford to do that. You gotta let your circumstances work for you, not against you.

What about my mother? said Bobby. She just faded away in the nursing home.

Harold told Bobby that she was just a simple country girl, that getting dragged all over the world and living the Army life had put her into a permanent state of shock. She was just heartbroken over how many different worlds there were in one life. When Robert disappeared, she was already used up. She just gave in and let her mind take her down. Sometimes, Bobby, you just got to go crazy to get folks off your back...

Harold lifted a bit and Bobby reached out. Who's my father? he said. Can you tell me?

Harold drifted higher toward the roof. He smiled a full smile and lifted his hands. I am if you want me to be.

Bobby nodded.

Harold ascended, and what was his essence dispersed from the earth into the great imagination of everything possible and otherwise.

Bobby did not want to go to Harold's funeral. He had grown fond of Harold, gotten to know him as up close and personal as any father and son could ever wish for. The specter of a funeral just seemed wrong to Bobby. Harold had saved the day, holding off Silliporn's father just long enough, just like a movie, just like a damn movie, a movie he didn't want to end. The doctor had clamped Bobby's chest tube and given him the okay to attend Harold's service.

The car doors slamming in the church parking lot beneath the flat, blue sky sounded beyond final. A single cardinal hopped to the pavement and picked a sesame seed from the white stripe. Silliporn guided Bobby by his elbow up the handicap ramp, followed by Bee holding Jenkins. Bobby stopped at the heavy wooden door, catching his breath, and tucked his borrowed dress shirt into the back of his black jeans, his nicest pair of pants. His breathing was still shallow, and he felt it. His eyes felt submerged, needing more light. The door opened, and the cold church air moved around his face, went down his collar, chilled the sweat gathered along his spine, and beaded across his stomach.

The church was packed with suits and summer dresses, patent-leather shoes, black pumps, colorful ties, and a finely laced bonnet or two. The aisle leading to the front seemed too short to Bobby. The *In Remembrance of Me* table sat off to the side, covered with potted mums. There was a casket there with the lid open, the centerpiece of an explosion of dahlias, roses, and daisies, yellow, white, and purple, Mr. Harold's favorite. Nadine sat in a folding chair beside the casket, small, fingering the scarf of a friend that had come off in her hands. It was natural for her to knead the fabric, to ply it between her thumb and forefinger.

The casket seemed to Bobby to come to him, to draw itself up the aisle and press it's cold, brushed steel edge to his palms. The pain in Bobby's neck melted away. Harold looked grand, solemn as a statue. The blue suit did him justice, put pounds on his frame, contrasting just right with his tan cheeks and hair thick enough to shame a teenage lifeguard. Bobby wept. He felt his hand reaching and let it go to the tie, just a bit skewed there around the collar. A minor adjustment before the body made peace with the earth.

Then, a man who was the preacher talked and praised Harold Suggs as it was his job to do. The lid was closed and Nadine wept with the finality, regretting that she'd hid the maple syrup, not regretting that she'd finally forked out for unexpired Ensure.

Through it all there was weeping. Bobby comforting Bee. Bee comforting Silliporn. Claudette with her arm on Nadine's sagging shoulder. Clara didn't weep, though. She'd been on the too-friendly end of Harold more than once but Chester, even though he knew the same, did cry, and with heart, because in the end Harold Suggs was a good man.

Come home, come home,
come home, come home,
Ye who are weary come home...
Bobby's heart...

Agents from the Canadian Security Intelligence Service and Royal Canadian Mounted Police argued with Sheriff Gaslight outside Chanarong Wongmalasith's semi-private room at Kuhlman County Hospital. International charges against the wounded man, *aka* Khun Phaen, included kidnapping, smuggling, human trafficking, and a rainbow of sexual offenses. Interpol was interested as well and monitoring the proceedings.

CSIS Agent Moriere shook his head. "You

cannot handcuff him to the bed. It is a violation of human rights."

"I can handcuff him twenty ways to Sunday," said Gaslight. "You can get back to Cancun and do it your way. When we got the bull by the horns, we like to reach under and grab its nuts. You ever see a man run with his nuts nailed to the floor?"

"We're from Canada," said the RCMP agent.

"You sure don't sound Mexican," said Gaslight.

"Scuse me." Sharla, the big-rig nurse, pushed through the group into the room.

"He cannot escape. It is impossible," said Moriere. "You are posting a guard to this door every minute, yes?"

"Don't need to. He's handcuffed to the bed," said Gaslight.

"What if there is a fire?" said Moriere.

"Well, I'll put some marshmallows on his bedside table," said Gaslight.

The two agents talked among themselves while Gaslight stepped in to look over his prize. The local paper had run a headline, "Sheriff nabs Chinese hit man," citing the capture as a "blow to communism."

Khun Phaen lay in bed with his left arm taped to his torso. Sammy's ax blow had snapped the shoulder blade in half and made a nasty gash. Khun Phaen smirked at Gaslight. He rattled his swollen, handcuffed hand, the one the turtle snapped. He was starving for Thai food.

Gaslight pulled out a peach-flavored cigar and lit it. He peeped around the curtain at the judge in the next bed. "Well, his skin looks better..."

"Sheriff, you can't smoke in here," said Sharla. She flexed her forearms.

"Oh, right," said Gaslight. "Old Judge here talking yet?"

"No and let's hope it stays that way, good buddy," said Sharla. "Gonna put some goodie down yer tube." She pushed a hundred ccs of Ensure through a feeding tube hanging from the judge's nose. He smacked his lips like he could taste it and frowned. His eyes rolled.

Gaslight moved back to Khun Phaen. He thought about how big China was, about how the people were like ants marching across the great empty places. "I got you behind the eight ball," he said.

Inside one of the deluxe cabins at Tippy's Sun-luvver Nudist Colony, Bee adjusted Silliporn's bikini bottom and matching veil. "You are so beautiful," she said. "Hot sexy mama. Gaybert's gonna pee himself when he sees you." Gaybert had asked Silliporn to marry him. He was in love, simple as that, and couldn't let her slip away to Thailand amid the insanity of the past two weeks. Her visa had been extended to testify in a federal grand jury against her father, first in Atlanta and then on to Canada for more of the same. Bobby had seen the writing on the wall, realized that he was not the father of Jenkins, and felt that his future was with Bee.

Sheriff Gaslight wanted to pursue murder charges against Khun Phaen for the death of Harold, but Nadine had put the nix on it. She'd have rathered Harold went out natural-like, the hero on his white horse, than cut short by some gangster from Taiwan.

Outside, the regular guests at Tippy's lazed around in hammocks and soaked up the sun in webbed folding chairs. A lively game of volleyball offset the cicadas lull and drone. In the Buick, Sammy and Bobby drank warm beer. They nodded their heads to the eternal heavy chords of Black Sabbath. Bobby's eyes misted.

"Almost like the old days," said Sammy. He stared at the galaxy of pins holding up the roof fabric.

"Yeah." Bobby looked away. His stab wound still looked angry. The steak knife had nicked his subclavian vein and punctured the top of his lung. It'd taken a week to re-inflate it and suction out the bloody clots. He thought about the lock of Harold's hair he had pressed in a book.

"Come on man, it's good times now." Sammy drummed his fingers on the dashboard.

"Yeah," said Bobby. "You gonna move in with Mrs. Nadine? She sure could use you."

"Hell no. Sister Haylie's…staying with her for awhile. I thought you and me, though, could move in the old cabin. Sister Haylie about said as much. What you think?"

"Well, it could be that the next wedding is

mine," said Bobby. All their HIV tests had come back negative and Silliporn had admitted that Jenkins belonged to her father. He had known it, but the dream, the possibility of it all, had seemed so real. "What about your place at Candy Mountain?"

"Hell, that's history. Bad habits live there. What about we go out west, maybe California. See some sights? You know Nadine's headed out there with, what's her name, Claudette?" He raised his eyebrows.

"Yeah, that's a hoot. But me and Bee, I don't know. It's like really going somewhere. Like I'm learning to walk all over again. Hard to explain."

Sammy resumed bobbing his head to the music. "Bobby, check it out."

An enormous naked couple from Vancouver wearing sun visors and flip-flops waddled across the graveled parking lot on their way to the outdoor cabana.

"It's the end times," said Sammy.

"Damn straight," said Bobby.

On a Plane Somewhere over Arizona...As the taped show aired nationwide, Nadine and Claudette drank little bottles of white wine and complained about how small the seats were. Sister Haylie clutched the armrest of her chair with one hand, putting her prayer beads through the motions with the other.

Missionary Thick...At the Suggs', Bobby and Bee crowded into Harold's old recliner. Gaybert sat in a kitchen chair beside Silliporn curled in Nadine's lounger. Jenkins cooed and gurgled in her lap.

Kuhlman...At home, Clara and Chester gripped the armrests of their loungers. The TV boomed.

Tippy's Sunluvver Nudist Colony...To the sounds of "All Shook up," Sammy poured up a pitcher of virgin margaritas for a lumpy couple from Saginaw, Michigan. Even with their private club license, alcohol sales at Sunluvver's didn't start till noon. He spotted the couple's buxom teenage daughter and forgot to change the channel to *The Price is Right* on the TV playing behind him.

"You gonna do your Elvis show tonight?" said the lady.

"Yes, muh ma'am," said Sammy.

Kuhlman County Jail...In the lockup dayroom,

Bobby's Uncle Lloyd braked his wheelchair, adjusted his snack tray of butterscotch pudding from a can, and grinned at the TV. He loved pudding from a can. Sheriff Gaslight stored his pistol and waltzed in, happy as a clam. He could still see the latest headlines with his photo, "International hit man captured, County Sheriff deals blow to global communism."

*Jefferson County Health Department…*The mid-morning crowd gazed at the waxed floor. "It doesn't feel safe without a condom," said the young woman in the video. The muscular man licked her neck. "But I want to feel you for real," he said, "from the inside." Back for another treatment, the old man in the shabby, blue quilted overcoat couldn't take it anymore. He stood in a chair and switched the channel to *The Price is Right.* Everyone clapped as the camera swept the colorful audience.

*Food Freezer…*Walter hobbled into his office on one crutch, fiddled with the tiny black-and-white TV, and funneled the sound to the speaker system. Smells of suntan lotion mixing with the asphalt of the new super-size parking lot wafted through the packed store. Wearing only red aprons, the Toms high-fived. "Dian," said one. "Kathleen," said the other.

*Federal Detention Center, Toronto…*Khun Phaen frowned at the cartoon playing on the TV in his medical holding cell. Agents from the Canadian

Security Intelligence Service had just finished grilling him. Interpol was on the way. A sling snugged his left arm and shoulder to his torso where the ax had blasted his shoulderblade. Twenty-two stitches laced the back of his skull. He motioned for the nurse to change the channel. Rod Roddy shouted, "Nadine Suggs! Come on Down!"

Bee jabbed Bobby in the ribs. "It's Mamaw!"

"Jealous Lice!" said Silliporn.

Bobby laughed, shook his head, and looked over his shoulder to the hospital bed stripped of sheets and lying flat. He saw Harold there on the edge, sipping a tall glass of ice water. He looked years younger. He gave Bobby a thumbs up and slipped through the wall. Bobby squeezed Bee's thigh.

"Ow," said Bee.

Hearing her name, Nadine rocked her seat in slow motion. A smile creased her face from ear to ear. She pushed and fell back. The audience's crazed enthusiasm hushed. Then she felt two, strong, familiar hands reach under and pull her to her feet. With tears in her eyes, she squeezed past Claudette and Sister Haylie to the aisle. She raised her cane into the air, almost fell, caught her teeth, and the crowd went nuts.

"She looks a lot bigger on TV," said Bee, and Bobby agreed.

The audience cheered Nadine all the way

to the front, and the first item up for bid was a bottle of Vermont maple syrup.

"She crying," said Silliporn.

Bobby watched Silliporn cuddling Jenkins and his stomach dropped, then lifted. He was happy for her, happy that Bee was there for him.

"Mamaw, they're bidding too high!" Bee clutched Bobby's arm.

Laughing, Gaybert leaned down and kissed the top of little Jenkin's fuzzy head.

"Nadine Suggs, what will you bid?" said Bob Barker.

Nadine considered the other three bids, squinted, and said, "One dollar."

Bobby gazed back at the empty bed. "Sprinkle cheese, mayonnaise, maple syrup, peanut sauce," he said to the room. "Stuff to make other stuff taste better. Makes it all easier to swallow."

"What?" said Bee.

"And the winning bid is..." Bob smiled. "One dollar!"

"Go, Mamaw!" said Bee.

Nadine trembled and tears wet her eyes as *The Price is Right* cacophony melded into a soothing commercial for allergy medication. A thin pretty girl with glasses was sad because she couldn't play with her shedding kitten in a field of goldenrod thick with pollen.

"That girl drinks too much diet soda," said Bobby. "Plus, her mother never let her get dirty when she was a kid. Now she's allergic to all creation."

"What?" said Bee.

Jenkins looked serious and made a spit bubble.

A dog food commercial came on. The camera zoomed to a mound of dry, brown chunks. "Basted with meaty juices," said a man's confident voice.

"Damn straight," said Bobby. He kissed Bee's cheek and nodded to the bass line playing in his head.

www.ingramcontent.com/pod-product-compliance
Lightning Source LLC
Chambersburg PA
CBHW051644180726
48284CB00006B/1858